CHASING VICTORY

The Winters Sisters

Book One

By

JOANNE JAYTANIE

Enjoy ~

Joanne Jaytanie

ISBN-10: 0-9967001-5-3
ISBN-13: 978-0-9967001-5-3

Edited by Ruth Ross
Copyedited and formatted by Self-Publishing Services LLC (self.publishing.services@gmail.com)

Dedication

Thank you, Shelia for introducing me to Ruth Ross, she is a brilliant editor.

To my husband, Ralph. Your unending love and support has always been my rock.

My beloved Dobermans; Taisha, Misty, Dax, Kes, and Captain. You have all left this world behind, and yet I feel your spirits beside me, always.

The Doberman on the cover is ~ *Dax*

American/International Champion Starlaine's Virtual Reality, CD, NA, NAJ, ROM

In the year of acquiring his Companion Dog Title (CD), Dax was the Doberman Pinscher Club of America (DPCA), Highest Scoring Dog earning a CD, where he placed first in his class. At the same DPCA Nationals, he also placed first in his agility class.

He was the first in his litter to achieve an AKC breed championship, (CH), and the first to be awarded a DPCA Register of Merit (ROM). In 2001 Dax was tied for the number three Novice Doberman for Agility in *Front and Finish Magazine*. Two months after we lost him, we learned that he was rated number six Doberman in AKC Novice Agility.

Dax was a wonderful dog. Dax and Ralph made an awesome team.

Table of Contents

Acknowledgements

Photographer of the Doberman on the cover is Denise Caley Stringfellow

Photographer of author ~ Sarah Burlingame

The Doberman in the picture is ~ *Jaytanie's Maiden Voyage ~ Anya*

Chapter One

A sudden breach in the forest's tapestry of sound caught Victory's attention. Victory's ultra keen sense of hearing instantly noticed the void. Her ability to interpret the reactions of the animals stopped her in midstride. Ever so slowly she turned toward the silence and walked.

The silence shattered and she could hear voices; one was Jeffery. He didn't say he'd be bringing others with him. His scream abruptly ruptured the cool morning air and flushed the birds from their perches. Victory dropped to her hands and knees, the tall sword ferns camouflaging her body. She froze.

"I told you I'd locate someone who could help with our problem," Jeffery whimpered. Blood ran from the gash on his lip and right cheek. "This is a field of the research I am not an expert in."

A big burly man, dressed in a neat black suit, lifted his massive hand to strike Jeffery again. "You were trying to run away."

"No, no I wasn't." Jeffery fell to his knees in an attempt to put distance between himself and the burly man's fist.

"Then why did you run to the forest?" A second man stepped from the shadow of the nearest evergreen tree. A shaft of sunlight shone directly behind him, making his image a dark silhouette. A tiny bright orange orb appeared as the man inhaled on a cigarette.

"I told you. I have a friend, she specializes in this field and I'm sure she could help me." Tears started to leak down Jeffery's cheeks, mixing with blood, and dripping onto his neatly pressed white shirt.

"Right. Out here. In the forest. With the birds and whatever. If you really were meeting someone, you'd be having lunch or coffee. You're not exactly the outdoors type, Jeff."

"I know, I know, but she is. I thought meeting her here would put her at ease, and I'd get more information and cooperation." He moaned as he threw his hands in front of his face.

"He's stalling," grunted the burly man.

"No, I'm not," Jeffery protested.

"You assured us from the beginning you were our expert," the man in the shadow said.

"That's it," Victory mumbled to herself. She knew she'd heard his voice before. It belonged to Detective Ken Howard. He was the homicide detective who led the investigation at Claremont when one of her colleagues, Lisa Evans, was found dead in the company's parking garage. Victory dropped to her belly and slinked closer. She stopped barely short of the group's sight, still hidden by the lush undergrowth.

"You're wasting my time, Jeffery." Detective Howard spat as he stepped back into the ray of sunlight. "So where's this woman of yours?" He nodded at the thug, who backslapped Jeffery.

"She'll be here; she said she would." Jeffery wrapped his arms around himself, and fell to the forest floor like a child.

"I don't believe you. Dr. Jeffery Maxwell, your services are no longer needed." Howard stepped back into the darkness at the same time the burly man pulled something black and shiny from inside his jacket.

Bang, Bang. The sound was sickening, something Victory would never forget. Jeffery rolled on to his back, his chest a dark crimson. Victory gasped. The two men spun around and scanned their surroundings. They could not see her lying on the lush green forest floor. Tears streamed down Victory's face as she lay deadly still. The birds and animals flushed themselves from the immediate vicinity. The two men continued to scour the forest until all the commotion passed and the forest fell deathly silent.

"You hear something?" asked the burly guy.

"I thought I did, but I don't see anything," answered Detective Howard. "Maybe one of us should take a walk, see if Jeff's girl is nearby," he cajoled.

"I'm sure I heard something. Stop being an ass; maybe it is the girl Jeff rambled on about."

"No girl would wander alone through the forest. I still say he was running. We've wasted enough time out here, let's go," Howard said.

Victory had no idea how long she'd stayed rooted to the same spot. The next thing she knew she was running. The trees and bushes tore at her clothes and pulled at her hair, making the tears flow once again. Consumed with panic, she didn't stop until safely locked inside her Jeep, and speeding down the mountain trail. She drove absently, replaying the scene over and over in her mind. *She should call the police. No, Detective Howard was the police.* She wouldn't be safe with them; she wouldn't know who to trust. She had to leave, get out, so that no one would associate her with Jeffery.

It had been a shock to hear from Jeffery after all this time. In college they were inseparable. Victory had been in love with him and thought he was in love with her. How could she not? They seemed to be the perfect match. They both majored in veterinary medicine and would spend their days and nights trying to dream up how to save the animal world. They'd planned to take on the future together. Then the week before graduation, Jeffery got approached by a corporate type with money to burn, and their dreams were dust. What a devastating time it turned out to be, to discover Jeffery's main priority was money.

Jeffery's phone call to her had been cryptic; he hadn't gone into any details. He only mentioned he needed her help and insisted they meet today. Did he sound as if he missed her? She wasn't sure; maybe all he needed was her professional advice. She closed her eyes for a brief second, replaying the cadence of the conversation in her mind. Jeffery had sounded upset. She would have helped him with whatever he needed. They may no longer have been lovers, they may not have stayed in touch, but she still felt a strong emotional bond to Jeffery. Now he was gone. Victory couldn't believe what she had witnessed really happened.

A half-hour later, Victory pulled into the parking lot of a shopping center. She turned off her Jeep and stared aimlessly out the window. After five long years, Jeffery had called her and asked to meet out at their old picnic area in the foothills of the Olympic Mountains. The two had spent one spring break together in her home town, and she was amazed he still recalled the spot. A few short hours ago she'd felt both nervous and a little giddy at the thought of seeing him again. Now, the only thing she knew for certain is she had to disappear until she could figure out what was going on. She couldn't leave a paper trail; she had no way to be certain Jeffery had not mentioned her name. Looking into her purse she counted out her cash. If she was careful she could make it to her sister without using her debit card, but it was going to be a long night without coffee. She got out of her Jeep, locked the doors, and headed to the coffee shop.

* * * *

Victory drove most of the night, but finally she had to take a break. She kept fighting off the urge to close her eyes. She pulled off the interstate at the next rest stop. She parked and grabbed a blanket out of the backseat.

"I need a few hours rest," she mumbled to herself and was asleep almost as she spoke the words.

BANG! Victory jolted out of sleep, shivering from the adrenaline rush caused by the replaying of the gunshot in her dreams. Panicked, she swiveled her head wildly, expecting to see Detective Howard and the man who shot Jeffery. Neither of the men was there. All she saw was the ebb and flow of travelers stopping to take a quick break and stretch their legs.

She glanced down at her watch and realized it was later then she thought, after eight in the morning. She reached into her purse, pulled out her phone, and punched the redial button. The phone rang three times; she heard her sister's voice telling her to leave a message. "Payton, its Victory. Change of plans, I'm on my way to meet you; I'll fill you in when I see you." She didn't want to upset her sister with any details. She would wait to tell her what had happened in person. She disconnected the phone and started the Jeep's engine.

Chapter Two

Tristan was irritated. If he'd been able to follow Jeffery as he planned, he wouldn't be looking into the cold, dead eyes of his only lead.

"Damn it, Wyatt."

"No need to yell, bro; I hear you loud and clear."

Wyatt was miles away, yet Tristan heard his brother's voice clearly in his mind, as if he stood right next to him.

"Yeah, and if you didn't take so many blasted liberties with your telepathic link, you wouldn't have heard me yell."

"I also wouldn't know what was going on, either," Wyatt said.

"That's why they made phones," Tristan snapped.

"Right, and we both know how good you are about using those."

"Don't give me grief. I would contact you as soon as I finished analyzing the scene. You are too damned impatient, is all. You were born impatient. You practically talked my ear off the whole way through the birth canal."

Tristan's mood had lightened slightly as he chuckled at his own joke. Wyatt always managed to lift his spirits. He turned back and looked at Jeffery's body, and became somber once again. "If I hadn't been sidetracked following up on your lead, I might have been able to save Jeffery." Upset with himself and his brother, he spoke aloud, the same time he sent the thought.

"Someone wanted Jeffery dead. I know this is difficult for you to admit Tristan, but you can't save everyone."

"Yeah, well there goes our only real lead," Tristan hissed while taking in his surroundings, trying to get a read on what'd taken place. "There it is again."

"What?" Wyatt answered.

"Shhh," Tristan responded. *"I'm not talking to you."* Flaring his nostrils widely to fill his lungs with the odors surrounding him, Tristan took several deep breaths, each time filling his lungs more deeply. He closed his eyes and focused on his breathing.

The scent from a person will travel in the wind forming a scent cone; these scents are picked up by bloodhounds and Tristan. He'd caught the identical scent while tracking Jeffery through the forest. He knew Jeffery's scent and the dead man's odor wasn't the only scent cone he detected.

Old Spice and sweat, accompanied by the distinct odor of cigarette smoke still lingered, along with scents that were uniquely human: stress and testosterone. These stenches littered the vicinity, and underneath them all, the strong scent of cordite given off by the gun and the blood-soaked ground. It was highly possible those were the scents of Jeffery's killers.

He turned slightly to his right and picked up another scent cone. A weak scent, but there all the same. Without thought he moved with his eyes still closed, off to the right. Lavender and chamomile. Someone else was here, a woman. By the weakness of her fragrance, Tristan surmised she stayed a long distance away from the action. He stood motionless and allowed the odors of the ghastly scene to penetrate his every pore.

He opened his eyes and continued walking, the lavender and chamomile growing stronger with each step. He'd walked about sixty feet when he found a patch of bent and broken ferns. It was a small depression, but the lavender-and-chamomile woman had definitely been lying among the ferns. Tristan crouched down into the depression and looked back to where Jeffery lay. He could barely see Jeffery, and he was sure whoever had been laying here could not have heard or seen anything except the gunshot that ended Jeffery's life.

"Tristan...what did you find?"

Tristan felt Wyatt's voice pushing into his mind.

"Someone else was here, but a good distance away from the action. I don't think she was a part of it," Tristan said.

"She. Are you sure?"

"I'm positive, looks like we have a new lead after all. With any luck the two guys who killed Jeffery aren't even aware they had an audience."

"Luck, we certainly could use that. If she was as far away as you say, then the odds are in our favor," said Wyatt.

"I'm going to head back down the mountain. I'll catch a ferry back to Seattle and go to Jeffery's condo and search it."

"Okay, I'll notify the police, anonymously of course, and I'll send one of the guys to stake out the lab and search Jeffery's office."

* * * *

As the sun slipped behind the treetops, Tristan quietly opened the bedroom window at the back of Jeffery's condo and slid inside. The room he entered was as neat as a model house and nearly as sparse of personal belongings. There were no papers lying around, no clothes, no coffee cups or other dishes, and the bed neatly made. As Tristan walked down the hall, he scanned the bathroom and noticed the towels were carefully hung. He passed the office, living room, and kitchen, each room as pristine as the last. This didn't look like a guy's place. After the initial once-over he began a detailed search, looking through drawers, closets, and cabinets, all the while being careful to remain invisible to any passersby.

As Tristan sat on the floor and leaned against the desk in the office looking through Jeffery's iPad, his phone vibrated in his back pocket.

"Find anything?" Tristan said into his cell.

"By the time we were able to access his office, it looked like a wrecking ball hit," Wyatt said. "Whoever tore the place apart had no trouble being there while there were still people around. Leads me to believe it had to be someone who works there or is known by the other employees. Anything on your end?"

"I only now found his iPad. There is one entry for today: "Eleven a.m., Vic." I wonder who Vic is? Maybe one of the men's scents I picked up in the forest; maybe a secret meeting gone bad?"

"Possibly. Or it could have been the woman. She could have lain in wait to ambush Jeffery," Wyatt said.

"So we have a long list of possibilities."

"That's not a whole hell of a lot to go on."

"More than we had two hours ago," said Tristan.

Tristan stuffed the iPad in his backpack and continued his search of Jeffery's home office. The room was lined with floor-to-ceiling bookcases wrapping around all four walls. He scanned the contents looking for something to jump out at him. He came upon a row of yearbooks from high school, college, and veterinary school, and pulled out the last book from the shelf. Handwritten notes to Jeffery were on almost every page, and he carefully read each entry. About half way through the book, he saw it.

"Watch out world, here we come. Together forever, Love Vic." Could this be the same Vic Jeffery had the appointment with? He went to the class section and started to scan the names of the students: Vicki, Victor, and a Victory. At least the scent he picked up left out Victor. He pulled out his cell phone.

When at all possible Tristan preferred normal channels of communication, it saved on his mental strength. The greater the distance between the two brothers, the more concentration they expended.

"I need a computer search."

"What do you have?" Wyatt asked.

"I have his yearbook here with a note from Vic. I know it's a woman and there are only two possible options in his class."

"Assuming they were in the same class."

"Don't give me grief, bro. At least it's a starting point. Plug in the names Vicki Burrows and Victory Winters."

"I'll call you back as soon as we have something. In the meantime I think you should get your ass out of there. More than likely whoever tossed his office will head for his place sooner or later."

"Always the big brother."

Tristan snapped his phone shut before Wyatt could respond, stuffed the yearbook in his backpack, and headed for the bedroom. As he entered the hall he noticed night had fallen and a flashlight beam passed over the front windows; the scent of Old Spice drifted in. He couldn't smell anyone else, at least the odds were even. He dropped to the floor and stayed in the shadows as he slithered down the hall to the bedroom window, where he'd entered the condo. He dropped down into the bushes and slid the window closed as he heard the front door click open.

After a few minutes of drawers opening and closets being emptied, there was an abrupt halt. "I'm at Maxwell's place," the intruder spoke into his cell. "No, I haven't found anything yet. Do you think he was really waiting for some girl when we confronted him? If that's the case, I gotta wonder how much he told her. Yeah, okay, I'll be out of here in about thirty minutes and then I'll head back to the office."

Finally, the first positive thing Tristan had heard all night. It appeared more like they might have a witness to the scene of the crime, instead of a third murderer. He realized this man had even less information than he had with regard to their mysterious woman. Tristan slowly crept away from the condo. The dusk of the early evening hid his departure as he crossed a number of well-kept lawns and headed back to his Porsche parked two blocks away.

Tristan sat in his midnight-blue Porsche 911 Turbo and stared at the yearbook. He tried to put the pieces together, but he couldn't get any of them to fit. He pulled out his phone and once again called Wyatt.

"Update."

"Nothing yet; why don't you go back to your place and get some rest. You've been up for over twenty-four hours."

"That sounds like a good idea. I'm getting a little sloppy. I missed the early signs of one of the guys from the forest breaking into Jeffery's place."

"Tristan!" Wyatt suddenly sounded worried.

"It's no big deal; I got out before he saw me. I'm simply saying I do need some downtime."

"Go home and straight to bed. Meet me at the base in five hours."

* * * *

At exactly six the following morning Tristan arrived at the front gate of the military base. After a hands-on inspection of his identification, he was saluted on base by the Marine at the gate. Tristan drove to the back of the base and pulled into a parking place directly in front of a nondescript gray building with the initials SOCOM posted over the door.

This building housed the Puget Sound satellite office of the secret Special Operations Command, made up of elite military personnel from the Army, Navy, and Air Force. This SOCOM satellite consisted of ten people in two teams; Tristan, a former Navy SEAL at the rank of commander, led Team Alpha.

Wyatt was his boss and officer in charge of both teams. As far as Tristan was concerned, joining SOCOM couldn't have come at a better time. While he loved the SEALs, he often found himself butting heads with the strict military rules. SOCOM gave him more flexibility, and this fit his personality much better. It also didn't hurt to have his brother as his boss, at least most of the time.

This transfer of both brothers was not coincidental. Ten years ago while in the Navy SEALs, Captain Roberts served as the commanding officer in charge of all SEAL teams. Roberts was known to have a "hands-on" way of running his teams. He made it a habit to personally know each of his men. Tristan and Wyatt caught Captain Roberts's attention with their extraordinary abilities and perfect mission records.

Roberts had tracked both brothers' careers and six months ago, now as the general in charge of SOCOM, he requested their transfer. Unwilling to commit his idea to paper, Roberts set up a face-to-face meeting with the Farradays. His plan was to form a special team using military personnel who displayed more advanced instincts. During this meeting the brothers revealed to him their heightened abilities, with a promise he would keep their secret.

Removing his hat, Tristan entered the large building and walked directly to his commander's office.

He stood in the doorway and saluted the man sitting behind the desk, whose attention was on his computer.

"Morning, sir," Tristan greeted the officer.

Wyatt looked up from his computer to see Tristan standing in the doorway. Studying Wyatt's face, Tristan had the sense of gazing into a mirror. Tristan had violet eyes and black hair, while Wyatt's eyes were blue and his hair dark blonde, but otherwise they were twins.

"You can drop the sir, we're the only two here," Wyatt said.

"Did your search uncover anything?"

Tristan tossed his hat into one of the two chairs in front of Wyatt's desk and himself in the other.

"Yeah, quite a bit actually," Wyatt responded. He stretched his full six-foot-two-inch frame leisurely back into his chair. "Vicki Burrows owns a small woman's clothing store. She's married, has three children, and lives in Maine. Not likely she's our woman, and I moved on to Victory Winters.

"Victory lives in Poulsbo, Washington, literally down the road from here. She is a veterinarian and a geneticist, and specializes in molecular biology. She works for Claremont Research located in Bellevue. She is the department head for some kind of research being done with canine DNA and its potential benefits in curing diseases in humans. I can't seem to find out much detail about the project. It does sound like her expertise and Jeffery's are quite similar. I did find an abundance of family background. Parents are Joseph and Susan Winters, of The Winters Corporation, a leading firm in cancer research, among other life-threatening diseases. Joseph and Susan were killed in an automobile accident about four years ago, looks like a hit and run. The company was left to their daughters, Payton, Victory, and Willow.

"Payton and Willow both work for the company, but Victory chose another path. She still serves on the board of directors, along with her sisters. The family owns a fifty-acre estate on the outskirts of Poulsbo. All three sisters list their parents' home as their home address," Wyatt said.

"I'd say it sounds like a good start. Both she and Jeffery are involved in DNA research. Now we need to locate Victory and find out why she was in the forest and if she saw anything," Tristan said.

"I tried to call her at work this morning. They say she called in and said she wouldn't be back in the office for two weeks; she has a lead on a current project. Sounds to me as if this is something she does quite often. I couldn't get any additional information, although I got the feeling her trip was all very last minute."

Tristan got up from his chair and poured himself a cup of coffee, his fourth of the morning. "The good thing is she called in. That means she got away, and the two guys who killed Jeffery are either not aware of her, or haven't identified her yet. I'm going to do more background research on the company," Tristan said. With his free hand, he grabbed his hat and headed to his own office.

Tristan sat down behind his desk. He skimmed the pile of mail and memos dropped on top of his desk since yesterday. None of it was urgent, so he stacked it all into a pile and moved the pile to the far corner of his desk. He turned his attention to his computer and sipped on his coffee. He typed in "Winters Corporation," which generated an immediate flood of information to fill his screen. He scanned the data and read about the formation of the company, the studies they participated in, and the drugs they created. He needed his own first impression, so he picked up his phone and dialed.

"Winters Corporation, good morning, how may I direct your call?" came a woman's smiling voice.

"Yes, I'm trying to reach Ms. Winters," Tristan said.

"Which one, sir?" the woman asked.

"Payton."

"I'm sorry; Ms. Winters is on vacation. Would you like her voice mail?"

"When do you expect her to return?"

"I can't give out any additional information, sir; would you like her voicemail?"

"No, thank you. Could you connect me to Willow Winters?"

"Ms. Winters is located at one of our international offices; would you like me to transfer you?"

"No, thank you, I'll call back. Goodbye." Tristan hung up the phone and leaned back in his chair to think. Wyatt appeared in his doorway. "They aren't easy people to get in touch with on the phone," Tristan commented.

"You called the company." Wyatt leaned his broad shoulder against the doorjamb.

"Yeah, Payton is also out of the office. Willow is out of the country at another location. I searched the airlines passenger manifests. I found no listing for Victory Winters, therefore we know she's still in the country, unless she has access to a private jet. I also Googled Victory and Payton. There have been a couple of newspaper articles about Victory. Seems she is a practicing vet, with a specialty in holistic remedies. She practices both acupuncture and chiropractic on her patients. The articles talk about two dogs that couldn't walk; she literally got them up and running again," Tristan said.

"It seems Payton has an avid dog hobby too. She is a professional dog handler. There were a number of articles about her and her Dobermans." Wyatt nodded his head at the computer. "Type in 'American Kennel Club'; let's see if we can find some kind of schedule."

Tristan typed in the information. "I've found it, the AKC. Wow, they have shows every weekend all over the country."

Wyatt's cell rang. "What do you have for me, Logan?"

Logan was one of Tristan's team members and a former Army Special Forces.

"I searched the property. The motor home you asked about is not on site. The only two people I saw looked like employees. I didn't see anyone matching any of the women's descriptions."

"Okay. I'd like you to set up a tap on the phones. Can you do set the tap now, or do you have to wait until dark?"

"Shouldn't be a problem, sir. Like I said, there are only two employees on the grounds right now. I'll get right on it, over and out," said Logan.

"Excuse me, sir." Wyatt turned to find Jack, another member of Team Alpha standing behind him.

"Yes, Jack."

"I've completed my work on Victory Winters' phones."

"Did you find anything?"

"She received a text message on her cell from Jeffery Maxwell two days ago. She placed two calls this morning. The first one to her sister Payton, at eight ten, lasting one minute; the next one at eight twelve to her office," Jack reported.

"Can you tell me where she made those calls from?" Wyatt asked.

"Yes, sir," Jack said, as he pulled his report out of his file to find the answer. "Approximately five miles south of Mount Shasta, California."

"Good work, Jack. Get the license on Payton's motor home and locate her vehicle."

"Yes, sir," Jack replied, as he left the office.

"Her receptionist said she is on vacation. You think Payton took off for a dog show and Victory is running scared after her?" Tristan asked.

"I think it's a good possibility, and as good a place to start as any. She's not at her office, didn't take a plane, and is supposed to be working on a project. Going to her sister would be a safe place in her mind. Of course the question is why she didn't call the police, if she did in fact witness Jeffery's murder," Wyatt said.

"There must have been a reason in her mind. Nevertheless it does seem strange she would watch her friend be killed and not try to contact the authorities," Tristan said.

"I need you on the road ASAP," Wyatt said.

"I packed this morning. I'm ready to leave anytime."

"Okay, follow her trail and see where it leads. I'll keep the others on standby and have them wait for any new intel. There are a bunch of dog shows in California.

San Francisco has a show on Friday. My guess is Payton took the time off to go. There are shows all down the state for the next three weeks. I'd say it's a good fit for her timeline." Wyatt turned and left Tristan's office. Walking away he had another thought. "And Tristan."

"Yes, sir," Tristan said, using Wyatt's proper title in front of the other men.

"Make sure you keep in touch. Or I will keep informed using my own means," Wyatt said, without as much as breaking stride toward his office.

"Yes, sir, always threatening," Tristan said, with a slight smile.

Chapter Three

Tristan's Porsche 911 maneuvered the highway with ease. Driving gave him the time he needed to work through the last few days' events; he was still trying to fit the pieces together. His cell phone lit up and he tapped the screen on his dashboard.

"Hey Jack, what's up?"

"I tracked an outgoing call from Victory's cell a few seconds ago. The call originated from San Francisco, looks like she is at the fairgrounds."

"So it's highly probable Victory has reached her destination and is meeting up with her sister at the dog show. Question is, how long will they stay put?"

"The show goes for two days. You think they will take off before that?" Jack asked.

"No telling. Depends on Victory's state of mind, and Payton's reaction to what happened to her sister. Thanks Jack, I'll talk to you soon." Tristan tapped his screen off, grabbed a Red Bull out of the cooler in his passenger seat, popped the top, and turned up the volume on the Phil Collins song.

* * * *

Two hours later at a private airstrip outside of Seattle, a black Lincoln Navigator with black-tinted windows pulled up to the tarmac where a Cessna 400 sat idling. Two men got out of the Navigator, and were greeted by a third man standing by the plane.

"Hey Max, sorry to pull you back from your day off, but we needed a man with your experience on this job." Dave Anderson walked toward Max and greeted him with an outstretched hand.

"That's okay, Dave. The boss said he would pay me double time. So, who are we tracking?" Max asked, shaking Dave's hand.

"We've been trying to locate this Vic. We think she is the woman Jeffery told you he planned to meet up with. We located a woman who we believe might be this person. Her name is Victory Winters."

"How much does she know?" asked Max.

"That's part of the problem; we have no idea. She could be totally in the dark," Dave said.

"Come on, guys," Jerry jumped in. "Are we going to stand out here all day shooting the breeze or get on the damn plane?"

"He's a little cranky," Dave snickered. "He thinks someone beat him to Jeff's condo and searched it before he got there."

"I know they did, and it was a pro. Couldn't tell anything got misplaced, but the hairs on my arms stood up. I'll bet I just missed him."

All three men loaded their bags and got into the aircraft. Ten minutes later, the Cessna taxied down the runway, lifted off and disappeared into the steely gray sky.

* * * *

Victory arrived at the San Francisco Fairgrounds and got the directions to her sister's motor home. She pulled up alongside Payton's forty-five-foot custom-made Prevost. With four sliders, a king-size bed, full bath, and washer/dryer, everything a girl could ask for. The interior was professionally finished in a warm shade of sage with a coffee-colored leather overstuffed sofa and two huge chairs to match. The floor was wall-to-wall light cherry hardwood. There was even a small office where Payton did all her work while on the road. She called it her own private island.

Victory opened the door and was greeted by a big black Doberman madly wagging his short stub of a tail.

"Hey there, Parker." She lovingly rubbed the top of his head. "You holding down the fort? I guess everyone else must be ringside." As if understanding every word she said, Parker responded with a whine. "I know it's terrible to be retired. Look at it this way; you get your pick of the furniture while everyone is out." Victory rubbed his head one last time and closing the door she headed to the show grounds.

The show grounds were humming with activity. People pulled carts stacked high with dog crates and grooming supplies in one hand and leashes with excited dogs in the other. The dog show scene was its own little world distant from the day-to-day responsibilities of everyday life. No wonder Payton loved it so. What could be better than spending the day with your dogs, not a care in the world, at least for that moment in time?

Victory followed the flow of people to the main building. As she stepped through the door, the activity magnified; she was enveloped by barking dogs in crates, vendors, a loudspeaker, and the flow of exhibitors and their dogs warming up around the rings. She stood in the doorway and studied the building's layout.

For the first time since Jeffery's murder, Victory felt a soothing feeling flood her body. Being around all the dogs gave her stability, made her feel safe. She wandered through the building and stopped every now and then to look at the different breeds of dogs and some interesting items at the wide variety of vendor booths. She could feel the excitement in the air radiating off the dogs. Dog shows were great socializing environment for dogs, and for the most part she could sense they loved the sport.

* * * *

Victory was so tuned into the animals she was totally oblivious to the people around her. Leaning against a far wall, away from the frantic pace of the exhibitors, Tristan remained motionless, only his eyes tracking Victory's movements. The second she walked into the building, he'd sensed her. Even amidst the potpourri of grooming supplies, perfumes, hair products, perspiration, and various other human and canine odors, he was able to distinguish her scent as she approached the building. When she entered through the main door, once again he got hit with the subtle aura of lavender and chamomile. He didn't need her description or picture; Tristan could pick her out of the crowd solely by her essence.

He remained deadly still so as to blend into his surroundings and scanned the entire building, looking for anyone who appeared out of place. Not seeing anyone who looked a threat, he refocused his attention on Victory. As she walked toward him, Tristan studied her. She walked with lightness to her stride. She was dressed in a sweater and jeans but radiated sophistication. Her eyes were a deep jade, and, for a fleeting second, he caught a flash of anguish. Her shiny golden brown hair had a natural wave and fell past her shoulders. Her skin was flawless with a touch of pink on her cheeks, and her smile could light up a stormy night. As Victory approached him, he found himself mesmerized by her natural beauty and lost all focus on his assignment.

"For crying out loud, I feel like a school kid," he muttered to himself.

"Geez, I started to get worried. Your thoughts are unfocused. I guess she's a real looker. I got a little warm flush going." Wyatt popped into his thoughts and broke the spell.

"It's nothing; I was daydreaming for a bit," Tristan said.

"Don't. This is no time for daydreaming. Keep on task. You're likely not alone."

"Yeah, yeah, I know; I'm fine. I've located our target."

"Good. Your only assignment is to keep tabs on her for now, don't engage," Wyatt said.

"Roger that."

As quickly as Wyatt entered his mind, Tristan could feel his presence fade. All their lives, they'd been each other's constant companions. Tristan counted on Wyatt being there, it was a wonderful feeling, but sometimes, like now, having another person in his head was a real pain in the neck.

* * * *

Whenever Victory found herself in an enclosed space or in a crowd of people, she would often get the feeling of being watched. Over the years she realized, it was merely her ability to sense people's emotions. Coupled with her sharper-than-average hearing and it could make anyone neurotic. Had she not taught herself years ago how to filter out the bombardment of noise and emotion which now encompassed her, she would have fallen to her knees from the deluge of sensations.

Victory felt a whisper of electricity run the length of her spine. She paused. She didn't hear a specific conversation, and yet she could feel a conversation; this was new—what kind of sensation was this? Slowing her pace, she glanced around, and surveyed her surroundings. People seemed to be going about their business, grooming dogs or talking with friends or studying the competition. For one brief instant, she saw the back of a massively built man with jet-black hair; her attention had been drawn to him. In the blink of an eye, he disappeared out the door.

"Geez, now I'm really getting jumpy," she muttered to herself.

* * * *

"Wyatt, she knows I'm here." Tristan's thoughts pushed to reach for his brother as he turned and left the building.

"She can't possibly know you are there, you said you saw no one there when you found Jeffery. How would she even know to look for you?" Wyatt asked.

"I didn't see anyone. She wasn't there by the time I reached the scene. Nevertheless, when you and I first communicated, I watched her pace visibly slow as she scanned the area."

"Really. That's interesting. Could be no more than women's intuition."

"I'm not so sure. It seemed like more than that. Get Jack to use those cyber skills of his and do some more digging, see if he can find anything more on Victory Winters. I think she may have telepathic skills."

"I'll get him right on it, but in the meantime, watch yourself," Wyatt said.

Chapter Four

Payton stared at Victory in disbelief, tears trickling down her cheeks.

"Poor Jeffery. Are you okay? I can't believe it. I spoke to him about one of my research projects only last week."

"Maybe I should have called the police. But seeing Detective Howard there really spooked me. I wouldn't know whom I could trust," Victory said.

"No, Victory. You did the right thing. You have no idea who else might be involved in this, or how high up the ladder this goes. You left the scene. You could be a suspect as far as the police are concerned. No. Whoever these men are, they are dangerous. They didn't see you, therefore you are safe. There's nothing you can do for Jeffery now. Contact the police and you could find yourself in real trouble. Getting away for a while and leaving town was the best idea," Payton rambled on, trying to soothe her own mind.

"Detective Howard was the officer who interviewed all the department heads after my work colleague Lisa was found murdered in the company parking garage. That can't be a coincidence. Somehow, these two events must be connected."

Victory slumped in one corner of the sofa. Her big red Doberman Dax lay next to her; he rested his head on her leg and stared up at her soulfully with his infinite dark chocolate eyes. She ran her hand down his head and neck and then started to rub his ears; his velvety soft coat flowed under her hand. This constant connection with him was helping her to get through the horrors of the past few days.

"I keep playing out what you told me in my head, over and over again. I can't believe Jeffery is gone," Payton said.

"I know what you mean," Victory said, as tears again welled up in her eyes, making it difficult to focus on Dax's ears. "I wish he would have given me more details on the phone, but I guess I'll never know how I could have helped him. I can't believe he would have willingly been involved in anything so dangerous. Associating with those men wasn't the Jeffery I knew." She wiped at her wet cheeks. "I realize it's been five years since we last saw one another, however at one time I believed with all my heart, Jeffery was the one."

"He hadn't changed that much. He didn't know how dangerous those men were," Payton said.

She sat quietly for a moment watching her sister stroke Dax. "Dax really missed you this time, sis. He sits by the door for hours, looks out at the yard, and waits for you to come home," Payton whispered, trying to ease the pain she saw shimmering in her sister's eyes. "I'm glad you will be able to spend time with him. Maybe you should think about taking him on your next project."

Victory's job had kept her moving around over the last year. The family home, now owned by herself and her two sisters, Payton and Willow, served as her home base. She was currently working on a research project that required constant travel. Since Payton could stay at the family home, she kept Dax, along with the three other family Dobermans and sometimes other canine guests.

"Wow," Victory remarked. "You really did a great job putting this all together," she said, as if she just noticed her surroundings in the motor home.

"Yeah, it has everything I could ever need, my home away from home. I'm really glad you decided to find me. I keep thinking about those two men in the woods. Do they know you were the one Jeffery planned to meet?"

"No, at least I don't think so. They were questioning him about me, but he never revealed my name," Victory said. She thought for a moment. "He tried to keep me safe." Her revelation made the tears fall even harder.

"When I spoke with him last week, I wish I would have asked him what his current projects were," Payton said. "Since the two of you were out of touch for so long, I can only assume he wanted your help with a current project."

"Five years," Victory repeated. "We didn't see each other or speak to one another for five years. I'm not sure what Jeffery wanted. He phoned and basically asked me to meet him out at the picnic spot. He didn't elaborate about what he wanted to talk about. I have no idea how our research projects would coincide with one another."

From habit she stared down into Dax's bottomless eyes. She could feel he sensed her distress; it radiated off of him. She was born with the ability to read animals' feelings. Her ability came as natural as breathing to her.

While practicing veterinary medicine at a cutting-edge clinic in Seattle, she worked on an Australian shepherd for a soft-spoken gentleman named Todd. No one had been able to diagnose the problem with his dog, Sassy. The only real symptoms Sassy presented were that she didn't want to eat or play.

Victory mentally connected with Sassy and discovered she had two ribs stuck out of place. After only one chiropractic adjustment and a few acupuncture sessions, Sassy began acting like a puppy again, playing Frisbee and eating with gusto. Todd was extremely impressed with Victory and marveled at the fact she diagnosed the problem quickly. Todd had taken Sassy to three other vets, and all did extensive tests and X-rays, but none of them could diagnose the problem.

"She told me." Victory's only response when Todd asked how she diagnosed Sassy.

Over the next few months Todd and Victory became good friends. The two met every weekend at Green Lake Park to walk Dax and Sassy, who also became good friends. One afternoon Todd began telling her about his work.

"I work for a private research firm. We recently started this new division, basically it entails looking into the possibility of using dogs' DNA."

Victory's face lost all color as she stared at Todd. "What do you mean? You don't hurt them or do experiments on them, do you?"

"No, no, nothing like that. I guess I'm not explaining it quite right. We are trying to find a genetic link between the canine world and the human world. We are investigating the possibility of incorporating canine DNA with human DNA. We hope to discover a beneficial link to aid in curing diseases in humans. Along with this we are also trying to establish a baseline, looking into the possibility that some humans may possess heightened abilities, thereby already linking them to canine DNA. As of yet, we haven't been able to tap into any definite connection and haven't found anyone with the natural ability to really understand dog behavior. Frankly, during our last board meeting I thought of you. I told the board how you cured Sassy. They would like to know if you would be interested in leading the new research department," Todd said.

It happened eighteen months ago. Since then, Victory's life had become a whirlwind, and she loved it. She felt like she finally found the path she was born to walk, and she enjoyed every minute, except for the need to leave Dax at the family home. She needed to change the current situation and have Dax be with her.

"Victory." Payton's voice pushed into Victory's thoughts, concern in her tone.

"Hmm?" Victory looked up at Payton and brought herself back to the present.

"I asked you about those men, the ones in the woods. You knew Detective Howard, but the other guy, the one who actually pulled the trigger, did you know him? I can't believe Jeffery would knowingly put you in danger."

Victory could feel Payton's panic. "I don't know the other man. I've never seen him before. I couldn't get a clear view of his face and his voice was unfamiliar. Jeffery didn't mention anyone else would meet with us. I know he wouldn't put me in danger intentionally."

"And why in the woods? Jeffery was never an outdoors man. You are really sure they were not aware you were there?" Payton kept repeating herself. Victory knew Payton hoped the repetition would dislodge new memories in Victory's mind.

"No, I stayed too far away to be seen. I'm sure they had no idea I was there. But that's why I came to you in California. So no one could place me out in the forest."

"Won't they miss you at the lab? Call your condo looking for you?" Payton asked.

"No, even when I'm in town I work away from the facility quite often. I didn't bring everything I needed, but fortunately I left my laptop in the Jeep. I called in to the office when I arrived in San Francisco and told my assistant I'd discovered a lead on one of my projects and decided to follow up."

* * * *

Payton studied Victory; it looked apparent that shock finally started to set in. Victory's glassy eyes and ashen complexion concerned her. "You're safe now. You look beat. Why don't you go back and grab a nap? Take Dax."

"I guess the events in the woods really drained me. I thought I would help you finish loading first."

"I'm pretty much done, at least until tomorrow. Are you sure you want to stay for the show tomorrow?" Payton asked.

"Yes, I don't want you to change plans at the last minute. Any changes could look as if we have something to hide. We need to continue on as if nothing happened. If you really don't need any help, I am feeling worn out."

* * * *

Dave Anderson and Jerry James sat in the coffee shop down the block from the fairgrounds. They had been there for over an hour, each on their third drink, they waited for Max to return from recon.

"You are absolutely positive there was no one else out there when you shot Jeff?" Dave asked.

"Not another soul. Me, Ken, Jeff, and all the dumbass birds, no one else," Jerry said.

Suddenly Max was standing beside their table.

"Jesus." Jerry jumped, spilling his latte down his shirt front. "For Chrissakes, can't you make some noise when you approach?" He spat the words at Max as he reached for the nearest napkin in an attempt to wipe some of the hot latte from his shirt.

"Damn Jerry, we can't take you anywhere." Dave laughed at the sight of Jerry, his crisp white shirt now covered in coffee.

"Sorry, I thought you saw me coming," Max said, knowing full well he'd not been seen.

"You know no one ever sees or hears you coming unless you want them too. That's one of the reasons we hired you." Dave attempted to stop his snickering at Jerry's misfortune. "So, did you find her?"

"I took a couple of pictures on my phone and sent them back to the office to verify our target. What's the next step if it is her?"

Both Max and Jerry looked at Dave.

"We are supposed to keep tabs on her, to shadow her. We need to know if she really knows anything and if so, how much," Dave said.

Forty-five minutes later, Dave's phone beeped and lit up with a message. "Got our answer; lab confirms her identity. The boss wants an update every day."

"This would be good downtime for me." Max stretched and rubbed his eyes. "I spoke with a couple of people while I scouted the fairgrounds. Looks like this dog show will continue for the rest of the weekend."

"Okay, then we'll take shifts. I'll go in first and keep an eye on her. You and Jerry head back to the hotel and get some rest. Jerry, you're next up. Meet me at the Denny's up the block at ten tonight," Dave instructed.

Jerry glanced down at his watch; he had barely four hours to get some rest. "Great, night shift," he grumbled.

"You got it. We need Max to get some rest. I want him at the top of his game when we need him."

* * * *

Tristan walked between the trailers and motor homes; he moved quietly and stayed in the shadows. The place was so buttoned up he could hear the traffic a mile out on the highway. It amazed him only two hours ago the place reminded him of a zoo, dogs barking, people laughing and talking, cars coming and going. Now there wasn't a soul around, and the dogs were all put to bed and quiet. He glanced down at his watch; only eleven o'clock. He walked to space eighty-nine and found a large custom Prevost. There wasn't a single light shining through the windows of the motor home, so he crept closer to get a good look around.

An instant later he picked up a fresh scent approaching from the west, and given the wind, heading his way. A familiar scent, human and male, stale coffee, and yeah, there it was—Old Spice. He slid under the motor home and lay flat on the ground behind the wheels.

* * * *

Jerry searched the fairgrounds looking for space eighty-nine. He knew the motor home Victory ran to was parked there, except he was having a hell of a time finding it. There weren't any clear markings around. The hell with it; he would look for a "big" motor home; those were Dave's exact words. He examined the parking area around him and spotted a likely vehicle one row up. That had to be it, one of the largest motor homes on the fairgrounds and very custom-looking.

He approached cautiously, taking in his immediate surroundings. He could swear he was being watched, only there wasn't a soul around. Probably coffee jitters; he'd spent hours in the local coffee shop today, and this wasn't his type of gig. He was much more the in-your-face and conquer kind of guy. This type of work made his blood run all right, but not with the high he loved.

He was standing in the shadow of the RV right next to Victory's when a light flicked on in her motor home.

"Aw shit," he muttered as he flattened himself to the back of the vehicle.

* * * *

Victory didn't know what troubled her, but something had woken her from her fitful sleep. The scenes in the forest kept playing through her dreams. There it was again, a sound, different from the ones she'd grown used to since she arrived here. It was a whisper on the wind, a rustle of movement, maybe someone rubbing against something. Whatever it was, it had woken her and she needed to get up and take a look around. She switched on the table lamp and got out of bed. Dax was awake and alert in the same instant.

"You heard something too," she said to Dax. "Let's go take a quick look around; if I don't, I'll lie here awake all night."

Without turning on any other lights she padded down the dark hall to the main door, unlocked it, and cracked it open. Dax thrust his nose in the opening and took a long sniff, as he tried to shove his way past Victory.

"Easy Dax; you stay right here."

With his head pushed against her leg, she could feel the vibration of a low, guttural growl coming from him.

"Shhh, I can't hear anything with you grumbling."

He stopped instantly and sniffed again.

Victory opened the door a little wider; at the same time, she gave Dax a hand signal to stay put. She softly stepped down the stairs. She could hear the gentle snores of numerous dogs and people, and a couple moving around inside their motor home. She stood on the bottom stair, closed her eyes, and blocked out all the familiar sounds around her. She searched for a sound that was out of place: breathing, movement, anything that would signal impending danger. She couldn't pick up anything sounding out of the ordinary. After a minute she turned and retreated back into the motor home.

* * * *

An instant later Tristan blew out the breath he started holding from the minute he saw the door open, and silently moved away from the motor home. When he'd walked far enough away from Victory, he reached out for his brother. *"Wyatt...Wyatt."*

"What's up? Do you know it's after midnight? What are you still doing up? Don't tell me something happened to Victory," Wyatt said.

"Yes and no. Did you find out any more information on her?"

"Not yet, but I've got Jack doing some digging to get more information on her current project."

"Something's definitely different about her. It's like she can hear the minutest sound, similar to my scenting ability. I was doing some recon when Mr. Old Spice joined me."

"His name is Jerry James and he works for Biotec, exactly like Jeffery did," Wyatt said.

"Really, so Biotec wants Victory."

"Looks like, but we aren't one hundred percent sure yet."

"Jerry slithered away as soon as Victory turned her lights on. I think they have been ordered to keep tabs on her for the time being. Probably trying to figure out how much she knows without alerting her to their presence. Let me know as soon as you find out any more information."

Tristan scouted the fairgrounds; he kept an eye out for Jerry and his crew. Two hours later all was still quiet, no sign of anyone in the area. Tristan walked back to his Porsche, started the engine, and headed for his hotel. Experience told him nothing more would be happening tonight. If Jerry meant Victory any harm he was given the perfect opportunity to grab her; of course he would have had to deal with a very large Doberman.

Chapter Five

At the crack of dawn, Victory was awakened by blow-dryers and barking dogs, as people and dogs got ready for their second day of showing. She rolled over to reach for Dax and realized Payton had taken him with her. She got out of bed, threw on an old pair of jeans and a sweater, and headed out to the main salon of the motor home.

The aroma of coffee led her to the half empty pot, a mug, a scone, and a note from her sister.

"About time you got up, sleepyhead. Yes, Dax is with me, along with all the others. I left you Parker, who's simply along for the ride. As soon as you have some breakfast, head out to ring number five; that's where my setup will be. I think the dogs could all use adjustments before they show. Luv ya, Payton."

As she read the note, Parker got off the sofa and joined her for breakfast. He sat next to her and pressed his head into her thigh in hopes of a pet and scones. Victory could hear his plea for both.

"I know you want some. Lay down next to me while I have some breakfast. If you are good, I will save you a bite or two."

Parker eased himself to the floor, looking up at her with longing, dark eyes.

"I think you will be my first patient of the day, Parker. You're very uncomfortable. Is your hip causing you problems again?"

Parker wagged his short tail.

Victory finished her breakfast and made sure she fulfilled her promise to Parker by sharing her scone. Then she set about realigning his hip bone. She ran her hands lightly down his black satin coat. She started at the top of his head and never removed her hands until she reached the tip of his tail. She noticed a few warm spots and adjusted his spine at those points.

"I think you have a few more trouble spots. Later this afternoon, I will pull out my needles and do some acupuncture on you."

Parker answered with a lick on her face. She gave him one last pat, slipped on her sneakers, and headed out the door.

Entering the main building, she was again amazed by the hum of activity. The building was more crowded today, with an influx of spectators admiring the variety of breeds. Victory looked down and noticed in her haste to leave the motor home, she'd forgotten to tie her sneakers. Without a thought she bent down to fix the problem and got instantly swallowed up by the crowd.

She was knocked off balance and started to fall. She immediately felt two huge hands slip around her rib cage, and she got pulled up to her feet. Simultaneously a warm current swamped her body.

"Thank you. I really should have moved out of the flow of traffic before attempting such a feat."

"No problem, glad I could help," a male voice answered.

By the time Victory recovered her balance and turned around to introduce herself, the man had melted back into the crowd. She was surprised he'd left.

"Huh, he must be late for his ring."

She looked into the flow of people and was sure she caught sight of the same tall man with glossy jet-black hair she'd noticed the day before.

Payton looked up at Victory without missing a beat of her dog grooming.

"You look much less peaked today, but your energy is still low. I was wondering if you would do me a favor and go over each of the Dobermans before I take them into the ring. But only if you feel up to it," she added.

"No problem; I'd be happy to."

As she had done with Parker, she ran her hands slowly down each dog, making slight adjustments where they were needed. Only after she'd finished the last dog did she turn to talk to Payton.

"It could easily be my nerves, but I'm having the strangest feelings."

Payton stopped grooming and looked up to give Victory her full attention.

"What do you mean strange, like funny strange or scary?"

"I'm having the distinct feeling someone is watching or maybe even talking about me. I can't get a clear link. By the time I feel them, it's almost like they feel my presence and shut down."

"You mean like you sensed them," Payton clarified.

"Sort of, but it isn't exactly the same."

Payton looked slowly around them.

"I know most of these people, have for a long time. Of course, I can't account for all the spectators, but I don't see anyone who looks out of place."

"The feeling's gone now. I did notice a man leaving the building yesterday when I first felt this way, but I only saw the back of his head. A few minutes ago, I tried to tie my sneakers and nearly fell. A man helped me up, and when he touched me I felt this electrical current run through me."

"What did he look like?"

"That's the tough part. He approached me from the back. I thanked him and he responded, but before I could turn around he disappeared into the crowd," Victory said.

"I think it's time we leave. I should be done showing in the next thirty minutes."

"So where were you planning on going next?" Victory asked.

"The next show isn't for three days and the site is no more than a couple of hours away. I have reserved a spot in the Redwood National Park and thought I would camp for a couple of days," Payton said.

"That sounds great. Let's stick to your plan and camp; it will provide the perfect opportunity to unwind."

Victory and Payton packed up the motor home in record time. They pulled out of the fairgrounds, taking no notice of the small Winnebago View pulling out behind them.

* * * *

"I wouldn't exactly call this stealth," Jerry complained as he looked around the Winnebago. "What's the top speed, fifty miles per hour?"

"Oh stop your bitching Jerry, it's great for sleeping." Max yawned as he stretched out on the sofa.

"Stealth is not what we're after," Dave replied from the driver's seat. "Our intel says the girls will be heading for another dog show. This is our best bet for staying close and blending in."

"How much longer do we need to tail them? When are we going to know our next move?" Jerry asked.

"For now we keep doing what we're doing. I will be talking with the boss tomorrow; we'll get any updates then," Dave said.

"Great," Jerry whined. "I love tailing a girl all day."

"What's it matter to you?" Max chimed in; his eyes were closed and at first glance anyone would have thought him asleep. "We get paid either way."

"I know. I'm getting antsy; I'm ready for a little action. I feel like I'm following my grandmother."

He failed to mention the he'd nearly been seen by Victory the night before.

"I'm sure we will have our fill of action soon enough," Dave said. "In the meantime, why don't you take Max's advice and grab a nap, since you'll have night watch tonight."

"Again," he moaned.

"I swear to God, the boss must think you're good at whatever it is you do, because I sure wouldn't put up with all your bitching," Max said.

Jerry glared at him through half-closed lids but thought it best not to respond. Instead he got up from the passenger seat and headed for the empty bed in the back.

Three hours later, they pulled into the Redwood National Park and followed the girls to the RV campgrounds.

"Good decision on the Winnie, Dave. We would have a hell of a time blending in with a Lincoln, and I bet there isn't a hotel within an hour of here," Max said with a smirk.

"Thanks. I'll go in and register."

Dave parked the Winnebago and headed for the office. Ten minutes later he climbed back in the motor home.

"Good thing the park ranger is chatty. He told me the girls plan on being here for the next two days."

"Great, out in the woods again. Not a coffee shop in sight," Jerry grumbled.

"You're lucky I thought to stock food before we took off. We have plenty to last for a few days," Dave said, and glared at him.

* * * *

A few minutes later, a sleek midnight-blue Porsche 911 pulled up to the main office. This was the kind of job Tristan loved. He'd packed his one-man tent along with enough provisions for a week. His past experiences in the service taught him how to be prepared and pack only the necessities. He knew he would be on the other end of the park away from the RV parking along with the other tent campers. He didn't mind. He looked forward to getting out and walking in the clean mountain air.

Tristan set everything up and headed out to canvas the campgrounds. It was early evening and the sun started to set behind the evergreens, giving off a warm golden glow. He came up to the Prevost. As he approached the motor home he noticed the door stood open to allow the Dobermans free rein to go in and out of the vehicle into an enclosure made of metal exercise pens that ran along the side and back of the vehicle. He saw two imposing Doberman males glaring at him. They didn't make a sound and didn't break eye contact with Tristan as he continued past the motor home.

Tristan caught the tip of a scent cone, and a familiar odor filled his nostrils; Old Spice. The odor intermingled with something new; Polo. The two scents intertwined, but Tristan knew they belonged to two separate individuals. He had become well versed with Old Spice, that scent belonged to Jerry. The other, Polo, must be an associate of Jerry's. Seems the girls did not arrive at the campgrounds alone. He followed the spoor down the road; the odor grew stronger with each step. Four sites away, he spotted a small Winnebago and a man asleep on a lounge chair beside it. Based on Wyatt's description, Mr. Polo had to be Dave Anderson, probably the ring leader.

Tristan ducked into the bushes; no time like the present to get a feel for the group. Quietly he moved in the shadow of the vegetation, not disturbing a single branch, and blended effortlessly with the foliage. He picked up the aura of two men inside the Winnebago. The familiar aroma of Jerry's Old Spice confirmed Tristan's suspicions that these were indeed the men tailing Victory. The third scent was new; the odor tugged at him. It belonged to a strong, confident, dominant individual. After a few more minutes he retreated from the motor home and retraced his path to his tent.

He stepped into his tent and grabbed his backpack off the sleeping bag. He dug through it and pulled out his phone, flipped it open, and punched in the office number.

"SOCOM, Noah here."

"Hey there, Noah, nice to have you back," Tristan said.

"Hey, Tristan. I finished my assignment yesterday. Caught up on my sleep and thought you guys could use my help," Noah said.

"Always welcome. So are you up-to-date on what's happening?"

"Yes. The captain briefed me first thing this morning.

"It looks like there is a crew tracking Victory, a standard three-man team. They have set up shop in a Winnebago a few spots down the way from the girls. Two of the men work for Biotec; my best guess is they are all employed by the company. See if you can do some poking around and find out about our third guy. His name is Max. I want to get a heads up on any special traits. I have a feeling he might be ex-military," Tristan said.

"Will do."

"Great. I'm getting a feel for the place tonight. All's quiet now, I think I will call it a day and hit the bunk early. I'm sure tomorrow will prove to be a long day," Tristan said.

"Roger, I'll talk with you soon," Noah said.

Early the following morning Tristan finished his breakfast and decided to check on the girls and their shadows. He strapped a hunting knife to his belt, put his hat and sunglasses on, and picked up his walking stick. He headed out of his tent once again in the direction of Victory and Payton's motor home. He strolled slowly and stopped every now and then to examine the foliage along the path.

Inside the exercise pen, a large black male Doberman and a smaller red female were stretched out on the ground, lying on their sides sunning themselves. Tristan slowly approached the motor home and presented a feeling of calm so as not to create a negative reaction by the two Dobermans or startle Victory, who was in the back storage locker digging through supplies.

Victory sputtered to Dax who was standing next to her wagging his tail.

"Your Aunt Payton sure knows how to pack a lot of supplies into this small storage, Dax, only she forgets all this stuff will need to come out again."

She was half inside the storage area trying to pull a bicycle out. She grabbed hold of the bike and pulled at it with all her might. Instead of pulling the bike free, her hands slipped, and she fell back out of the storage area and slammed on to the ground.

"Looks like you could use a hand," Tristan smiled, trying to stifle his laugh.

* * * *

Victory snapped her head around toward the male voice. She found herself gazing up into magical violet eyes, smooth olive skin, a straight nose, and high full cheekbones. All were exquisitely framed by shiny black hair cut right above his collar, his hair looked a little unruly with a natural wave. His body was broad and from what she could tell in excellent shape. He stood tall; at least six foot four and astonishingly quiet on his feet, since she didn't hear his approach and her dogs had not alerted her. She stood up and casually brushed the dirt from her jeans and hands.

"Thanks, I guess I could use some help. My sister believes in cramming as much into a small space as absolutely possible," Victory said, a slight tinge of pink flushed her cheeks.

Tristan extended his arm out over the exercise pens, showing no fear of the dogs. Victory reached out to take his hand.

"Hi, I'm Tristan Farraday."

"Nice to meet you, Tristan, I'm Victory Winters. Have we met before?" she asked, having the strangest feeling she had met this man.

"No, and I can honestly say I would certainly remember meeting you," Tristan said as he smiled down at her.

Dax poked at Tristan's arm. Tristan reached down under his chin and scratched.

"Dax likes you," she said, with surprise in her voice.

"I have that effect on dogs. Guess it's true dogs can sense who likes them." Tristan continued rubbing Dax.

The two dogs that were lying in the sun both lifted their heads in unison and looked up at Tristan.

"The big black guy sunning himself is Parker and the red girl is Kes."

"Wow, you have a lot of Dobermans."

"We have one more, Asia; she's out taking a walk with my sister."

"Would you like me to get your bike out?" Tristan asked.

"Yes, thanks. See where the clips hold the pens shut?" Victory said, as she pointed up near the front of the Prevost. "Go ahead and come on in; the dogs won't bother you."

Tristan walked down to where Victory told him to enter. As he opened the pens, both Parker and Kes got up to greet him.

"Parker, Kes, sit," Victory commanded.

"They don't bother me. I love dogs."

Tristan walked to the back of the motor home and looked into the storage area. "Wow, looks like you packed for a month."

"Yeah, Payton likes to be prepared."

"Payton, oh your sister?" Tristan asked.

"Yes, Payton is my sister."

A few minutes later Tristan had rearranged the storage area and carefully slid the bike out.

"Thank you so much," Victory said. "That could have taken me hours, and I don't even want to think how many times I would have ended up on the ground." She looked up at Tristan, grinning.

"I wouldn't want that. Glad to be of service." He walked the bike up to the side of the motor home.

"I could use a cold drink. Would you like to join me, that is, if I'm not keeping you from anything?" Victory asked.

"Nothing that can't wait; I would love a drink."

Victory disappeared into the motor home and returned with two tall glasses of iced tea. It surprised her that Tristan managed to dig out two of the folding chairs and a small table while she poured their tea and came back out. He was relaxing in a chair with his feet stretched out in front of him. Parker lay at his feet while both Kes and Dax rested their heads in his lap, clearly enjoying their ear rubs. Victory reached out to the three Dobermans with her mind and found calm and contentment.

"Boy, my guys like most people, but they don't usually warm up to them this fast," she said as she handed Tristan a glass.

"What can I say? I guess I'm simply a likeable kind of guy, as far as animals are concerned." He sipped his tea and then put the glass on the small table. "So, what brings you here, vacation?"

"Sort of. My sister shows dogs, and I'm here to help her out on the circuit. We have a couple days break and thought this would be a nice place to unwind." Victory picked up her drink and took another sip. "How about you?"

"Working vacation. I'm studying the local foliage and it's a great time for me to get my camping fix," Tristan said.

"Oh, you're a botanist," Victory said with excitement. How interesting. She would enjoy talking to Tristan.

* * * *

"Yes, I am," Tristan wasn't lying; one of his three degrees was in botany, and it served him effectively on many assignments when he needed plants for healing or poisons.

"Botany is one of my favorite hobbies. I use it often," Victory was as excited as a child at Christmas. "I would love to pick your brain while I'm here." Victory smiled at Tristan.

Wow, her smile is mesmerizing, Tristan thought.

"Sounds like fun. I have no set schedule, so any time." Having researched her background he knew this would be a great way to stay close to the women.

Tristan and Victory chattered for hours about the local foliage and Tristan's research. Victory invited him to stay for dinner, as a thank you for helping her. Suddenly all three Dobermans alerted, posed like sentinels, not moving a muscle. In unison three stubby tails started wagging feverishly and they began whining. Payton appeared, beside her a small black Doberman bitch carrying a red Kong in her mouth. Tristan's attention was drawn to the sight of the three guardians.

"Boy, I guess nothing gets by them," he said.

Victory's gaze followed Tristan's. "Not a thing. That's the bonus with having Dobermans, forever on guard."

"I left for only part of the day and you found a new friend," Payton said as she approached the Prevost, with a dazzling smile on her face. Tristan could easily see the resemblance between the sisters, even with Payton's deep auburn hair and hazel eyes, the two girls were no doubt related.

"Hey sis, have a nice walk? This is Tristan. He was nice enough to use himself as a human can opener to pry out my bike and chairs from the back storage. I swear to God, I don't know how you can possibly pack so much stuff into such a small space." Victory shook her head at her sister.

"Believe me, it's an art." Payton opened the exercise pen and let the little black Doberman enter first. The other three all ran up to her and gave her the smell test to find out where she'd been. Asia ignored them and walked up to Tristan. Both Payton and Victory looked at one another, dumbfounded.

"It seems you have a way with our dogs. Asia is usually very standoffish with strangers, mainly because she is still young and unsure," Payton said.

"Nice to meet you, Asia," Tristan said and reached down to scratch under her chin.

"It seems dogs really like Tristan," Victory said, staring in surprise at Asia.

"So it seems," Payton said. "Hi Tristan, I'm Payton, Victory's older sister."

"Funny, you don't look older," Tristan said, as he grinned at the sisters.

"I like him already. I'm not that much older, about ten minutes."

"You're twins?"

A unique detail that had been overlooked in their initial research.

"Actually, we're triples. Willow is the baby."

"Really." Tristan found himself a loss for words. He knew what it felt like to be a twin, but wondered how different it would be to be one of three. "Will Willow be joining us for dinner?"

"No, she didn't come with us on this trip," Payton said.

Tristan noticed Payton wasn't quite as forthcoming and open as her sister seemed to be.

* * * *

"Status," Max barked as Jerry walked in the door of the Winnebago.

"Not much. The girls are having dinner with some local camper," Jerry said.

"What's he look like?" Max asked.

"Just some local yahoo. They've been talking bushes and stuff, nothing worthwhile."

Jerry inhaled a deep breath through his nose, savoring the smell of steaks that were on the table. "They're not going anywhere. Can I stay and have dinner now?"

Dave looked up from his newspaper into Jerry's pleading brown puppy dog eyes. "Shit. Jerry, you act like you haven't eaten in a week. Yeah, sit down. We should be hearing from the office first thing tomorrow."

Chapter Six

At eight in the morning Dave was on his laptop engaged in a conference call with headquarters. He insisted on being alone in the Winnebago so Jerry and Max were exiled, left to wrap themselves in blankets and huddle around the fire pit in the chill morning air. One hour later the door to the RV swung open and Dave emerged holding a large steaming mug of coffee. The two men looked at him with murder in their eyes.

"You guys look cold. You should come in and get some coffee."

Jerry and Max looked at one another, got up, and headed into the RV.

"Took ya long enough," Max grumbled on his way in.

Jerry and Max got their coffee and joined Dave around the table.

"Headquarters researched Victory; she has the expertise we need, and they want her to take Jeffery's position. In fact, they feel she probably has more knowledge and will be a better fit."

"So, now she has to be convinced to come to work for Biotec," Max said.

"Yes, currently she's working for a competitor. HQ wants me to contact her via email and see if I can sway her to come on board."

"And if not?" Max asked.

"Then we go to plan B."

"I'm hoping the plan is to start right away. I hate camping," Jerry said.

"I'll be sending her an email this morning."

* * * *

Victory loved being away from her everyday responsibilities. In an effort to clear her mind of Jeffery, she got up at first light, took out her bike, leashed up Dax and Asia, and went for a morning ride. The park was beautiful and so peaceful, she could hear the sound of every bird, animal, and insect. She returned to the motor home, made coffee and breakfast, pulled out her laptop, and sat down in one of the overstuffed chairs in the main salon.

Being away was good, but she still needed to stay in touch with the office. She read and answered her email until she came to an unfamiliar address and a subject line surprising her. Knocking her coffee onto the floor, she grabbed her computer and ran to Payton's bedroom.

"Payton, wake up. You have to see the email I received. You won't believe this."

"What time is it? It can't be morning yet. What are you doing up? This is supposed to be our vacation,"

Payton said, as she stretched and rubbed the sleep from her eyes.

"You have to see this now. And yes, it is morning."

Payton took the laptop from Victory. She placed it on her lap and turned to stack some pillows behind her back.

"Payton," Victory whined impatiently.

"Okay, okay. 'Dear Ms. Winters, My name is Dave Anderson. I am an Executive Vice President for Biotec. Ms. Winters, you were referred by Jeffery Maxwell. I would like to arrange an appointment to talk about the possibility of you coming to work for our company. Jeffery has been working on a project and unfortunately the company transferred him to one of our satellite offices. He believes you would be highly qualified to become lead project manager for the project he has left behind. Please contact me at your earliest convenience.'"

Payton finished reading the email and looked up at Victory, her hazel eyes shining bright and huge.

"Yeah, right. Jeffery was 'transferred.' You are *so* not going to fall for this."

"We have no idea who murdered Jeffery, except for the fact that Detective Howard was there. I heard nothing to indicate his company was behind the murder. We have no way of knowing if he might have been involved in something on the sly. We've both known good people who were swayed by money. Dave Anderson is probably in the dark about Jeffery's whereabouts and believes he was transferred. But before I tell him no, maybe I can pull some information out of him about what project Jeffery was working on," Victory said, as she typed out a response and sent it.

Victory's computer beeped, alerting her of an incoming email.

Payton pulled the laptop away from Victory and read the new email.

"'Dear Ms. Winters, I can't really get into the details of Jeffery's project over the Internet because of his highly classified work. Suffice it to say, your skills and past experience would be a good fit,'" Payton said.

"That's very gray. I have worked on hundreds of different projects; it looks like we're not going to get any information from Mr. Anderson. Time to mention I already have a job I love, thank you very much," Victory said.

"A good start, but I bet it isn't enough to make them go away. Based on what you heard in the woods, it sounds like there are not very many people available with the type of skills they need. However, I find it difficult to believe Biotec would be involved in Jeffery's murder," Payton said.

"I'm not interested in the position anyway."

Victory took her computer back from Payton and started to type. "Dear Mr. Anderson, Thank you so much for your invitation. I am flattered. However, I have a job I like very much, with a company I love. Therefore, I will have to turn down your offer. Thank you for thinking of me." Victory pushed the send button without another thought.

"Don't you even want my input?" Payton asked.

"Sorry, sis. I ripped the bandage off, short and sweet."

Payton looked at her sister sitting next to her on the bed and smiled.

"Fine. Then get out of my way. If I have to be awake at this ungodly hour of the morning, I hope you made coffee."

She gave Victory a little shove and slipped on her hot pink sweats and gray sweatshirt.

"A whole pot, minus one cup that's currently soaking into the carpet," Victory said.

The two of them wandered down the hall to the kitchen, followed closely by four Dobermans.

"I'll feed the kids so you can have your breakfast."

"Thanks, sis," Payton said.

"No problem, I already ate."

Fifteen minutes later Victory's laptop beeped. She opened it up and started to scroll through her inbox.

"Man, he's going to be persistent; listen to this. 'Dear Ms. Winters, I think you would find this project extremely interesting. Could we please meet to discuss the project? We would be willing to pay you whatever you think is fair. Maybe you could take a year leave of absence from your current company, or possibly we could work something else out and you could do both. At least give me a chance to buy you a cup of coffee–that's all I ask. Dave Anderson.'"

"Boy, they really want you. Now what are you going to do?" asked Payton.

"I don't know. How many ways can you say no? Maybe I should say I can't meet because I'm out of town. Or maybe I should meet with him and see if I can get any information or feelings from him. He might know something about what happened to Jeffery," Victory said.

"Don't even go there, Victory. You are going to get yourself into trouble. Like you said, we don't even know who murdered Jeffery. Maybe Dave Anderson is looking for witnesses."

"I've been searching for news about Jeffery on the web and so far no mention of him. It's like he fell off the face of the Earth. That's not right. His family will start asking questions soon," Victory said.

"Let them ask. Then maybe someone will start looking for him. We'll do what we can, but I don't want you mixed up in it," Payton said.

"I'll send back an email and tell him I'm out of town and see what he says, no harm in that," Victory said.

Payton looked at her sister with concern on her face.

"I know how you get when you decide to take on a cause, nothing can stop you," Payton said. "I just don't want it to get that far."

Victory started typing. She'd barely hit the send button when she got a reply. "'I do hate to disturb you while you are on vacation, but the nature of this project demands action sooner rather than later. If you are at least willing to meet with me over a cup of coffee, I can be in any city of your choice, with adequate notice of course.'" Victory finished reading the email and looked over at her sister. "I've got him hooked."

"Yes, you do. So how are you going to play this out?"

"Tomorrow we head out for the Sacramento shows. But you don't show tomorrow; you're only setting up and grooming dogs."

"That's right. The first show is the following day."

"I thought if you didn't need me, it would be a good time for me to get together with Dave."

"This whole idea is making me nervous," Payton said. "The last thing I want is for you to become involved with someone who might know something about Jeffery's murder."

"I'll be fine, sis," Victory said.

"Okay, but you need to play this safe. You make sure to pick somewhere with a lot of people and keep your phone with you," Payton said.

* * * *

Tristan sat inside his tent. He'd finished his breakfast and was updating his daily logs when his cell rang. He looked at the ID and flipped it open to answer.

"Hey Wyatt, I'm hoping you have some news on your end."

"That's my line. It's been kind of strange not 'talking' to you."

"Yeah, I know. But I don't want to freak Victory out or give her any reason to question me. I'm sure she can sense our telepathy. What I'm not sure about is how close to her I have to be to have her sense us; so for now, better safe than sensed."

"I have to agree. We don't want to spook her, so back to the initial question," Wyatt said.

"I had dinner with the girls last night. I didn't get a lot of time to wander freely. But we did have some good conversations, and Victory told me bits and pieces about her position with Claremont. Nothing in great detail, as it is classified, I know she loves her job and is loyal to the company. I believe she was not involved with Jeffery at the time of the murder. He must have thought she was the only one who could help him with his project. Don't know yet how she ended up at the scene of the murder, but my gut tells me the part she plays is an innocent one," said Tristan.

"That's basically what we have deducted here. The only question now is, do we pull the plug on Victory Winters' tail, or do I leave you in the field for a few more days?"

"The fact still remains, she has three men from Biotec camped out a few spots down the way from her, and it doesn't look like they are going away any time soon. They are obviously interested in her. Besides, it's not like we have any other leads at the moment," Tristan said.

"You have a point. Okay, I'll give you three days. If nothing happens in that time, I need you back here. And Tristan: keep me updated. Don't make me have to call you, via phone or thought."

"Got it; talk to you tonight." Tristan snapped his phone shut. He set about organizing and packing, since he knew the girls would be heading out for Sacramento tomorrow, and he wanted to be ready to leave on a moment's notice. Today, he would wander around the park and eventually end up at the girls' motor home.

* * * *

"It took some doing, but I got her to meet with me." Dave was on his phone to his boss at Biotec. "She thinks I am flying into Sacramento tomorrow. How do you want me to play this?"

He listened intently and responded, "No, she hasn't seen me out here; I've made sure of it. I sent the guys out to keep tabs on her while I kept a low profile. Yes,

I'll get it done. The Cessna will be waiting for us in Sacramento."

Dave got off the phone and looked at Jerry and Max.

"Tomorrow you two really start earning your money. Victory has agreed to meet me for coffee in the middle of downtown Old Sacramento. By the end of the day we have to get her into the Cessna without being noticed by anyone; it won't be a problem, will it?"

"No problem at all," Max said. "This is exactly the type of work I live for."

Chapter Seven

Early the next morning, Victory and Payton finished their last round of dog walks. They did their final check around the Prevost and headed to Sacramento. Ten minutes later a midnight-blue Porsche 911 pulled out behind them and shadowed them down the road.

Tristan felt antsy this morning. He'd scouted the park the night before and noticed the guys packing up and getting ready to head out. He got more than close enough to discern the notable stench of adrenaline. Unfortunately they were conversing in low murmurs, which had made it impossible for him to hear what they planned. At one point he did catch snippets of their conversation: something about a lot to do before Thursday and a busy place. Tristan had no concrete evidence, but he'd bet money they were arranging something that revolved around Victory. He kept watch on the crew until they headed out a few hours later. Now he was agitated because for the first time, they were one step ahead of him. His priority now was to make sure he didn't lose Victory.

Tristan tapped the screen on his dashboard and called the office.

"SOCOM, Logan."

"Morning, Logan. So you're riding the desk. You mean to tell me there isn't anything exciting the captain can send you on back there?"

"Funny. Nope. Seems he thinks you might need a babysitter. Of course, I'm the best man for the job."

"I don't need a damn babysitter," Tristan snapped.

"You never know, and you usually do."

"Very funny; I need to speak with him."

"Okay, hold on for one sec. You haven't lost your women have you?" Logan asked.

"No. We're on our way to Sacramento. Right on schedule."

"Okay, but if you need me, give me a call."

"I'll keep that in mind."

"Tristan, what's your status?" Wyatt asked.

"The Biotec guys pulled out last night. I think they made contact with our target and have a plan in place for Sacramento."

"You called that one. Jack tapped into Victory's emails last night. Dave Anderson from Biotec has made contact with her. He was adamant about meeting with Victory to discuss a special project they would like her expertise in. She told him no a couple of times, but he kept coming at her. If I were to hazard a guess, I would say her curiosity finally got the best of her, and she wants to know why her friend got killed. She's playing with fire, Tristan. Make sure you stay on top of the situation. They made her a job offer on a very important contract. Someone at Biotec seems to feel Ms. Winters is the best candidate."

"Or they're trying to lure her in and clean up any loose ends," Tristan said.

"That is certainly a possibility. Our job now is to keep her alive, away from them, and find out what this project is about. I think you might need some backup. It's looking more and more like we were on the right trail, and Biotec is somehow involved in this DNA manipulation. This could get really ugly. Biotec is a powerful company," Wyatt said.

"Let me scout it out and get a feel for their plan. Then we can decide who we need to send."

"I'll give you twenty-four hours, no more."

"I need more time, Wyatt."

"Commander Farraday, twenty-four hours. I'll have Jack send all the details of the meeting place to your email. I'll expect your call."

"Yes sir, captain." Before he could finish, Tristan heard a click on the other end and the line went dead. It was great to work with his brother most of the time, unless he pulled rank, and then he was pretty much screwed. Even so, he did get a lot of leeway and used it to his greatest advantage.

Up ahead, he saw the Prevost exit at a rest stop. He entered the other side of the rest stop; he needed to stretch his legs, grab some lunch, and keep an eye on the women. He figured it would take them a while to walk all the dogs. What he did have to be careful about was to stay downwind of the Dobermans. Now that they knew his scent, he didn't want them to alert on him and signal the women.

Tristan sat in the passenger seat of his Porsche with his legs stretched out the door and watched the Prevost at the far end of the rest stop. He leisurely ate his lunch as Payton and Victory took their time walking each of their dobes. They gave them all a bowl of water, and what looked like some kind of a treat.

"Wow man, I don't think I've ever seen a Porsche 911 Turbo with all the bells and whistles; it's cherry, man."

Tristan turned to see two guys staring at his Porsche.

"Thanks."

"I bet it can really fly."

"Sure can, it gets me where I want to go."

"Come on guys, stop bothering the poor man," said a girl as she came out of the restroom.

Tristan turned back to check on the girls and noticed Victory started to scan the vicinity.

"I'll be damned," he mumbled to himself.

He slid down in the front seat of his Porsche in case her gaze came his way.

Fifteen minutes later they were headed down the road and Tristan called the office.

"SOCOM, Logan."

"Hey, it's Tristan."

"You must really miss me."

"You're a comedian. I think we have another little twist; can I talk to Jack?"

"No, he took a late lunch; I can take the information for him," Logan said.

"Okay. I need him to do more digging on the Winters sisters. All the way back to birth if need be. Victory is showing signs of heightened hearing. I had a feeling she had keen hearing, but this is unreal. At first I thought she possessed only telepathy, but it's both, telepathy and heightened hearing. I'm sure of it now."

"How heightened?" Logan asked.

"The sisters parked their motor home at the far end of a rest stop. I had a clear sight line, still I parked at least four hundred yards away from them. Some guy came up and commented on my car. I said thanks, and when I turned back, Victory was scrutinizing the rest stop."

"I'll be damned. That is some good hearing. I'll get the info to Jack as soon as he is back."

"Thanks Logan. The sooner I know the playing field, the better off I'll be."

* * * *

Max spent the entire day in Old Town Sacramento. The coffee shop Victory picked out was located on Front Street close to the river. Max figured his best plan was to get Victory out by boat. The tricky part would be to get her from the coffee shop to the boat. He needed to leave that part of the plan up to Dave, and it worried him. Max was someone who liked a clear plan and total control. Not to say he couldn't change on the fly; he could, but he always started with a clear idea. His phone vibrated in his pocket.

"Max here."

"Hey Max, Jerry. Dave wants to know how your plan is coming along. You've been gone all day and we haven't heard from you."

"Actually I need a boat, something quiet and fast," Max said.

"You plan to get her out of there by boat?" Jerry asked.

"Don't talk about it on the phone." Chrissakes, he hated amateurs. Didn't they know anyone could listen in on cell calls? "I'm about finished here. We need to meet. Let's have dinner."

One hour later Dave, Jerry, and Max were sitting down for dinner at a neighborhood Mexican joint.

"I got you that boat," Dave said.

"Jerry will be the lookout for the job. I want him in the boat and coming up the river one hour before you meet with the girl," Max said.

"One hour before, what am I supposed to do all that time?" Jerry asked.

"Go buy a fishing pole, some bait, and a six-pack of soda, and go fishing. It's your job to be the lookout and to keep the boat available to me as soon as I need it. This is going to be sticky. Dave, it's your job to get the girl as close to the river as possible and away from as many people as you can. The fewer people, the fewer witnesses," Max said.

"Maybe I can talk her into a boat ride with me," Dave said.

"If you can the entire plan would move along smoother. We'll play it on the fly. After dinner, you need to go down to the docks and reserve a slip, Jerry. If Dave can talk the girl into a ride, I will call you and give you a heads up."

"Sounds like a plan," Dave said.

"Let's hope it goes smoothly. There will be a lot of people milling about," Max said.

* * * *

Victory opened the door of the Prevost and walked down the steps. Payton was engrossed in the bathing of her current Doberman.

"Hey Payton, I'm off for my date; I'll bring you back a treat," Victory said as a taxi pulled up alongside the motor home. "Great, right on time. I shouldn't be too long, not more than a couple of hours at the most I wouldn't think."

"Give me a call if you are going to be longer than that, so I don't worry. Before you say it; yes, I am acting like a mother. But these guys are dangerous. For God's sake Victory, don't forget that."

"I know. That's why I'm meeting Dave in a very public place, Old Town Sacramento. Don't worry sis; I'll be fine. See you soon," Victory said, as she closed the door to the taxi.

* * * *

Tristan sat in the bookstore two blocks down from where Victory was going to meet Dave for the last two hours. From the intel he received, the meeting would be taking place in about thirty minutes. Those Biotec guys were good; he hadn't seen Max or Jerry since he'd been there. Odds were Jerry played the lookout and wouldn't actually be involved in the plan, whatever the plan might be. Of course, there was always the possibility Dave really did want to offer her a job as his emails had said, but it didn't feel right to Tristan. Something was up. He always followed his instincts, and he would see this meeting out to the end.

A black Lincoln Navigator with matching tinted windows pulled up to the front of the coffee shop. The passenger door opened, and Dave got out.

A few minutes later, a taxi pulled up in front of the coffee shop. Victory got out of the back of the vehicle. Tristan's breath caught in his chest as she bent forward to brush the wrinkles out of her jade linen shorts. As she inspected the block, the rays of the early afternoon sun shimmered through her caramel-colored hair.

* * * *

Victory walked into the coffee shop. She casually looked around at all the tables. A man in the far corner popped up and waved a hand at her.

"Ms. Winters," Dave yelled.

She wasn't close enough that day in the woods to get a good look at the man who killed Jeffery, but she'd heard his voice clearly. She knew this was not the voice of the man who pulled the trigger, but all the same this voice sent icy fingers down her spine. Victory smiled at Dave and remained glued to her spot, trying to compose herself. It suddenly struck her this masquerade would be harder than she thought.

Dave approached her. "Ms. Winters, I'm Dave Anderson. It's such a pleasure to finally meet you in person."

Dave stuck out his hand to shake hers, and it took all her power to keep the smile on her face and shake his hand.

"I have a table already. Would you like to go have a seat and I can order you a drink?"

"Thank you. I think I will go up to the counter and order my coffee and then come over to the table, if you don't mind." She needed to pull herself together right now if she wanted to make this work.

"Whatever you would like, I'll be waiting at the table."

Dave gave her a slight nod and went to sit down.

A few moments later, drink in hand and her composure in check, Victory joined Dave at his table.

"I really am glad you decided to take the time out of your vacation to meet with me. Jeffery has spoken so highly of you," Dave said, as he rose and pulled out a chair for Victory.

"I haven't spoken to Jeffery in years. I guess our careers keep us both so busy. How is Jeffery?"

She abruptly picked up her drink, took a sip and averted her eyes as tears threatened to fall.

"Oh, he's doing fine. He is out of the country on another project, like I mentioned in my emails. Before he left he said you would be the person we would want to get to replace him on the project he left behind."

"Really," Victory said.

"Yes. This is an extremely important project. The first milestone is due at the end of next month so we are running against the clock."

"I see. Surely there are others who would be interested in your project. Is there no one internally you can promote?" she asked.

"Unfortunately no. I'm sure there would be others interested, Ms. Winters, except we have not located anyone as qualified yet," Dave said.

"If this is such an important project, why did Jeffery get sent out of the country to another project?"

She knew she challenged him, but the words were out before she could stop herself.

"Ah, well, ours is not to question why. The powers that be believed he was needed elsewhere and so off he went," Dave responded lightheartedly.

"What can you tell me about the project?" Victory asked.

"Regrettably I can't give you too many details because it is highly classified. What I can tell you is you would be working with animals and probably doing similar work as you are doing now, only with state-of-the-art equipment," Dave said.

"And how do you know what I am working on now? It is also classified," Victory said.

"I realize I am taking time out of your vacation," Dave said, ignoring her previous question. "I think I can show you something that would change your mind, something truly astonishing. It will answer all of your questions. Please remember what I want to show you is highly classified.

"Biotec has a satellite lab right across the river from here. I came over to meet you on one of the company's boats. I thought I would take you over to the lab and give you a short tour. Part of Jeffery's research is contained there, so it would give you an idea of what you would be working on. In the end if you still chose not to work for us, you must tell no one about what you saw. Would you like to take a short walk with me?"

She hesitated briefly, thinking about the Taser she had placed in her purse after Lisa Evans was found dead. Finally she responded, "Let's go."

She grabbed her purse and headed for the door without a second thought. Victory was bound and determined to find out what got Jeffery killed. Besides, what could happen? It was in the middle of the morning, they were in Old Town Sacramento, and people were everywhere.

"Great. I need to make a quick call. I'll meet you outside."

"I need to make a call too. My sister expected me back in less than an hour. I don't want her to worry." Victory walked past him and went out the door.

She turned and walked away to call Payton as Dave came out of the shop. A man in a hat and dark glasses bumped into Dave. For a split second she had a sensation she knew the man. The impression passed quickly when Payton answered the phone, Victory's attention being refocused on her sister.

"Hello, Victory, are you okay?" Payton asked.

"Yes, I'm fine. I might be later than I thought."

"So things must be going according to your plan."

"Dave is giving me a tour of their satellite lab which is right across the river," Victory said.

"I don't really think going across the river with him is a good idea," Payton said, concern flooding her voice.

"Yes, okay, I'll see you in a few hours. 'Bye." Victory snapped her phone shut before Payton had a chance to argue with her. She looked over at Dave.

"My sister is planning on me being home for lunch, so she doesn't want me to be too late."

"No problem. We should have you back in plenty of time; this way."

Dave gestured down the docks toward the moored boats.

"It only takes about fifteen minutes to cross the river, and the lab sits on the river bank. I promise you, you won't be sorry. There are some pretty exciting things being done there," Dave said.

What harm could there be in taking a peek at the lab? Besides, she still wanted to get more information about Jeffery, and getting into one of his labs was probably a one-time deal.

* * * *

Tristan saw Victory walk out of the coffee shop alone and let out a breath he was unaware he held. It surprised him she'd got done with the meeting so soon. It must not have gone well. Then Dave walked out the door and the two started down the sidewalk together. He still hadn't seen Max or Jerry, so he needed to stay out of sight. He waited until Victory and Dave passed the first block, then he walked out of the bookstore and started after them.

They walked together down the pier to one of the slips where a small motorboat was tied up. Dave stepped onto the boat and held his hand out to Victory. She reached out for his hand and stepped into the boat. He untied the boat and pushed away from the pier, started the engine, and headed away from the shore.

* * * *

Dave slowed the boat. "Did you hear that?" he asked.

"Hear what?" Victory asked. She sat on one of the bench seats.

"I heard a sputter, or a pop, I couldn't tell for sure. I had a little problem with this boat on the way over to meet you. I think it's time for an engine overhaul."

He turned away from Victory, lifted the bench top on the other side of the boat and began digging around inside it.

"Great, I thought he said he put it in here," he said, as if talking to himself.

"What are you looking for?" Victory asked, beginning to get edgy.

"I had a couple guys take a look at the boat before I came to meet you. They said if I heard the noise I should put a can of oil in her, but I can't find the oil."

He closed the lid of the bench and looked at her. "Would you mind taking a look in that side? Maybe they couldn't tell their left from their right," he said, with a slight smile on his lips.

Victory rose from her seat, turned, and raised the lid.

"What does this—"

Before she could finish the sentence she felt a prick at the back of her neck. It felt like a bee sting. Instantly her world turned to black.

Dave dropped the syringe and grabbed Victory before she hit the deck. Carefully he placed her on the closed bench.

"Sweet dreams, Ms. Winters."

Chapter Eight

"Damn it, what is she thinking? Is she really going to get on a boat with that guy? Shit," Tristan sputtered to himself.

"Wyatt."

"I'm here, Tristan," Wyatt responded almost instantly.

"Victory left the meeting place. She got into a boat with Dave, one of the Biotec guys."

"She did what?"

"You heard me. I'm going to see if I can get myself a boat. I need the team here now."

"I can send Logan in the helicopter stat. He can be there in two hours. You can't lose sight of her, Tristan."

"Tell me something I don't know," Tristan said, as he ran to the docks. *"Send Noah to keep watch on Payton. I don't know how much you want to tell her about what's happened to Victory. But she is going to panic when Victory doesn't return. And for all we know, they might go after her next as leverage."*

"You're right. I'll send Noah now and fill him in by the time he gets there. Keep me in the loop," Wyatt said.

Tristan ran down the docks and saw the boat rental sign. A man was tying up a small speedboat—that should do the trick.

"Hi there, how much to rent by the hour?" Tristan asked.

"No hourly rental, half-day or whole," the man said.

"Fine, take this," Tristan tossed him a credit card. "I'll pick it up on my way back," he said, as he started to pull the line of the bow from the man.

"Wait, I need to inspect it first. It was just returned from another renter," the man said with exasperation.

"I'll take full responsibility. If I have any problems, you can charge my card."

"Okay, buddy, it's your dime." He released the line and stepped away.

The engine came to life and the boat took off. Tristan could narrowly make out the outline of Dave's boat docked on the other side of the river. He estimated at his current speed, he should be there in less than eight minutes. Then the black Navigator appeared, son of a bitch. If she got into the vehicle, he would lose them for sure. He saw Max get out of the SUV and go down to the boat. A minute later Dave got off the boat, followed by Max who carried something large.

"Shit."

Tristan grabbed his binoculars and took another look. He studied the object and saw a leg, along with a jade pair of shorts, peek out from under the blanket.

Tristan managed to reach the docks as the Navigator pulled away.

"Wyatt run this plate: BY73397; it's a Washington plate. I've lost Victory."

"Got it," Wyatt said.

"Dave drugged her, or knocked her out on the boat ride across the river. He had Max wait for them in a black Lincoln Navigator. They loaded her up and took off. I don't see any other vehicle right offhand, but I could keep looking."

"No. Head back to your car. The guys have left in the helo already. Call Jack as soon as you can. I gave him the plate number to research. He'll let you know where the guys will be putting down," Wyatt said.

Tristan dug his phone out of his pocket and punched in the speed dial button for the office. He turned and headed back to the boat.

"SOCOM, Jack here."

"Jack, I need an answer on those plates." Tristan said, never breaking stride.

"Vehicle is registered to Biotec, part of the fleet out of Washington," Jack said.

"It wouldn't be very practical for them to drive her clear back to Washington State; they won't be able to keep her drugged for all those hours. Where are the guys flying in with the chopper?" Tristan asked.

"They can fly in almost anywhere. I have them coming into a field about three miles from the dog show RV parking. But there is another small airport in addition to the Sacramento Airport located a few miles west of town."

"Best guess, Dave is flying Victory out of here and he will be using that small airport; it's much less conspicuous. I'm heading back to my car. Get into the flight plans for the airport and see what might be flying out in the next couple of hours and where the destinations are."

"I'm on it. I'll get back to you as soon as I have any information," Jack said.

Tristan reached the pier and stuck his phone back in his pocket. The man who had rented him the boat already stood there.

"Hey, man, back so soon?"

"Yep, she runs like a dream," Tristan said sheepishly.

"I charged you for a half-day," the man said, and handed Tristan his card and receipt.

"No worries. I still used your boat. Thanks." He grabbed the card and receipt and took off at a run up the docks. He covered the entire length of Old Town and reached his Porsche as his phone rang.

"Yeah, Jack, tell me you have something."

"A Cessna 400 registered to the Biotec Corporation took off from that airport eight minutes ago."

"And you got the destination?" Tristan asked.

"It's a private plane. They didn't have to file their flight plans because they flew VFR," Jack said.

"VFR?" Tristan asked.

"Visual Flight Rules. Means they are flying by sight. If they flew by Instrument Flight Rules, or IFR, we would have a destination. I'm trying to track them now. As soon as I get them I'll let you know," Jack said.

"Okay, I'm on my way to the field right now. By my estimation they should touch down in about ninety minutes. Keep me updated on the Cessna. Transfer me over to Wyatt, please."

"Will do."

Tristan heard a click as Jack transferred his call.

"Hey Tristan. Tell me you have a plan," Wyatt said.

"I'm going to meet the guys when they come in. I want to know where the Cessna is heading. My gut says they are taking her back to their headquarters in Washington. I will leave my Porsche with Noah. Logan and I will head back to Biotec. As soon as Jack locates the Cessna, have him do a search on the layout of Biotec."

"I'll have him get right on it. Good idea for Noah to take care of your Porsche. That way I can leave him with Payton for now. I may have Noah bring Payton in and put her in a safe house," Wyatt said.

"Don't forget. She's got four Dobermans. She won't leave them. You will probably have to get them all home and leave the dogs with the housekeeper. She may agree to that, but she won't leave them behind," Tristan said.

"Great, this keeps getting better and better," Wyatt said.

"Yep, and then there's Willow."

"I almost forgot about Willow. Well, let's take this one step at a time. Noah will stay with Payton for now. Hold on Tristan, Jack has something. I'm going to put you on speakerphone," Wyatt said.

"Hey Tristan, I've got their Cessna on radar and I'm tracking it. I've also tapped into their communications. They are landing at the small airport west of Seattle, due to touch down in ninety minutes. I'll send you the coordinates," Jack said.

"Good work, Jack. Hope you didn't have a hot date tonight. The captain is going to keep you really busy. Call me as you get updates."

Tristan pulled up to the field where his team's chopper would be landing. By his calculations he still had almost forty-five minutes to wait. He turned off his engine, reclined his seat, and closed his eyes. He knew the next twenty-four hours would be nonstop. His years in the military had taught him the art of sleeping anywhere in order to survive and function in the field. This would be his only time to recharge.

Tristan woke to the whop, whop, whop, sound of helicopter blades growing louder as the team approached. He sat up and rubbed the sleep from his eyes. He got out of his car the same time the helicopter touched down. The door to the chopper opened, and Noah jumped from it.

Seconds later the engine shut down, the blades spooled to a stop, and Logan got out of the pilot's seat.

"Tell me it's so—Jack said I would be driving your Porsche." Noah knew the car was Tristan's prize possession.

"That's right, and if I find one scratch or dent on her you're a dead man," Tristan said.

"Don't worry, I'll take good care of her," he teased as he patted the hood of the shiny sports car.

"Okay kids, we're kind of pressed for time here, so let's get to it," Logan said.

"Always the party pooper," Noah joked. "I know I'm only here to babysit. At least tell me she's pretty."

"Keep her safe, Noah. Remember the Winters are a very prominent and influential family," Tristan said.

"Yeah, yeah, I'll be good. Give me the details."

Tristan spent the next ten minutes reviewing the packet of information he'd put together over the last couple of days pertaining to all three of the Winters women. He included pictures and every detail, right down to the personalities of every Doberman. He pulled out all the information on Payton and put it together.

"This should be everything you need. I don't know how much detail Wyatt decided you should give her, but Payton seems pretty together. Naturally she will be shaken at first, but after the initial shock wears off, I believe she will be more than willing to work with you to help get her sister back safely," Tristan said.

"All right then, I guess I'm off. Ah, Tristan, keys? I don't want the bad guys to beat me to her," Noah said.

"Remember what I said," Tristan said, as he tossed the keys into Noah's outstretched hand.

"No problem. Man, I've been waiting forever to drive this baby. You guys take care. See you back at the ranch."

Noah grabbed his gear, threw it into the back of the Porsche, jumped into the driver's seat, and started the engine. A huge smile spread across his face as he put the car in gear and peeled out of the field.

"Jesus, Tristan. You really think you'll get your car back?" Logan said, as he shook his head.

"I sure as hell better, and in the same shape it left this field, or he'll be sorry he was ever born. Let me grab my gear and we can head out."

As Tristan walked across the field to pick up his packs that he left where the Porsche had been, his phone rang.

"Hey Jack, I'm ready for your update."

"There's more chatter coming from the Cessna, and it seems Seattle is not the final destination," Jack said.

"Tell me you know where they are going."

"Pretty sure. They have a small helicopter waiting at the airport for them. A few years back Biotec bought one of the smaller San Juan Islands off of the Washington coast. They have since built a satellite compound and lab there. It's all highly top secret and very secure. I believe that is where they will take Victory. You only have two ways to get there, by water or air," Jack said.

"That means we will have to leave the helicopter on the mainland, get as close as we can by boat, and then scuba in at night," Tristan said.

"That's probably your best alternative. Security will be tight. Employees are ferried over on company-owned boats. I'm still trying to pull up blueprints on the lab, but so far no luck. I'm confident we will find something; we are digging deeper."

"It sounds like we are going to get wet," Logan said.

"Yup, and there are a few little glitches. I'll fill you in on the way back," Tristan said.

"All right then, let's get this party started," Logan said, as he jumped back into the pilot's seat.

Chapter Nine

Victory began to awake and felt as though she had a major hangover. A voice inside her told her that wasn't the case. The last thing she remembered was being on a boat with Dave, and they were on their way to tour a lab. Where was she now and what time was it? Never mind that, what day was it? She sat up ever so slowly and looked around the room. She sat on a queen-size bed, still made, with nightstands on each side of the bed. A desk sat in one corner of the room, an overstuffed chair in the other, next to a bookshelf full of novels and an adjoining bath. There were no windows, and that made it feel like a cell, even with all the homey touches.

All of a sudden, she felt like the room closed in on her.

"Get a grip, Victory," she mumbled to herself, "lots of rooms don't have windows."

She swung her feet off the bed and headed for the door. She tried to turn the knob, but it wouldn't budge. It must be stuck. She tried it again. It wouldn't open. Now she really did feel like the room was closing in on her. She stepped back from the door and reached into her pocket; her phone was gone.

She walked back to the desk, pulled the chair out, and sat down. There was a click at the door and it swung open. Dave walked in with the same smile he had when he met her at the coffee shop. *He is one creepy guy,* she thought.

"So glad to see you are up and about," he said.

"Thanks, the nap was great; what did you inject me with?" Victory snapped. She needed to fight the urge to keep herself from springing across the room and wringing his neck.

"Nothing that will hurt you, but you might feel like you drank all night. Mr. Braxton is waiting to see you. Everything you need to freshen up is in the bathroom. I'll be back to escort you to your meeting in fifteen minutes." He turned and left the room. The door shut behind him and she heard the click of the lock as it snapped back into place.

Mr. Braxton was here to meet with her, *the* Mr. Braxton. Lawrence Braxton—the owner and founder of Biotec. Maybe now she could get some answers as to why she'd been drugged and locked in a room. Victory went into the bathroom and found everything she needed and readied herself for her meeting. Unfortunately, she found nothing to use as a weapon.

Dave promptly returned fifteen minutes later and escorted her from her room. As they walked down the hall she saw no one. They entered the waiting elevator and Dave pushed the button for the tenth and top floor. She noticed as they entered the elevator that they were on the basement level. No wonder her room had no windows.

The doors to the elevator opened and revealed a gleaming black marble floor. The exterior wall contained glass from floor to ceiling, and it showcased a breathtaking view of the ocean. Far off in the distance she saw a tiny outline of land. They stepped out of the elevator and walked down the hall until they reached a desk where a prim woman with red hair, glasses, and a smart navy suit sat typing away on her computer.

"Good afternoon, Sarah," Dave greeted her.

She looked up and nodded at Dave. "Good afternoon, Mr. Anderson. Mr. Braxton is expecting you. Go right in."

"Thank you," he answered.

He headed for the door, opened it, and motioned for Victory to enter. The enormous office sat on the top corner of the building and flaunted the same awe-inspiring glass walls on two sides of the room. Even with the afternoon light the room was darker than the hall had been, giving an eerie glow to the interior. Dave turned a knob and the windows lightened, letting in the sun's full force.

No expense was spared in this office. The floor was teak with cherry inlays that trimmed the edge. The desk was an antique, probably cherry, and looked massive even within the large space. There was a built-in bar on one wall, housing a variety of high priced wines and brandies. At the far end of the bar stood a gleaming Waterford water pitcher accompanied by an assortment of glasses. Across the room stood four tapestry wingback chairs and two antique mahogany side tables, Victory estimated were made sometime around the 1800s and were very rare. There were at least eight priceless pieces of art she saw, including vases, sculptures, and three paintings on the back wall. She'd no doubt this office could rival any museum.

"Ms. Winters, so good to finally meet you," Lawrence Braxton said, as he turned his desk chair around to face her. He rose from the chair and walked toward her with his arm extended. "My name is Lawrence Braxton; I am the CEO of Biotec."

"Yes, I know who you are Mr. Braxton. I'm sure you don't remember, but we met at the Governor's Ball a few years back. Tell me, do you drug all of your interviewees?"

"Drug you?" Braxton said, with surprise on his face as he turned to look at Dave.

"Sorry, sir, but you did say to get her here by any means necessary. It seemed to be the best way at the time," Dave said sheepishly.

"I see. I think we have everything under control, Dave," Braxton said, with a wave of his hand. Dave turned and left the room.

"I am truly sorry about you being drugged. Sometimes Dave takes things too literally. Please sit." He motioned to one of the wingback chairs. "May I offer you a drink or something to eat?"

"As long as it isn't spiked," Victory said. She still wasn't certain about the whole situation, but would play along with it for the time being. She knew they wanted her expertise, and she intended to find out what they wanted her expertise for.

Braxton passed his hand over the top of his desk and a panel lit up.

"Sarah, please bring two mint juleps and an assortment of fresh fruit and cheese."

"Right away, sir," Sarah said.

"I hope you like mint juleps. They are so light and freshening, perfect for a late afternoon, don't you agree?" Braxton asked.

"That sounds fine," Victory said.

She was certain Braxton wasn't the kind of man used to being disagreed with, so she would bide her time.

Sarah entered the office with a large tray containing two wonderful-looking mint juleps, and an assortment of fruits and cheeses that made Victory's mouth water. She walked over to the large coffee table and set the tray down. Two thoughts came to Victory: *First, this woman was good, someone to watch; she was sure she got a glimpse of a gun inside Sarah's jacket as she bent to put the tray down. Second, she couldn't remember the last time she had eaten.*

"Thank you, Sarah," Braxton smiled at her.

"You're welcome, sir. Will there be anything else?"

"Not at the moment," Braxton said.

Sarah took her leave. Braxton picked up one of the drinks and held it out to Victory.

"Come, sit, enjoy, and let's have a nice visit. I'm sure you will be interested in what I have to tell you."

Victory took the glass from Braxton, took a napkin from the tray, and a few pieces of cheese and fruit. She sat in one of the chairs and began to nibble on her cheese while she waited quietly for Braxton to start talking.

"I understand you are employed by Claremont Research, and you seem to be very loyal to them," Braxton said.

"I am not only loyal, but I love my career, and the people I work with."

"That can only take you so far. You are the department head leading the research for a possible genetic link between canines and humans. You have also spent field time out of the lab, to try to locate humans who might possess heightened senses. I believe you have started dabbling in incorporating these canine heightened senses, on a purely cellular basis, of course."

"Dabbling!" Victory nearly yelled. She was appalled at his cavalier attitude about her work, and besides that, how did he know the details? "What I do or don't do is not *dabbling*. It is classified, and consequently I will not confirm nor deny your description of my employment."

"Fair enough." Braxton picked up his drink and took a long slow sip. He put the drink back down, dabbed his lips and locked his gaze on Victory's. "However, Claremont is going about this research all wrong. Biotec is currently working on the same type of project. We have the equipment, the people, and the financial backing. All I need now is you, Victory. You are the one I want to take the lead and get this research to the next level. I'm not asking for much; give me three weeks of your time. I'm not asking for you to quit your current position. I am positive we can work something out."

"What if I say no? Will you let me walk out of here and go home?" Victory asked, testing the waters.

"I guess I would have to. But it would be in your best interest to give me the three weeks. Dave has kept close tabs on Payton and Willow. If you are not interested in this position, then I'm sure we could persuade one of your sisters to come work with Biotec."

"They don't have the experience I have."

"Humm, I see. Then it might be a problem, for them," Braxton said.

Victory was indignant. How dare this man threaten her.

"Who do you think you are, to drug me, bring me here against my will, and to top it off, threaten my family?"

Braxton sat back in his chair and looked her up and down.

"My dear, I do not threaten. I merely made a statement of fact. I can prove my point, if you like. Isn't your sister Payton in Sacramento at a dog show with her motor home? It would be a shame if her brakes gave out as she came down Mt. Shasta on her way home."

Victory fully understood the gist of his statement and felt a cold shiver run down her back. She set her glass and napkin down on the table. She took a hard look at Lawrence Braxton. The gentleman's demeanor had slipped for a split second, and she saw the dead cold eyes of a killer, one with no soul. In a flash it was gone, and staring back at her was the business tycoon.

"Don't give me your final answer now. I'm on my way off the island for a meeting. I'll be back in thirty-six hours; I'll expect your answer then."

Braxton walked back to his desk and ran his hand back over the panel.

"Dave, Ms. Winters is ready to return to her room."

The door to the outer hall opened, and Dave walked in.

"This way, Ms. Winters."

Victory felt like she was in a dream, or maybe more like a nightmare. Lawrence Braxton had directly threatened her sisters. She followed Dave in a daze to the elevators; he held the door open for her to get in. The ride back down seemed shorter. The elevator stopped and Dave led Victory down the hall. She was still disoriented, but even so, this hallway didn't look familiar. He stopped at a door, opened it, and gestured for her to enter. The room was beautiful, with cherry wood floors sprinkled with plush throw rugs. A king-size poster bed, a writing desk, two huge overstuffed chairs, and one whole wall of windows containing a balcony complete with table and chairs.

"We have provided you with a wardrobe for your stay. You will find everything you need in the bathroom and closet. Your meals will be brought up to you, unless you would prefer to eat out in the gardens," Dave said, looking down at his watch. "Dinner started fifteen minutes ago and will be available for the next hour."

Victory's face lit up at the thought of getting outside.

"Are you saying I'm allowed to go outside?"

"Of course, you're not a prisoner." Dave smiled a wicked smirk. "Besides, you are on an island. Enjoy." He turned and left the room.

Victory listened for the longest time until she could no longer hear Dave's footfalls in the hall. Then she waited a few minutes longer. She walked up to the door and tried the knob. It turned smoothly. She walked out of her room and began her exploration.

* * * *

Logan had landed the helicopter at the nearest helipad on the coast. As he and Tristan got out, they saw a Humvee approach.

"He's right on time," Logan said.

"Would you expect anything else?" Tristan asked.

The charcoal Humvee came to a stop directly in front of them, and Wyatt got out.

"Nice to see you, Tristan, and you too, Logan. I brought all of your gear. This is an under-the-table mission. Biotec is a very prominent company and until we have something concrete on them, we have to tread very lightly."

"Of course we do. Why is it people with money always get special treatment," Tristan spat.

"Don't start, Tristan. I've been on the phone all day with General Roberts at the Pentagon, trying to convince him to let the two of you go over to the lab, so don't make a mess of this," Wyatt said.

Tristan rolled his eyes. "Fine, we'll watch our step."

"General Roberts is not convinced that Biotec is behind any of this. The company has a pristine history of being on the cutting edge of disease research. Their primary goal is to improve quality of life," Wyatt said.

"What better way to improve quality of life than to mess with our genetic makeup, right?" Tristan asked.

"I suppose that's one way of looking at it. If manipulating DNA is really what is going on there, we need to know how they are doing it, and who is working with them. We can safely assume they are not in this alone. You guys need to get going, and I'm sure I don't have to say this, but be careful and don't get caught," Wyatt said.

Logan and Tristan pulled on their wetsuits and air tanks, packed up their gear in their waterproof backpacks, and headed out to the ocean. They climbed into the dark-blue high-speed boat. The sun had begun to set, casting a sparkling purple and pink glow over the water. This lighting provided them with a natural camouflage to any passersby looking out at the ocean.

A few miles away from the island, they anchored the boat. They rechecked all their gear and dropped into the frigid water. Tristan and Logan approached the island from the farthest side from the lab.

"Let's take our gear up and find a place to stow it," Logan said, as he peeled the mask from his face.

They moved quickly from the shore, getting out of sight as soon as possible. Together they ran for the tree line without a single word, searching for a place to hide their gear.

"Here," Logan grunted.

He was one of the best for finding cover on the fly. He found a small cave right inside the tree line, perfect for getting to and from the water and just large enough for the two of them to squeeze into. They stripped off their scuba gear, unpacked their dry bags, and prepared to head for the lab to scout it out.

"I think our best bet is high ground," Logan said.

* * * *

Victory sat alone on the edge of a bench under a big evergreen tree. Her back to the lab and she looked out at the Pacific Ocean, tears trickling down her cheeks. She wiped her cheeks dry, angry at herself for allowing Lawrence Braxton to affect her in this way.

"Victory," came the quiet whisper of her name.

Eyelids sparkling with unshed tears, she looked up and then around her, expecting to see someone.

"Don't look around; you can't see me. I'm on the bluff immediately off to your right, but don't look over," Tristan said.

* * * *

Tristan and Logan had crawled up the side of a bluff overlooking the gardens of the lab. They both were lying flat on their stomachs with bushes, twigs, and other vegetation covering their bodies. Each of them held binoculars up to their eyes. They weren't far from Victory or the lab, but easily out of earshot.

"Tristan, Logan. I have an update," Noah's voice sounded in their ear buds.

"Go ahead, Noah," Tristan whispered.

"Payton became hysterical over Victory's kidnapping and insisted on calling the police. It took some doing, but I talked her down. She explained to me what Victory witnessed in the forest." Noah described the scene as Victory experienced it. "Here's the interesting part, Payton told me Victory possesses an ultra-keen sense of hearing."

"Your timing is perfect. Thanks Noah," Tristan said. The day in the forest finally fell into place for Tristan. Now he understood how the scene played out.

"Tristan?" Victory murmured, sheer surprise on her face.

Now that he could understand.

"Yes, it's me. That's the only thing I will understand. You can hear me, according to your sister

Payton, but unfortunately, I can't hear you. Your sister also told us you know sign language. I happen to have a friend here who also knows sign. Keep your hands low, in your lap. My friend Logan will read for me."

"What are you doing here? I don't understand. Who are you?" Victory signed, total confusion and anger showing in her face.

"It's a long story. I work for SOCOM, a unified branch of Special Operations encompassing the Navy, Army, and Air Force. We were already on Jeffery's trail when you came into the picture. What you need to know right now is, we are with the government, and we are here to get you out."

"What makes you think I believe you? You told me you were a botanist," she signed.

Logan turned to Tristan.

"Seems we are in for a challenge. She doesn't believe you, Tristan."

"I'm telling you the truth, Victory. We are here to help you. Why else would the two of us be here?"

"Why don't you tell me?" Victory signed back. "Maybe you want my research too."

"We aren't here for your blasted research. We are here to help you. We don't have time for this now. We need to get you out as soon as possible," Tristan said.

"No you can't. Braxton has threatened my sisters," she signed.

"Victory, you need to stay calm. You don't want to draw attention to yourself. What do you mean, Braxton threatened your sisters?" Tristan asked.

Victory closed her eyes, took a deep breath, and then relayed the entire conversation between herself and Lawrence Braxton.

Tristan and Logan looked at each other. They didn't say a word, but they both knew Braxton had absolutely threatened Willow and Payton.

"Okay, don't tell anyone about your decision. Meet us back here tomorrow at ten in the morning and we'll have a plan."

Tristan could see she still didn't trust the two of them, but at this point Victory's options were limited.

"Is Payton okay?"

"She's fine. We have one of our best with her," Tristan said.

"What about Willow?"

"We had Payton call her at the office. She's okay. Tomorrow, ten, be here, Victory. You need to be very careful. The men you are dealing with are extremely dangerous. We have good reason to believe Lawrence Braxton is the person who ordered Jeffery's murder."

Chapter Ten

"No Tristan," Wyatt said, for the fourth time in the last ten minutes.

Tristan paced the SOCOM office. Logan and Wyatt sat in chairs across the room from him.

"Wyatt, stop. Take a breath and think about it. We have tried to get a lead on this for weeks. We knew Jeffery was somehow involved, but not who his contacts were. We were heading in the wrong direction. It doesn't look like this is being run by a foreign organization. It's looking more like someone in our own backyard, and that in itself makes it top priority. We need to get a handle on this and quickly. This situation literally dropped in our laps, and it's the break we've been looking for." Tristan pulled out all the stops.

"Do you have any idea how many things could go wrong with this plan?" Wyatt asked.

"What else is new? We're always hanging out on the line," Tristan said.

"Can you really handle this cover on the inside? There's a ton of information you need to know," Wyatt said.

"I'm not stupid, Wyatt, and I'm not your average Joe. I do have a few degrees, including biology and chemistry, so I understand about science. I also have Victory on the inside. She can help me if needed," Tristan said.

"You hope. But only if she can keep it together."

"She can. I've watched her for the last week. She can handle this and will do it because it means keeping her sisters safe."

"Okay Tristan, you win. Let's get the team together. We have a lot of work to do, especially Jack, and we only have—," Wyatt looked at his watch, "about twelve hours to get this crazy plan worked out."

A few minutes later Jack, Logan, Wyatt, and Tristan were gathered around the large oval table in the Situation Room.

"Okay guys, we're one man down and I really think Noah needs to stay with Payton for now. Especially since Braxton has threatened her. We may try and move her to a safe house after she gets back from California, but for now we are one man short. Braxton wants Victory to give him three weeks on the project. Tristan has come up with a way in. He wants Victory to tell Braxton she will give him the three weeks, but only if he brings in her lab assistant," Wyatt said.

All three of the guys looked at Tristan. Logan was the first to speak, a smirk filling his face.

"Tristan—an assistant?"

"Yeah, you don't think I can assist. I can assist," Tristan shot back.

"Enough guys, we don't have time for this." Wyatt knew he had to stop them now or this bantering could go on forever.

"Jack, you are the lead for this part of the project and are going to be ultra busy. We need an ironclad background. We know Braxton will have his people do an extensive background search on Tristan. No slipups. Tristan, Logan, you guys are backing up Jack. Our drop-dead time is oh seven hundred. By then, Logan and Tristan need to head back out to the island to make contact with Victory. That's it. Let's go to work."

* * * *

Nine forty-five the next morning, Victory walked out of the building and casually strolled to the gardens. She didn't want to draw anyone's attention, so she stopped every now and then to look at a flower or greet the employees she met on the grounds. Out of the corner of her eye, she caught movement heading her way.

"Ms. Winters, Ms. Winters."

Victory turned to see Sarah, Braxton's secretary running toward her. She stopped to let Sarah catch up to her; she certainly didn't want this woman following her to her destination.

"Yes, Sarah?" Victory said, and greeted her with a smile.

"Sorry to disturb your walk, but I've heard from Mr. Braxton. He will be arriving at noon and he wishes to meet with you as soon as he arrives."

"At noon? I thought I had at least another four hours," Victory said. She was red-faced and exasperated.

"I'm very sorry, but Mr. Braxton's schedule often changes on an hourly basis. I won't keep you any longer, as I'm sure you have thinking you need to do," Sarah said.

Victory glanced around her to make certain no one was near. She closed her eyes, took in a deep breath, and listened. She heard the chirping of the birds, the sound of the breeze blowing in from the ocean, and bits and pieces of different conversations, but no one took notice of her. She opened her eyes and looked at her watch.

"Shoot, it's ten past ten," she muttered to herself.

Picking up her pace, she headed for the bench overlooking the ocean. When she finally arrived, she sat in the same spot she had the day before. She fixed her eyes on the rolling waves.

"There you are. We thought you were going to stand us up."

Tristan's warm, soft voice floated into her thoughts. Suddenly her controlled façade fell away and panic set in. She frantically started to sign about her run-in with Sarah and having to meet with Braxton in two hours.

"Calm down, Victory. We have a plan. Everything is going to be all right," Tristan said.

"We? Who's we?" She signed.

"All your questions will be answered. But right now we are short on time; we have to make this fast. I'm hoping you will be able to retain everything I need to tell you," Tristan said.

"I'm one of the best research specialists in the world. What do you think?" She flashed a glance in his direction.

"I'm glad to see you still have your sense of humor. Take your left hand and slid it down the inside leg of the bench until you find a small—,"

"Yuck," Victory said out loud. "Sorry about that," she whispered.

"No worries. There is no one within one hundred and fifty feet of you, and yes you have found what I want you to. A synthetic chewing gum, pull it free and be careful; it is encapsulating a tiny earpiece."

Victory pulled apart the gum and found the earpiece. She looked around and then quickly placed it in her ear.

"It's sound activated. Say 'go' when you want to start the recording; 'back' to rewind, and 'stop' to end the recording. Got it?" Tristan asked.

Victory hand signed the instructions back to Logan and Tristan word for word.

"Okay. You need to memorize the plan recorded in this earpiece before you go back to the lab. We can't take the chance they might have sensors able to detect electronics. So when you are done with the earpiece, put it back in the gum and throw it out into the ocean."

"Tristan, who are you? You're certainly not a botanist," Victory said.

"We're the good guys, Victory. I told you, part of a U.S. military team. It will all become clear after you listen to the recording. Learn the plan, and stick to it, verbatim; don't deviate from it at all. And Victory?"

She hazarded a brief glance in his direction.

"Good luck," he murmured.

* * * *

It was a few minutes before her meeting with Braxton. She got up from the bench to walk back to the lab and took a few steps toward the edge of the cliff to toss the gum into the water.

She had to get back to her room in time to splash water on her face and take a breath without fear of being watched. She wiped the water from her face when there came a knock on her door.

"Boy, they are nothing if not prompt here."

Victory hung her towel and headed for the door. Before she could answer a second knock sounded.

"Ms. Winters, Mr. Braxton doesn't like to be kept waiting," Dave said, from the other side of the door.

Victory swung the door open before he finished his sentence. "Ah, Mr. Anderson, my favorite kidnapper. Shall we go?"

She walked right past Dave without a second glance. For the first time since she walked into the coffee shop two days ago, Victory felt more in control of her situation.

They got out of the elevator on the top floor and walked down the same stunning black marble hall to Braxton's office. Dave knocked on the door, opened it for Victory to enter, and closed it behind her. Braxton put down his cell phone and continued to work on his computer. Victory had picked up a few words of his conversation as she approached the door, but none of it made any sense to her; something about a meeting with kaleidoscope?

"Good afternoon, Ms. Winters. I trust you have enjoyed your time on my lovely island," Braxton said from behind his antique cherry desk, without bothering to look up from his computer.

"Considering I had no other option and I can't leave the island, it was fine," she said.

Her abrupt response caused Braxton to stop typing, but his gaze remained on his screen.

"Good. Have you made your decision about whether you will come to work for me?"

"I will give you three weeks under one condition," she said.

That got his attention. For the first time Braxton looked up and actually made eye contact.

"And what might that be?" He raised one eyebrow and asked more out of curiosity than compromise.

"I need my lab assistant. He has been with me since the very beginning of my research. He understands my shorthand, my train of thought, and my idiosyncrasies. It will take me longer than three weeks to get any of your people up to speed."

Braxton sat back in his oversized leather chair with a sneer on his face. He didn't say a word for almost one whole minute. Then he asked, "Is that all?"

"Three weeks. Not a day longer. And you have to leave my sisters out of this." Victory stared Braxton in the eyes.

"No problem."

He had no intention of honoring his promise. But being the smug man he was, Braxton knew he would be able to convince Victory to stay of her own accord before the three weeks were up. If not, then he would again threaten her sisters.

"I need to able to speak to my sisters. I will tell them I got called away on research."

"Of course, as long as you don't give them any of the details of the project you will be working on. And as far as your assistant, it would be best for him if he too remained in the dark."

"My thoughts exactly. The less he knows, the safer he will be," Victory said.

"Good, I'm glad we are on the same page. Give Sarah all the contact information on your assistant on your way out."

"I need to call him first and let him know he will be coming out here to work for three weeks."

"Yes, you do need to contact him. But he won't be working here," Braxton said.

"We need to work together," she quickly responded, slightly less brazen.

"And you will be. Call him on your way out and tell him to pack for warm weather. He is to go to the airport tomorrow morning at nine. There will be a private helicopter waiting to bring him out here. Good day, Ms. Winters."

Braxton returned to his computer and Dave entered the office.

"I'll see you back to your room," Dave said, as he nodded to the hall.

Victory gave one last scowl in Braxton's direction and headed out of his office.

"I need to give Sarah some information, and then I have been given permission to make some calls," she hissed at Dave.

Sarah looked up, ready to receive her instructions.

"Sarah, I will be joined by my lab assistant, Tristan Grant."

She recited from memory every exact word she'd heard on the recording.

"Thank you, Ms. Winters. I'll take care of all the details," Sarah said.

Victory prayed his cover was good and would hold up to Sarah's scrutiny. At this point she didn't trust anything Tristan told her.

"That's fine. Mr. Braxton said I could phone both Tristan and my sisters."

"Yes, there's a phone right over here." Sarah led her across the hall to a chair and a side table with a phone on it. Victory looked at the phone and then back at both Sarah and Dave. Obviously they weren't going to let her speak to anyone privately.

"Is this the only phone I can use?" she asked.

"It's this or nothing," Dave snapped before Sarah spoke up.

"Fine."

She sat in the chair, turned her back to them, and dialed Payton's cell phone. Payton answered on the second ring. She knew the plan, but in case their call was overheard, Payton needed to convince the kidnappers she was in the dark.

"Hello," Payton answered.

"Hi, Payton, it's Victory."

"Victory! Thank God you're safe. Where are you? Why did you disappear? Are you okay?" She rambled on; it wasn't a stretch trying to act upset. Knowing the plan didn't make her any less distressed with the idea her sister had indeed been kidnapped.

"Calm down, Payton. I'm okay. I should have called you earlier to let you know I needed to deal with a bit of a misunderstanding with one of my business associates. They insist I stick around and help them work out a problem."

Dave gave her a bit of a frown.

"How's Dax?"

"He's okay. He was really agitated for the first day or so after you left, he has finally started to settle down now."

"Give him a kiss and a big hug for me and tell him I'll be home in three weeks. Tristan will be heading out to join me tomorrow. You know how I can't get anything done in my lab without him."

"Ahh, yes, I do know. I'm really glad he will be there to help you," Payton said.

"I need to still call him and Willow, so I guess I had better get moving."

"Okay, Victory…"

"I know, sis; I miss you too and all the doberkids."

"Please, take good care of yourself, and call again when you can," Payton said.

"I will."

"I love you, Victory." Payton whispered into the receiver.

"Right back at you. 'Bye for now."

Victory hung up the phone. For a short span she sat, her eyes closed, as she centered herself and replayed the recording in her mind. Then she opened her eyes and picked up the phone. She punched in Tristan's number as if she'd done it a million times before.

"Yep, what's up?" Tristan asked.

"Hi Tristan, I'm sure you've missed me," Victory said, as if they had known each other for years.

"Hey, doc. I haven't heard from you in one whole week. That's a change; you must actually be enjoying your vacation for once."

"About that. I have a new project for us, starts tomorrow."

"Of course it does. You never have been one to give much notice," Tristan said.

"Nature of the beast, why change now? Make sure to drop the boss an email to let him know we will both be out of the office together. Pack up all our gear. If you could make a stop at my place and get me some clothes, I would really appreciate it. We'll be in a warm climate, so pack accordingly."

She glanced over her shoulder to see if Dave was still there. He chatted with Sarah and remained glued to the same spot. If she wanted to do it, this was her chance.

"I also have a small jar of crystals next to my bed; can you bring those too? They look like a kaleidoscope." The last part she barely breathed out. "Thanks," she said in her normal voice.

"Will do; name the place and time," Tristan said.

"Nine tomorrow morning at Boeing Field, there will be a private helicopter waiting on the tarmac for you."

Victory thought this first conversation was going very smoothly, as if they had indeed worked together for years. This wasn't as difficult as she'd imagined it would be.

"Wow, this one sounds like a first-class kind of job. I think I'm gonna like this," Tristan said.

"I'll see you tomorrow, Tristan."

"See you tomorrow, doc. Take care."

Chapter Eleven

Tristan hung up the phone and looked around the Situation Room.

"She seems to be keeping it together. She gave us a couple of good leads. They will be moving us to somewhere warm. She also mentioned kaleidoscope."

"Are you sure she said kaleidoscope? I could hardly hear her," Jack said.

"Yes, I'm sure. I heard her plain as day. She said her crystals remind her of a kaleidoscope," Tristan said.

"Jack, get on your computer and pull up all of Biotec's properties and labs," Wyatt said. "That might give us a starting point as to where they will be taking Tristan and Victory. But the real problem is, we still don't know who else is involved with this group. You could be shipped anywhere in the world depending on who Lawrence Braxton is in bed with. Logan, you work on the term 'kaleidoscope;' see what you can come up with. Tristan, you need to head out to get all your stuff together. Spend some time at Victory's place, and see if there is anything there she might need or anything you can use. That's it guys; let's get started."

Four hours later the group was back together for an update in the Situation Room.

"Give us an update, Jack," Wyatt said.

"Captain, seems Biotec owns or has shares in a vast number of properties, over three hundred of them. I have compiled a list and ranked them according to the likelihood of priority. Then I took the top twenty that are located in a warmer climate."

"Let's hear your educated guess," Tristan prompted, trying to wait patiently while Jack rambled on.

Jack handed them each a page of the top twenty locations. Each location had a detailed accounting, which contained the number and type of projects, specific buildings, and number of employees currently working at each site.

"Great, this gives us a starting place," Wyatt said.

"Wait. Captain, it gets even better than that. Tell them what you came across in your search Logan," Jack said. He pushed at Logan's shoulder with a big smirk on his face.

"Logan," Wyatt said.

"I plugged in kaleidoscope in all our search engines to see what kind of hits we would get. We pulled up thousands, but one really jumped out at me," Logan said.

"We're all ears," Wyatt said, and took a sip of his coffee.

"Biotec owns one of the smaller Hawaiian Islands where they recently completed a high-tech lab last summer. Two months ago they sold their island and lab to the Kaleidoscope Group."

"There you go," Tristan said. "We finally have our first big lead."

"The Kaleidoscope Group is very clandestine. I can't get a real lead on any of the players in this group. If they can keep themselves this under the radar, I believe we are working with people who have, or are being backed with, a lot of money," Jack said.

"They would have to have a lot of money to be able to purchase an island and build the facilities you are talking about," Logan said.

"No, you don't understand. I don't just mean have money. I mean unlimited amounts of money," Jack said.

"Seems like that should help us narrow the playing field," Wyatt said. "There are a limited number of people who are mega-millionaires. I think the island looks like our best target.

"I'm going to call Noah back in. I've lined up a four-man team for Payton; she will have two guards twenty-four hours a day. I think she is safe for now, but if anything changes with Victory, we will move Payton to a safe house. Noah and Logan will head out to this island tomorrow and do some recon."

"If this is the place, I should be touching down about the same time the guys hit the shore. Should I try to make contact?" Tristan asked.

"No. Your priority is to keep your cover. I don't want to give them any reason to doubt you are who you say you are. Okay, go through the gear you will be taking. Our next job is to integrate some must-have equipment into the gear. Remember, guys, they have a couple ex-military working for them, so we have to be extra careful and extra clever," Wyatt said.

* * * *

Victory sat out in the gardens and heard the distant sound of the helicopter approaching. As if on cue, Sarah walked up to her.

"Ms. Winters, your helicopter will be here in five minutes. Would you like to follow me to the helipad, please?" Sarah asked.

Victory rose and followed Sarah to the other side of the gardens. They approached a twelve-foot chain-link fence with a locked gate. Sarah opened the gate by inputting a combination into a keypad. They both stepped through the open gate and it swung shut and locked behind them. A shiny black helicopter with gold letters spelled Biotec on its side panel came into view. It touched down scant yards away from where they stood. Sarah escorted Victory to the helicopter, the door slid open, and Tristan jumped out to greet her.

* * * *

"Hey, doc, what a great ride. You're gonna love it."

He threw his arms around her like they were long-lost friends and hugged her. Two sensations ran through him. First, the same zip of electricity he felt at the dog show when he caught Victory sizzled up his spine. Second, she stiffened in his arms the instant he touched her. Seems she really didn't trust him, and he was in for a challenge. He whispered in her ear, "Don't forget, I'm here to help you, so lean on me, act like we've known each other for years and try to *pretend* you like me." He pulled back away from her.

* * * *

Victory's questioning gaze locked into the depths of his violet eyes, but she recovered quickly. She smiled brightly, and leaned in to give him a quick peck on the cheek.

"Glad you enjoyed it. I know what a thrill seeker you are," Victory said.

"Okay you two, enough with the hellos; get in the damn helicopter," came a gruff voice from inside the craft.

Victory abruptly went rigid; an icy chill flooded her entire body. In a heartbeat the day in the forest played back in her mind. The memory of the bullets blasting away startled her. She spun back around and faced Tristan with a shocked look and mouthed the words, "He shot Jeffery."

Tristan looked inside the chopper. Jerry was engaged with the pilot. Tristan took Victory's hand and whispered, "Put it out of your mind for now. Don't think about the shooting. You can do this. You can't let him know you know."

Jerry turned from the pilot and refocused his attention back on them.

"Let's go! We're burning daylight and fuel. You'll have all the time in the world to catch up when you get there. Get your asses in this chopper right now."

Tristan made sure he got in first and placed himself between Jerry and Victory. He reached out his hand and helped Victory inside. For the entire trip she kept her attention on the scenery out the window or on Tristan.

"As you can see, we have the entire place to ourselves," Jerry said, as they approached the island. "The company bought the lab along with the island; it makes for the ultimate facility to work on R and D."

The helicopter took one pass around the small island and then landed on the helipad inside the main gate.

"Everything you need for your work will be provided in the lab," Jerry said.

A Hawaiian boy approached them as they got out of the helicopter.

"This is where we part ways. Go with Andy; he will show you both to your rooms." Jerry reached into the helicopter, grabbed his bag, and walked away.

"Guess, security isn't an issue here," Tristan said.

"This way," Andy said, and gestured with his arm. "I will take you to your rooms. You can get settled."

Victory and Tristan followed along behind.

"So Andy, how long have you worked here?" Tristan asked casually.

"I helped build the place," he said.

"Really. So you must live on the island?"

"I used to. But when Biotec bought the island, they moved my whole village to the next island over. The elders were upset at first, until they saw the new village Biotec built for us."

Tristan and Victory glanced at one another.

"So, you think Biotec is pretty great people," Tristan said.

"The elders think so," Andy said. "Here are your rooms. Miss Winters, you are here; and Mr. Grant, you are across the walkway."

Andy handed each of them a key card.

"If you need anything else, there is an inter-island phone in your room; press zero to reach me." He gave them a slight bow and turned and left.

Victory stood silently and stared down at her key card.

* * * *

"You look beat. Why don't you go in and get settled, take a nap for a couple of hours? I'll find out where and when dinner is, and wake you later this evening," Tristan said, gently leading her to the door to her room.

Victory glanced up at Tristan.

"Shouldn't we talk?" she asked.

"We'll have plenty of time for that. Besides this is not the place or time." Tristan stepped close and hugged her. Again he felt her tense in his arms. "The walls may have ears," he murmured. "I need to get the lay of the land." Then he backed away from her. "Really Victory, I won't let you miss dinner. I'll come and wake you in a few hours. Go and rest now; you're no good to anyone when you're this worn out." He smiled at her as if he'd known her for years.

"I guess you're right. Promise you won't forget me. I know how you get when a meal is on the line." She tilted her head up to look into his smoldering eyes, the molten violet color intensifying to a midnight blue. A shy smile lifted the left corner of her mouth.

Tristan could swear his pulse almost doubled as he gazed down into her sleepy face. Even with the stress of the last couple of days beating down on her, Victory's dazzling jade eyes sparkled up at him, framed by her silky caramel-colored hair. Coupled with the subtle fragrance of lavender and chamomile, it was all he could do to keep from running his hands through her beckoning locks. Tristan swore he would never get her scent out of his head or his blood.

"Tristan," Victory said.

"Hmm?" He shook his head trying to clear his thoughts.

"You will wake me, right?"

"Yes. I said I would. Now go take a nap."

He took her key card from her hand and inserted it into the door, opened it, and handed it back to her.

"See you soon." He turned and walked away, leaving her standing in the doorway.

Tristan strolled around for over two hours and no one made the slightest effort to stop him. The compound was massive. It was thoughtfully laid out; it contained dorms, labs, offices, test areas, and a mess hall. They even had a community center. The center looked huge, and housed a theater large enough to seat seventy-five people, a bowling alley, a canteen, and a coffee shop that would rival Barnes & Noble. The coffee shop housed thousands of books. While chatting with the barista she informed him he could borrow as many books as he'd like and as often as he wanted. There was a pool, a spa, a weight room, and basketball and tennis courts, even an indoor running track.

Each building and trail was clearly marked with what looked like hand-carved signs. The local foliage was expertly placed throughout the entire compound, giving it a flare of authentic island flavor.

Tristan was the new guy here and acted the part. He wanted to get a "feel" for the place. In fact, several people greeted him along the way, giving him the opportunity for conversations with some of the employees. He noticed one fenced-in area with "security clearance" and "high-voltage stay clear" signs posted at the gate and what looked like a fingerprint scan lock. He gave the area a wide berth, but he peripherally plotted its layout in his head, which he thought contained at least two large and three smaller buildings.

Victory opened her eyes to what sounded like hammering.

"Who's making that God-awful noise?" she asked herself. She woke to pitch-black around her, and a sudden panic shot through her. "Where am I?"

"Victory, Victory, are you awake? Are you in there?" Tristan nearly yelled at the door. Damn, he'd stood here for over ten minutes knocking on her door. Now the knock had become full-fledged pounding. He started to worry. Had she wandered off, or did someone take her from her room when he left her there. "Vic—"

"Stop making so much racket. Do you want the whole facility to hear you?" She pulled the door open during his last panicked banging and stood in the doorway, all fiery five feet of her. Her hair tousled, hands on her sexy hips, a slight tint of rose-colored glow on her milky smooth face, and her eyes a blazing deep aquamarine. Tristan was being pulled into the abyss; he had never seen eyes change color with a person's mood the way Victory's obviously did.

"I've been standing here for over nine minutes. I really started to worry," he replied in little more than a mumble, marveling at the intensity of her eyes.

"Oh, sorry. I must have been more tired than I thought; I didn't hear you," she said. Her voice dropped decibels to match his, her cheeks immediately pinking darker from her embarrassment. "If you give me a sec, I can get myself together, and we can go to dinner." Victory switched on the light in her room and headed for the bathroom. "Don't stand there, come in, and have a seat; I'll be ready in a second or two, really."

Tristan blinked at the bright light and rubbed his face. "Damn," he muttered to himself. It had happened again. He was going to have to really work at staying focused and in the present when Victory was around. "Damn," he said again. He felt like some sixteen-year-old kid with his first crush.

"Did you say something?" Victory asked. She knew what he said. Now that she felt back in the land of the living she could hear a pin drop in the next room, but she didn't want to intrude.

"Holy hell," Tristan mumbled under his breath. He had forgotten about her hearing; he wouldn't make the same mistake again, he hoped. "Nope, only talking to myself; your lights are really bright." *Idiot, was that the best you could do,* he thought to himself.

Victory reappeared from the bathroom. If he hadn't seen it himself, he would not have believed it.

"Let's go; I'm starved," she said.

In less than five minutes, she had changed and fixed her hair and her makeup, although he thought she looked great the way she was when she answered the door. Now this was his kind of woman.

"Okay then, after you." Tristan opened the door and held it for her. "Dinner it is."

Chapter Twelve

"Wow," Victory exclaimed as she entered the lab slated to be her new workplace for the next three weeks. "This is really some kind of facility. I thought Claremont had all the new bells and whistles, but this place is even ten times nicer than my—our lab."

She almost made her first big blunder by excluding the fact Tristan was indeed supposed to be her real assistant and therefore knew what their lab looked like. He'd filled her in last night on what he discovered. The lab was bugged and had a video feed. The main living space in both of their rooms was bugged, but their bedrooms and bathrooms were clean. They could have a conversation in their rooms, but they would have to move into the bedroom or bathroom to keep it private. Talking in either of those rooms would be an awkward situation. All the outdoor areas had small cameras every twenty feet, and the community center was also heavily monitored.

"I know you like all the latest and greatest Victory, but I like our own lab. I know where everything is and how everything works," Tristan said not missing a beat.

Maybe this wasn't going to be as impossible as she first thought. He was good, a quick thinker on his feet. Victory hoped he had some knowledge and understanding of the work she was doing.

"Let's get started." She walked over to the main computer and turned it on, sat in the chair, and began to read all the data and experiments Biotec had compiled.

* * * *

"Victory, you've been at it for five hours. It's time to take a break. Let's go grab some lunch and stretch our legs along the water," Tristan said.

Victory looked up at Tristan. He towered over her, one hand lay on the desk, his other hand casually draped on the back of her chair, his fingers brushed lightly across her back. She startled and flushed at his sudden nearness. When had he approached her? With her extra-keen sense of hearing no one had ever startled her, until now.

* * * *

Tristan's gaze locked on hers. He could see the sadness radiate from her expression. A number of times during the morning she made tiny gasps while reading the detailed accounts of the experiments conducted. He caught bits and pieces while working around the lab, and reading over her shoulder when he felt her sadness. Some of the experiments done in the name of science had been brutal and ill-prepared. No wonder they wanted Victory.

"Come on, one hour out in the sunshine and then you can get back to your computer." He smiled down at her, and as he did, he flipped off the computer and gently reached for her hand. He led her out of the lab.

* * * *

Noah and Logan lay on their stomachs camouflaged by the local vegetation. They'd been doing recon on the facility for the last three days. They drew detailed maps of the security system and tried to locate any weak spots. After hours of complete silence between the two, Logan finally whispered.

"Man, they got this place locked down tight and security continues out to the beach and into part of the forest."

"Every system has a weak spot. It's entirely a matter of identifying it," Noah said. "I think our best bet is around back, where they load all the incoming supplies."

"Yeah, I agree, fewer civilians around to contend with too. Let's head back to camp and work out the details. We can contact HQ tonight."

The two men blended back into the bushes.

* * * *

Victory and Tristan shut the door to the laboratory and stepped out into the fresh evening air. The long, draining day was reflected on Victory's face.

"How about a short stroll around the campus and then off to dinner?" Tristan asked.

"The walk sounds good, but I don't think I'm up to facing all the people who will be in the mess hall," Victory said wearily as she rubbed her tired eyes and then shoved her hands into her jeans pockets.

"Yeah, today proved to be a tough day. Unfortunately, it won't be getting any easier," he said.

"I know. It's going to take some getting used to. Those men must have been in tremendous pain during those experiments and for days afterward." Victory blew out a disgusted breath. "This research is nowhere near ready to implant into humans. I don't understand the hurry or what Braxton's ultimate goal is," she said.

"You have to eat, Victory. You need to keep your strength up if you want any chance of seeing this through to the end. I'll take you back to your room and then go and get us both something to eat."

"That's not necessary," she said.

"Yes, it is. I won't have you wearing yourself out. You do that and you won't be good to anyone, including yourself," Tristan said.

* * * *

They ate their dinner and carried on idle conversation about the day's events, playing their roles for the listeners who monitored Victory's room. Twice during the meal, Victory noticed Tristan putting his hands up to his head as if he might be experiencing a headache.

"Are you all right?" she finally asked when he shook his head as if trying to clear his thoughts.

"I'm fine; I have a bit of a headache," he said.

"Would you like something for it? I have pain medicine I think might help."

As she rose to leave the table, she noticed he followed her. As they entered the bedroom, Tristan quietly closed the door behind them. She turned back toward him with a hesitant look. He put his finger up to his lips and gestured for her to remain quiet. Then he walked around the room, checking to see it was still clear of bugs. Victory sat down on the small love seat across from her bed. A few minutes later he sat down next to her.

"I have this connection with my brother. For as long as I can remember, we have had both the ability to read each other's thoughts as well as the ability to communicate telepathically. We try not to read one another's thoughts, it's a real invasion of privacy, especially the older we get. But it still happens every now and then."

Tristan spoke quietly, looking straight into Victory's gaze. Outside of his team, he'd never told another soul about this ability, but he felt she might understand.

"Since we have been in the compound, I haven't been able to reach him. Every time I try, I get a buzzing sensation flooding my brain." Victory looked stunned. Triston wondered if he had made a mistake in telling her his secret. Then he thought he saw a sliver of excitement dance in her crystal-green eyes.

"Wow, a natural telepathic connection. I've always had a sense of oneness with nature, but not a true telepathic connection. Can he read all of your thoughts? Is he there all the time? Does it feel like two people inside of your brain?"

She was so excited, Tristan didn't have a chance to answer any of her questions.

"We have developed a conduit between us and learned not to intrude in one another's private thoughts. We have to focus on only that particular channel to communicate. So no, I don't feel like I have two people inside my head. I guess we have grown accustomed to it. We have learned to give one another space and privacy. Although Wyatt does tend to butt in every now and then. Of course, he doesn't think so," Tristan said with a smile. "Lately, I would love to hear him say hey."

"Braxton must have a high-tech security grid encompassing the compound. It would make sense, with the types of experiments they are performing, he wouldn't want any subjects able to communicate with the outside world," Victory explained as if she were thinking out loud. "Oh no, I just had a terrible thought. We can't let Braxton find out about your abilities. I'm sure he would love to use you in his sick experiments."

"Don't worry. I have no intention of letting him find out. I'm being very careful when I try to reach Wyatt. I really could use something for this blasted headache though."

"Sorry. You totally distracted me. I'll go and get you something for the pain." She got up and headed to the bathroom. She turned back with another thought. "But don't keep trying to reach him. You won't be able to get through, and it will intensify the pain in your head. We need to find out what type of grid he is using. He might even have the ability to pinpoint who is using their psychic powers. That's another reason not to keep trying to contact your brother. We need to keep this on the down-low."

She continued into the bathroom and returned with a bottle of pain medicine.

"I started working on a sort of detection system. I am close to being able to pinpoint psychic powers and locate any animal or person giving off psychic waves."

Victory handed Tristan a couple of pills and a glass of water. He tossed them into his mouth and followed with a large gulp of water. He stared at her briefly. They had spent only a few days together and already he admired her and her seemingly unending abilities. This woman who stood before him was a very rare find, in more ways than one. No wonder Braxton went to such lengths to secure her. Victory gazed back at him, puzzlement playing across her features. He shook his head slightly and attempted to refocus his thoughts.

"Does anyone know about your new research?"

"No, I don't think so. This is something I have been working on all on my own. Psychic abilities are something I am personally interested in; I guess you could call it my hobby. I am working on trying to detect the subtle ripples in energy someone or something gives off when using their abilities. I keep all my research on my personal laptop. I didn't even want to introduce it to my department until I worked out all the bugs," Victory said.

"With any luck Braxton didn't think there was any need to confiscate your laptop. Make sure you don't mention this while we are in the lab. We don't want to give him any more information than we have to." Tristan looked at his watch. "We have been in here for over an hour."

"So?" she said.

"To keep our cover we need to appear as more than work companions," Tristan said.

The color drained from her face and turned it ashen; at the same time, her neck flushed a bright crimson.

"What are you trying to say?" The tenseness returned to her body.

"Sorry Victory, I know this might be uncomfortable. But we need to act like we have an ongoing secret relationship. Otherwise our peeping Toms might begin to wonder what we are doing in here."

"Great."

She dropped down onto the end of her bed. She stared down at her hands. She wasn't going to tell him, faking a relationship with him wouldn't be a real problem for her. She found his smoldering violet eyes, midnight-black hair, and five o'clock shadow tantalizing. Yes, he was stunning, but that by no means meant she trusted him.

"Fine, if it gets us out of here and keeps my sisters safe, I can do it," she said, trying to sound like this would be a real effort.

"Okay, I'm going to go back to my room now and get some sleep. You need to get some rest too." Tristan got up and headed for the door, his head still pounding. Shit, he hoped the medicine kicked in soon or it was going to be a long night. The intense pain made his jaw clench.

"Tristan." He turned to find her right behind him. "Take this bottle with you. You can take two more pills in an hour if you aren't any better."

Wonderful, he must look as bad as he felt.

"Thanks."

He opened the bedroom door, but then turned back. He smiled and before she knew what happened, he leaned in and kissed her on the lips, ever so lightly.

"I'll see you first thing in the morning. I'll come back here and go with you to breakfast."

He headed straight for the hall, leaving Victory frozen at the threshold of her bedroom.

"Make sure you lock the door as soon as I leave," he casually tossed over his shoulder.

"I will," she stammered.

Had sparks flashed from our lips? Tristan wondered. He knew full well no lock would stop Braxton or his people if they wanted to enter her room. He walked out into the hall and waited for the click of the lock. He was bewildered by the electricity that sparked between them at the second his lips touched hers and wondered if she had felt the same sensation. He really needed a little downtime if he was going to be any help to Victory.

Chapter Thirteen

Buzz, buzz. Logan shook his head and rubbed his still sleepy face. He surveyed the confined camp he and Noah had set up in the back of a small cave. They'd found a great location, but the bunks left a lot to be desired. Buzz. "Moron." He grumbled. He'd almost forgotten the reason he woke up. He rolled over and grabbed the sat phone.

"Logan."

"Dammit Logan, you two still sleep like rocks. This is the second time I tried to reach you," Wyatt's voice vibrated through the phone.

"Sorry, sir," Logan said. "What time is it? I feel like we hardly hit the bunk."

"It's Oh five thirty," Wyatt continued, not waiting for a response. He heard a groan in the background that brought a small smile to his face. "Have you made contact with Tristan yet?"

"No, sir. But we have seen him in the compound every day, and it looks like he has the situation under control," Logan said.

"They must have some high-tech grid over the entire facility. I haven't been able to contact him either. I was getting worried, but as long as you have eyes on him, I won't worry yet."

"Wow, must be some kind of security to be able to keep you out." Logan yawned and rubbed his face once more. The sun was beginning to rise. It gave off an eerie glow over the island. Logan was barely able to see the tiny speck of light from deep inside their cave.

"We knew going in we would be dealing with a group on the cutting edge of technology. I guess they are proving us right. Are we still on point?" Wyatt asked.

"Yes, sir," Logan said. "We found our way in late yesterday. We will map out our entry and hang tight for Tristan's go."

"Good. Make sure you keep us in the loop. We can ship another teammate out to you if you need the help."

"We've got it under control, captain. We'll report to you each evening," Logan said.

"Okay, good luck." Wyatt broke the connection.

Logan looked over at Noah, who was inside his sleeping bag with it pulled up over his head. Man, that guy could sleep through an atomic bomb, if he wasn't on duty. Since there was nothing to be done for the next couple of hours, Logan decided to catch a few more hours sleep.

* * * *

"Good afternoon, Victory," Braxton greeted her as he strolled into the lab. "This must be your assistant," he said. He glanced at Tristan with a sneer on his face.

"I'm Lawrence Braxton, your boss while you are both guests on my island. And your name?"

Tristan looked up from the data on his computer at the infamous CEO of Biotec.

"I'm Tristan Grant." Tristan had no doubt Braxton already knew all about him, including how long he and Victory had worked together, along with the entire resume Jack meticulously created for this occasion. "It's very nice to meet you, sir," Tristan continued, extending his hand out for Braxton to shake. After all, he wasn't supposed to know what kind of scum Braxton really was. As far as he knew, this was only another consulting job for him and his boss.

* * * *

The door to the lab swung open as Detective Ken Howard walked through. He stopped short when he spotted Victory. For a heartbeat a look of concern flashed across his face, quickly disguised by a mask of arrogance.

In an attempt to gather information for Braxton, Howard had an affair with Lisa Evans, a Claremont employee. He had sworn Lisa to secrecy and convinced her their relationship could affect his position in the police department. Ken's original plan involved using Lisa and then breaking off their affair. Unfortunately, one evening Lisa had caught Howard copying Claremont company files from her home computer. He couldn't leave any loose ends, so he strangled her. He loaded her body into his car and dumped her in the parking garage of Claremont Research, making her death look like a mugging gone wrong. This change in plans actually aided Howard. He was the first detective to respond to the scene of the crime. This allowed him the opportunity to interview every employee. However, this twist of fate brought Howard to his current predicament. Victory knew Howard was a detective.

"Allow me to introduce my travelling companion. Ken Howard, meet Victory Winters and her lab assistant, Tristan Grant," Braxton said.

"Yes, we've met," Victory rallied back. "Detective Howard came to Claremont to investigate the murder of Lisa Evans, a work colleague of mine."

* * * *

Braxton continued on, as if Victory had not uttered a word.

"I trust you have had adequate time to familiarize yourselves with this project. It's time you start to move ahead. I want you to proceed with testing today. I will be on the island for the next two days and checking in regularly. After which time I will be contacting you via Skype each afternoon." Braxton moved around the laboratory taking mental notes of their progress.

"What type of testing?" Victory asked hesitantly.

"You will be receiving two vials of serum and a test subject." Braxton looked down at his wristwatch. "The test subject is receiving the serum right about now; this way, please." He gestured to the back of the lab where a large mirror covered the upper half of the wall.

As they approached the mirror, lights came on and illuminated a room behind the mirror. Tristan had assumed this was a one-way mirror, but he thought it was for Braxton's people to watch him and Victory. He was taken aback to see what looked like an examination room, complete with exam chair, monitors, and other medical equipment. It wasn't all the equipment he found disconcerting. A man sat strapped to the exam chair, shirtless and showing off his defined muscles, his steely black eyes burning holes through the window.

"What are you doing?" Victory nearly gasped, her face pale, appalled by what she saw. "This formula is nowhere near ready for human test subjects. You didn't tell me I would be using human subjects." Terror and anger totally overwhelmed her. She turned on Braxton, her eyes threatening to spill over with the tears she could hardly hold back. Tristan's heart nearly split in two at the sight.

"I'm not a physician," she continued. "I can't help this man if anything goes wrong."

"I'm not asking you to treat him, Ms. Winters. We have our own physicians on staff. I want you to study and improve upon what has been started." Braxton threw her a predatory look. "Don't be so naïve; you are here because you are a world-renowned Ph.D. in genetic work."

He turned his back on the two and walked to the door, which Howard held open. "I will be back at the end of the day and expect some results," he said, without so much as a backward glance.

Howard shot Victory a menacing glare and then followed Braxton out of the lab.

"Are you—" Tristan started. He stopped abruptly as Victory looked up at him. He didn't want her to say anything that would give them away. Tristan saw the etched shock on Victory's face and reached down for

140

her hand. "Come on, Victory, we are going to have a long hard afternoon. We need to take a break, have some lunch and maybe a short walk." He nearly dragged her from the room.

"The man is insane," Victory said, as she walked along the beach absently kicking at the small pebbles in her path.

Tristan felt like a huge weight lifted from his shoulders as she finally spoke. They had gone to the mess hall and eaten lunch, during which time Victory hadn't uttered a single word. Finally her initial shock had worn off.

"I realize Biotec is a huge corporation, still I can't believe they are so powerful they could get away with all this," she said, swinging her arms out in front of her. "Detective Howard investigated Lisa's murder. He told us Lisa got accosted by a drug addict looking for money. Now I wonder if he didn't kill her himself." Her pain was once again turning to pure anger.

"What would make you think that?" Tristan asked.

"Lisa and I would have lunch together every now and then, but we weren't what you would call good friends. About a month before her death, she told me she was seeing someone in the police department. When I asked her who, she wouldn't tell me," Victory said.

Tristan processed this new information. "There is a very good chance you're right. Howard could have murdered Lisa. He works for Braxton. It would make sense for Braxton to send in a spy to gather information about his competitor. What better way for Howard to obtain this information than by dating an employee.

And as far as Biotec being so powerful, it isn't solely Biotec," Tristan said.

Victory stopped and looked up into his face, unspoken questions reflected in her expression.

"We did some digging before I came out. Took your lead, remember? You whispered 'kaleidoscope' during our phone conversation. This facility is owned by a corporation called Kaleidoscope Group," Tristan said.

Confusion ran across her face. "But why would anyone want to kill Lisa? She was such a sweet, gentle person. I don't think she had an enemy in the world."

"Best guess: Howard used her to gather information, and once he had everything he needed, he tied up his loose ends."

Sadness and hatred warred in Victory's eyes. "Poor Lisa, she deserved so much better. Wait, did you just say kaleidoscope? Yes, I heard Braxton mention that word. I've never heard of them."

"No one has. This highly clandestine corporation has stayed under the wire, until now. Our best guess is Kaleidoscope Group is owned by a cartel of ultra-rich business tycoons throughout the country, possibly throughout the world," Tristan said.

Victory stopped dead in her tracks, a shocked look flashed across her face.

"Keep moving, Victory. I have a feeling we are being watched." As he said that, he reached for her hand and pulled her along with him. "We believe someone in the government is involved in this conglomeration, or at the very least, aware of its existence. That is the only possible explanation as to how this facility has stayed under wraps for so long."

"So, what you are saying is there is more than one insane person involved in this project. Isn't that wonderful? It makes me feel so much better," Victory said.

"What it means is—we are dealing with a very powerful group of people. They feel they are untouchable."

"Yes, they do and at the cost of how many lives? Jeffery, Lisa, and the man in the lab. Those are only the ones we know of," she threw back at him.

Victory knew she needed Tristan here to pull off this scheme and keep her sisters safe. Still, she didn't trust him and wasn't sure what his end goal might be.

"Much fewer than if we didn't get involved," Tristan rallied back at her.

She glared up into his eyes and retreated a small step, her angelic peach complexion reddened. She dropped her eyes and stared down at her fidgeting hands.

"I'm sorry," Victory all but whispered. "I didn't mean any of this is your fault. It's—who is that poor man in the chair, Tristan? How did he get involved with this maniac, and does he have any idea what Braxton has planned for him?"

"I'm sorry too. I didn't mean to get cross with you." He was only too aware she didn't fully trust him, so he attempted to lighten the mood. "Hey, I think we had our first lovers' quarrel."

* * * *

Victory turned apprehensively and looked back up into Tristan's now serene eyes. She noticed the inky color she'd seen only moments before was now replaced with a vivid violet. His sharp features had softened, which made him quite breathtaking. All were framed by his stunning blue-black hair.

"What I mean is, we are supposed to appear to be more than work associates. This little disagreement reinforces the façade to anyone watching. And believe me, there is always someone watching around here," Tristan said.

"You really think so?" Victory asked shyly.

"Boy, for such an intelligent person you can sure be naive." His comment had slipped out of his mouth before he had a chance to censor it.

"Thanks a lot," she commented rather tersely.

"I don't mean it as a put-down. In fact, at times I think it might be really nice to not be aware of all the crazy and sick people in this world. You seem so innocent."

As they walked along the beach, she could feel the heat of his body beside her, and she forced herself to continue looking straight ahead.

"I know there are bad people in this world. In case you forgot, I witnessed Jeffery being killed and a corrupt police detective took part in his death. I guess I choose to see the good in the world. Sorry if I sound naïve. Right now I have to deal with the really ugly Braxton's in this world. I haven't done enough research to be certain what ramifications could result from injecting the serum into a live human. Worst-case scenario? It could kill him. Best case, it will permanently change his genetic makeup." Victory stared out at the ocean; *when would this nightmare come to an end,* she thought.

* * * *

Tristan stopped, grabbed hold of Victory's shoulders, and slowly turned her to face him. When she kept her head down to avoid his gaze, he gently placed his hand under her chin and tilted it up until she was forced to look directly at him.

"You are the very best at what you do right?" He saw the question play across her face and then she gave a slight nod. "You know more about genetic testing and the possible ramifications than anyone else in your field. That gives this guy the best possible chance of making it though this mess."

Before she could respond he continued, "You are ready to deal with this, Victory. You have to be. People are counting on you, including your sisters. I know you can do this. Let's go back to the lab and get this started so we can finish it. One day Lawrence Braxton will get what's coming to him."

He didn't give her a chance to answer. Tristan took her hand and headed for the compound.

* * * *

Braxton pulled his ringing phone from his breast pocket.

"Yes."

"You were right, boss. The scientist and her assistant share more than a workspace. I've watched them since they left the compound. There is positively more going on than a work relationship between the two," Max said, still looking through his high-powered binoculars toward the beach.

"Good. It will give me one more tool to use if I can't get her to cooperate. Keep track of them until they return to the lab," Braxton said, and ended the conversation.

Braxton looked up from his desk and watched Howard pace back and forth like a caged lion.

"Why didn't you tell me that Victory Winters was the woman you brought here?" Howard scoffed, barely able to keep his anger in check.

"Why didn't you tell me Victory had done extensive research in genetic manipulation?" Braxton fired back without any hesitation. "That's why I sent you into Claremont in the first place. To find out if any of their scientists had gotten involved in this type of research."

"When I interviewed Victory, all she would tell me is she was a research specialist. She wouldn't reveal any specific information. I tried to push her, but she informed me her research was classified. She said if I wanted to know more, I would have to get a court order. I questioned Lisa about Victory, and she gave me the same research specialist line. I didn't think it was relevant at the time, so I left it alone."

"I don't pay you to think, Detective Howard. I pay you for information, and you failed to provide pertinent information."

Howard realized he had pushed too far, so he decided on a new route.

"Victory is an intelligent woman. She is eventually going to put two and two together and figure out I killed Lisa."

"No matter," Braxton said. "As long as I hold the fates of her sisters in my hand, Victory will do as I wish. Besides, she will never again be a free woman." Braxton looked down at his watch. "It's getting late. The helicopter will be ready to leave soon. Get yourself together and get back to the helipad. You don't want your department to wonder what happened to you."

Howard stayed rooted in his spot and momentarily contemplated continuing the conversation, but thought better of it and headed for the door.

"Fine. I'll touch base with you after you get back to the mainland."

* * * *

Max entered the laboratory, where he found Victory intensely studying something on her computer and Tristan sorting through paper files.

"I'm glad you are here," Victory said, without looking up from her computer. "I need access to the patient in order to move forward in my work."

"I can't let you in there. Mr. Braxton has not given you permission to enter the exam room," Max said.

"If Mr. Braxton wants me to formulate any conclusions, I will need access to the patient," Victory said.

Max stared at her, blatantly he ran his gaze up and down her entire body. Tristan could feel the hairs on the back of his neck stand on end. It took all his will not to punch this guy. As if he read Tristan's mind, Max glowered at Tristan and frowned. Then he turned and left the lab. A few minutes later he returned.

"You can have access to the subject, but not alone. I will be in the exam room with you. You are not allowed to enter the exam room without me."

"Fine. But stay out of my way." Victory was determined not to let Max bully her. She turned to Tristan. "I need you to prepare six vials and accompany me into the exam room."

Tristan nodded and readied the equipment.

Max unlocked the door to the exam room and held it open for Victory and Tristan, and he followed them into the room. As he entered Tristan was inundated by the stench of pure rage vibrating off the man strapped to the exam chair. Tristan stopped abruptly, shook his head to clear his thoughts, and inhaled a cleansing breath. He opened his eyes and was met with threatening dark-brown eyes. He could swear he picked up an ever-so-slight scent of wolf.

With a syringe in hand Victory cautiously approached the man. Instantly the man's full attention refocused in on her.

"Victory, be careful," Tristan warned.

She turned and looked at Tristan. "I know what I am doing Tristan; don't worry. It's your responsibility to make sure everything is ready."

She could hear the man's heartbeat accelerate as she approached him and a low growl vibrated from his very core. She tried to calm him and sent waves of sympathy his way. His heartbeat wouldn't slow, and she could feel his anger being directed toward her. She cleared her mind, and turned her entire focus on him in an attempt to communicate telepathically, as she had done hundreds of times with hurt animals.

"We aren't your enemy. We are trying to help you."

Both Tristan and the man in the chair shot her a look of surprise. Victory noticed the man's heartbeat began to slow slightly.

"What's taking you so long?" Max shot at her. "Get the damn blood and get out."

Victory cautiously approached the man. When he didn't show any signs of aggression, she wrapped the tourniquet around his upper arm and inserted the needle. The entire time the man's glare never wavered; it bore directly into Victory's eyes.

Chapter Fourteen

"What did you think you were doing today?" Tristan asked, after securely closing the door to her bedroom.

"What do you mean?" she asked, with a dumbfounded look on her face.

"In the exam room you attempted to communicate telepathically with that man."

She looked at him, shock on her face. "You knew?"

"Yes, I heard every word," Tristan said.

"What do you mean you heard every word? I can only communicate using feelings and thoughts. Not words, not sentences. I have never had a human hear me," she said in amazement.

"I got every word, and from the look on the guy's face, so did he. You need to be careful. We have no idea what is really going on here."

Tristan was angry with her behavior, but there was something underneath the anger, something he didn't want to confront. Could it be fear?

"One thing I do know is he was enraged and distraught. His heartbeat elevated and I could swear I heard a slight growl come from him. I only wanted to calm him. I don't understand how you both could have heard my thoughts. I've only ever been able to communicate feelings. At least that's what I have always thought. Hmmm. I wonder if telepathy is linked with the DNA that was injected into him. But it still wouldn't explain how you could have heard my thoughts," Victory said, as she studied his face.

"I can communicate telepathically with my brother. But I have never been able to communicate with anyone else. As far as our friend, my best guess is the serum too. When I entered the exam room, I caught the scent of wolf. Do you know what type of DNA got injected?"

"According to the file, canine, but it didn't specify what exact type." Victory was astonished. She didn't know which astounded her more: The fact that Tristan had smelled wolf, or that he, and very possibly the man in the lab, had heard her thoughts.

"Then the serum must be taking effect. Can his genetic makeup actually combine with the canine DNA?" Tristan asked.

"That's the problem," Victory said. "It is too soon to conduct this test on humans. For all we know the canine DNA could completely take over his system, and destroy his original genetic makeup. His body would try to fight it off, react to it as if it were another disease, which might even kill him. This has never been done on this scale, only on mice. Many of the mice totally changed their behavior; they became aggressive and turned on each other. And now we are dealing with human intelligence. There is no telling how human intelligence could be affected by the DNA clashes. Part of my research involves attempting to create a genetic buffer between human DNA and foreign or canine DNA. I am trying to create a linked pathway between the two, to allow both to coexist in one host, without negative reactions."

"And have you succeeded?"

"According to all my data, it is possible, at least on paper."

"Victory, I have a feeling Braxton is aware of your research. This whole setup seems all too convenient."

"Then maybe I should ask him to retrieve my laptop. It could save me some time. I have an excellent memory, but I'm sure I have forgotten some of the minor details."

"No. We don't want him to have any more information than we possibly need to give him," Tristan answered abruptly. "You will have to rely on that beautiful brain of yours." He stopped talking and cocked his head toward the hall door. He inhaled and filled his lungs with deep full breaths.

Victory grew quiet and watched him.

He looked at her, noticed her usual peach complexion etched with dark lines of worry and exhaustion.

"There are a couple of guys standing on the path close to your door. I haven't encountered them before; both of their scents are unknown to me."

She was surprised these men had approached without her hearing them. She attributed it to the intense conversation she and Tristan were involved in. Now she listened. She focused only on the intruders.

"Yes. They are debating who will stand first watch," she said.

"Don't worry about them. They aren't a threat; they are our watchdogs for the evening. You need to get some sleep; you look exhausted."

"Gee thanks. Is this your roundabout way of telling me I look like crap?" she joked lightheartedly. She felt worn out, but this brief span of playful banter between them gave her a feeling of release.

"No. You always look great. But anyone can see you are in need of sleep."

"I've had a hard time sleeping here. I spend all my time worrying. I know I shouldn't ask—but would you mind staying until I fall asleep?"

Tristan stared at her for a heartbeat, confused for only an instant about what she was asking.

"Ahh, I guess we are supposed to be a couple, so it would look more authentic if I spent the night, so to speak," he replied with a boyish grin.

* * * *

"Tristan."

There is was again. Maybe it wasn't a dream.
"Tristan."

Tristan's eyes flew open, and he bolted up and looked around the dark room. For a split second, he was disoriented. Then he felt the warmth of Victory curled up next to him. A shaft of moonlight streamed through the window blinds and landed on Victory. It illuminated her honeyed-colored hair fanned out on her pillow and her heart-shaped face, free of all lines of worry. He noticed the creamy peach color had returned to her face.

"Tristan, can you hear me?" Wyatt's voice rang clear in his head.

"Wyatt. You finally made contact, but how is it possible? I know the grid is still in place."

Then he felt it, a strong vibration of telepathic energy flowed through him. He glanced down into Victory's serene face; it had to be her.

"I've been trying to reach you since you went in. I couldn't push hard enough to get through the grid. But tonight I felt your presence. I thought you might have located a breach in the grid," Wyatt said.

"No. Something even better, I think I have stumbled on a psychic amplifier," Tristan said.

"Not possible. True amplifiers are extremely rare. If that is the case, you should have used this person's ability sooner."

"Believe me, I would have had I known. Even she doesn't know she is an amplifier."

"She?" Wyatt asked.

"It's Victory. She's sleeping next to me. When sleeping her barriers are down and her natural psychic energy is rippling through. I knew she had psychic ability, but I didn't realize her ability was this strong," Tristan said.

"Victory. You're sleeping in the same bed as Victory. Great. I hope you are only trying to put on a good show. This is not the time for a fling, Tristan. You two are in serious danger." Wyatt was certainly not happy about the situation.

"It's not like that. Never mind; you will have to take my word for it. Nothing is going on; it's all for show. The woman doesn't even trust me, much less like me."

"If you say so. Fill me in on what you found."

Tristan and Wyatt communicated until right before the sun came up. Then Tristan lay back down next to Victory and studied her. She was breathtaking, with her flawless complexion, shimmering light brown hair, and her creamy neck. As he drew his gaze back up to her face, Victory's jade eyes met his. Without a thought he leaned into her and brushed the lightest kiss across her lips. She pulled him to her, the softness and warmth of her body hypnotizing him. He claimed her lips and as she responded to him, he coaxed her lips apart with his tongue and thrust into the warmth of her mouth. It felt soft and warm, like heaven.

* * * *

Abruptly Victory pulled back, her eyes large and glassy. "I'm—I'm sorry," she stammered.

What on Earth had she been thinking, kissing this man? For all she knew, the only reason he was here helping her was for her research.

A small smile caught at the edge of his mouth.

"For what? I could get use to waking up like this."

"I don't know what I was thinking. I just—"

"Don't worry about it, Victory. I personally enjoyed it; don't tell me you didn't," he teased her.

Victory slipped out of bed and headed to the bathroom.

"It surprised me to see you still here. Guess I thought you would have left after I fell asleep." She called back over her shoulder as she closed the bathroom door behind her.

Actually he had planned to leave right after she fell asleep last night. He didn't even remember what

155

happened. One second he was watching her fall asleep, and the next Wyatt was waking him. Frankly, the entire chain of events was totally unlike him. He never let his guard down.

Twenty minutes later Victory walked out of the bathroom freshly showered and dressed. Her hair pulled back loosely with a barrette, exposing the soft pink skin of her neck. Tristan sat as still as a stalking cat sizing its prey. A tiny shiver ran up the back of her neck.

"I'll go make some coffee; feel free to use my shower." She felt like a teenager unsure of what to do or how to act. She headed out to the kitchen, needing to escape Tristan.

"Wait," Tristan said. He reached out to grab her arm before she left the bedroom. He gently pulled her back into the room and quietly closed the door. "I have to ask you something."

She stood still facing the door, deliberately not looking anywhere near his direction.

"You told me you can only communicate with animals," Tristan said. "Have you had this telepathic ability since birth or is it something you developed later in life?"

"I don't understand what you mean. I told you before, I'm not telepathic. I can only transmit feelings to animals. I can't communicate with people." She turned to Tristan with a look of confusion.

"You can communicate telepathically. You may not have had the opportunity to practice it, but not only are you telepathic, you are a conduit, a person known as an amplifier in the world of telepathic communication," he said.

She contemplated what he just said. "There is no such thing as an amplifier. That's a complete tale."

"They are very rare, but they exist, and you, Victory, are one."

He explained the events of the previous evening.

She walked over to the love seat and sat down. She tried to process what Tristan had told her. It might be possible. Specific past events flashed through her mind; could there be a link? "It's possible," was all she said.

"It's not only possible, you are an amplifier."

"Last summer I took a few weeks' vacation and spent them at our family home with my sisters. Payton was in the process of remodeling the entire house. We had finally decided the time had come to move on with our lives. Losing both our parents almost destroyed us and it took us years to start to move forward. Anyway, Payton finally agreed to remodel the house. But she wanted to keep Mom's office exactly as Mom left it. Willow and I convinced her she needed to make the space her own. So I took on the project of refinishing Mom's desk. I was preparing to strip it down when I noticed a bottom trim piece had come loose. I pulled on it, and it opened like a small door. Inside I found a thumb drive taped to the back of the trim." Victory stopped; she replayed the scene in her mind.

"What did you find?" Tristan asked gently, trying to prompt her to continue.

"My mother's personal diary or at least part of it. Mom had a tough time conceiving. She didn't get pregnant with us until the age of thirty-four. In her file I found a brief mention of her work on the fertility drug she used. I assumed she fine-tuned the drug to her specific DNA for maximum benefit."

"Your mother was a geneticist?" Tristan asked.

"A brilliant geneticist and molecular biologist," Victory said proudly.

"Doesn't seem like fertility drug would play into your psychic abilities at all," Tristan said.

"You're probably right. But what if they did more extensive changes?" she asked.

"They?"

"She and Dr. Ryker."

"Dr. Ryker?"

"Yes, he was also a masterful molecular biologist. Mom mentions his name a couple times in reference to her pregnancy."

"So you have a lead, someone else who might know about what happened. When this is all over, go and ask Dr. Ryker," he said.

"I can't. He left work to go on vacation in England fifteen years ago and disappeared. No one has heard from him or seen him since," Victory said.

"No friends, no family, no one has ever seen him again?" Tristan asked.

"As far as I know he had no living immediate family and his only friends were work colleagues."

"I see. So now you are beginning to think maybe these abilities of yours are somehow linked to this genetic tinkering?" Tristan asked.

"It's certainly possible." Victory sat silently and stared out into space.

"What do your sisters think about this whole thing in your mom's files?" he asked.

Victory sat a while longer and stared. Then she turned and looked at Tristan.

"I never told them. They were so freaked out when I first explained to them about how I could communicate with animals I couldn't bring myself to tell them about Mom's files and how it might somehow affect them."

"Do they have any special traits?"

"Nothing that I am aware of and nothing they have ever mentioned."

"Then it's possible this is just an ability you were naturally born with," Tristan said.

"I suppose anything is possible, but I am beginning to suspect the fertility drug was tampered with and I am the result."

Victory was astounded at the rate of cellular change in her samples. She wasn't sure what the outcome would be for the man in the lab. If this rate of change kept up, obvious mutations would manifest in the subjects soon, although she had no way of predicting what they would be. She rolled her shoulders for about the hundredth time in the past hour and rubbed her temples, trying to relieve the obsessive buzzing that had taken up residence in her head.

"You look tired, doc," Tristan said.

"Not really. But I have this nagging buzzing in my head. Not quite a headache but irritating all the same," she said.

"I'm sorry," he said.

"Thanks." She looked up at him from across the counter.

* * * *

Tristan tried to make a telepathic connection with Victory on and off all afternoon, but all he seemed able to accomplish was to cause her pain. He could see from her expression he needed to back off, to either take a break or try a new approach. He got up from his chair and walked around to the side of the workstation where she sat.

"Take a little break," he said to her as he approached from behind. He put a hand on each side of her temples. "Close your eyes, and clear your mind for a minute. Think of the ocean, the waves rolling on to the beach; hear its gentle sound in your mind and take deep cleansing breaths."

Victory did as he instructed and thought of the waves, and she forgot all the pressure of the experiment for the time being. The buzzing continued, only now it seemed to have dropped into the background, all but disappearing.

"Victory, can you hear me?" Tristan tried again to establish a telepathic connection with her.

"What the—" she responded rather curtly. She put her hands up to her temples and yanked his hands away from her. She opened her eyes and looked up at Tristan. Max had sat quietly in the far corner reading a magazine. Victory's outburst caused him to look over at them, a note of question in his glare. "Thanks for the break; I feel better, but we have a ton of work to get back to."

Did he finally make an initial connection with her? Tristan wanted to continue, but since they drew Max's interest, he felt he should leave any further communication attempts until they were out of anyone else's earshot. This would give Victory time to recover from his morning attempts.

* * * *

The day seemed long and trying. Tristan left the lab early. He claimed there was nothing left for him to work on for the rest of the day. She knew better. He would wander about the compound to do some recon.

Victory decided to take a walk. The fresh air would clear her mind and a little exercise would do her good. She'd been walking for at least an hour when she realized she had left the compound and wandered deep into the lush forest that covered over half of the island. At home, Victory made it a habit to take a walk in the forest by herself. So being out here on her own didn't immediately concern her. It was, however, getting close to dusk, and for her own safety, she knew she should start back to the compound within the next thirty minutes or so.

As she finished the thought, she felt a wave of agitation from the animals in the forest. She stopped, took in a deep breath, and focused on the local inhabitants. She picked out a group of wild goats a few yards away; all of them displayed signs of stress and tension. She felt a strong breeze blow along the jungle floor. That must be the problem. She had overheard people in the compound talking about a storm blowing in later today.

Victory turned around and headed back to the compound. She would pick up her pace and be back in time for dinner. In mid-stride, she froze. The same group of goats started to head away from her, and she gauged them to be approximately three hundred yards from her. There it was again. She wasn't merely imagining it; utter panic engulfed the group. Goose bumps rose on her arms. Their behavior wasn't about the storm; something menacing had entered the vicinity. Before she realized what she was doing, she dropped down to the forest floor and tried to camouflage herself against a large tree dripping in moss. She slowed her breathing and listened to the animals. A threat. Whatever approached was a threat, and she was right in its path.

Victory remained on the ground against the tree for what felt like an hour, but she knew it was only a fleeting period of time. The forest around her had gone eerily silent. A low guttural growl came from the direction of the wild goats. She couldn't tell for sure what made the sound, maybe a large cat or even a wild boar? Whatever it was, she decided her best bet would be to try and link to the animal telepathically and steer it away from both her and the goats.

She closed her eyes and concentrated. Her thoughts located the source and she tried to comfort the animal. Her eyes flew open and absolute terror flooded her. It was here; she was being stalked by something threatening, furious, and a little too intelligent. She tried to turn the animal away from her, but its approach was imminent. She must get out of here, but her legs seemed embedded in the ground. She had only one thought: *"Tristan!"*

Chapter Fifteen

The meeting with Logan and Noah was productive. The two men had located one weakness in the security grid. They updated Tristan and set in place their escape plan for if and when the need arose. Tristan in turn relayed all the information he'd acquired. He was heading back to the lab and glanced down at his watch. With any luck he would be back in time to join Victory for dinner. Suddenly terror flashed through his mind and caused his heart to gallop.

"Tristan!"

He heard Victory and she was terrified.

"Victory, what's wrong. Talk to me." He already changed direction, heading straight into the forest.

"Tristan, can you hear me?" Tears coated her words. He never heard her so distraught before.

"Yes, I hear you. Where are you? What's wrong?" Tristan asked without breaking his stride.

Victory lay deadly still, her mind feverishly searching for a means of escape.

"I'm out in the forest; something ominous is stalking me."

She wasn't sure Tristan could hear her or understand what she attempted to tell him. Each time she listened for a response, all she heard was a loud buzzing in her head. Could it be Tristan? Maybe he could hear her.

Tristan ran full out, but he wasn't sure exactly where she was. He knew as soon as he got away from the compound he would easily pick up her scent, except for the moment there was a flurry of odors, simply too many other scents to single her out. She wasn't responding to him, which probably meant she was not able to understand his thoughts, but he heard hers.

"I'm trying to send him away, but he keeps coming. He's something very intelligent, and I can't steer him away. Can you hear me, Tristan?"

Victory felt panic begin to overtake her. She had to control her panic. Without control she couldn't reach Tristan. Also, panic would trigger her adrenal glands and give off a stronger scent to the approaching predator.

Tristan finally put enough distance between himself and the compound. He stopped, cleared his mind, and filled his lungs with a deep breath as he took in all the scents of the forest. He caught her scent cone, but something lingered over the top of it. Animal or man, he couldn't figure it out. This was impossible; he could distinguish everything by its scent. The only explanation that seemed plausible was that both an animal and a man were somewhere close. The two scents were so intermingled it was impossible for him to separate them. This meant they had to be right on top of one another; maybe someone else stalked this animal. He turned in Victory's direction and ran as if her life depended on it.

Victory could hear branches snapping and the rustling of vegetation as someone or something crept through the forest. A cold sweat broke out on her body and a single tear trickled down her cheek.

"I could run," she thought.

She didn't realize Tristan had heard her. A blanket of warmth wrapped around her, grounding her, urging her to stay put.

"Tristan?" It had to be him. She couldn't understand the thoughts he tried to send her, even so she understood his meaning. He desperately tried to comfort her, to let her know she wasn't alone and to keep her from running. She knew that, knew she shouldn't run. Whatever or whoever hunted her would be on her in an instant. He—she was sure now it was a he, was intelligent and a cunning hunter. He was trying to flush her out. She felt that for certain, but still the need for flight tugged at her.

"Please hurry."

The terror in her mind tore at Tristan's heart in a way nothing ever had before. He needed to be there soon, or this thing would be on her. He could smell the scent strongly now, but he was still unsure of what it was. He did know it was only approximately ten yards away from Victory. Tristan stopped. She should be here. Where was she?

"Victory, where are you?" He whispered into the wind. Tears and fright were filling her mind. He might lose her connection any minute if her anxiety broke their connection. "Victory, focus. Listen to my voice. I need to know where you are."

"There's a large tree covered with moss..."

The tree stood right in front of him. Where was she? Her scent permeated the air around him, yet still he couldn't locate her. He caught a slight movement on the trunk. She almost completely blended in with her surroundings. He had never seen—or not seen anything like it. He reached out and grabbed her with one hand, and at the same time covered her mouth with the other so she wouldn't scream.

"Thank God, Tristan," she gasped.

"Use your mental link. We're not out of danger yet." He breathed the words in her ear.

Had he been alone, he would have turned and faced the oncoming threat. But right now his only thought was to get Victory out of the path of danger. He picked her up and headed for the river. Using his keen sense of smell, he honed in on the approaching predator. He'd quickly closed the distance. Then Tristan saw the river, and, as if on cue, the sky opened up and dumped sheets of rain. The air split with the boom of thunder as a jagged bolt of lightning went to ground.

Something howled. Was it a man or some kind of animal? Tristan placed Victory on her feet and looked around for two long pieces of reed.

"What are you doing?" Victory asked. She shook uncontrollably from fear and the chill air.

"I'm looking for reeds."

"Now is not the time to go botanist on me," she hissed.

"Unless you have fish bladders for lungs, we need reeds! That thing could track us forever, even through this storm. Our best chance is to get in the river and wait for it to pass us. The water will block our scent," he said. "Here," Tristan thrust a reed in her hands. "Stay close."

They waded out into the river. Victory's teeth immediately began to chatter.

"What do you think will get us first?" she asked. "Hypothermia from this ice cold river or the monster chasing us?" She glanced his way one last time, and then dropped down into the water.

Tristan refocused on the predator's scent cone to gauge how long they would have to stay under. No, it couldn't be possible. The thing was only steps behind them.

"Victory wait," he said, as he grabbed her by her shoulder right before she submerged her head.

Victory pulled the reed out of her mouth.

"What's the matter? Tell me it's not too late."

He pulled her back up toward him. "Listen, and tell me what you hear."

She listened carefully, blocking out all the sounds around her except for the predator. "He's turned back and is heading away from us."

"That's what I thought; it—he is moving away from us," Tristan said.

"Why? I'm not complaining, but he seemed pretty persistent," she said.

"He's moving away. I don't know why, but let's take the cue and get out of here. We should head back to the compound from the opposite direction."

"I can't see three feet in front of me with this deluge of rain pounding down on us," she said.

"I can get us back. I have scouted out the entire layout. We should reach the compound in slightly over an hour in this direction." Tristan pointed off to his left, the totally opposite way from where they came.

"Okay, I want to get back and soak in a hot bath for hours," Victory said.

The rain didn't let up for their whole walk back, and the wind started to kick up as they reached the compound. There wasn't a soul in sight as they entered through the back gate.

"Let's get you back to your room and out of these soaked clothes. I'll go back to my room, take a quick shower, and then head to the dining room and pick us up some dinner," Tristan said.

"You don't have to do that; I can go to dinner," she said.

"No, you can't. You're white as a sheet and you might be going into shock."

"I'm fine, really," she protested.

"Victory, trust me. We don't know what or why that thing was stalking you. We don't know if someone sent it out after you. You need to rest and recover your strength before facing anyone."

It began to look to Tristan as if there were more experiments taking place here than just Victory's.

* * * *

It pinned her against a wall of solid rock. Its eerie, yellow eyes glowed; blood dripped from huge canines. Victory let out a blood-curdling cry.

"Victory, Victory. Wake up. You're having a bad dream." Tristan gently shook her shoulders, trying to break the nightmare that had her in its grip.

Victory's eyes flew open. She felt Tristan hands shaking her, his violet eyes swimming with concern. Without a second thought, she threw herself into the warmth and security of his arms.

"Oh God, Tristan, it was awful." She wept openly.

"Shhh, it's okay. You're safe now. It was only a dream." He rocked her gently. It felt so natural having his arms wrapped tightly around her.

"No, not a dream—a terrible nightmare," she sniffled into his shoulder. She lifted her head and looked around the room. It was pitch-black, save for the small desk lamp. "Did you bring dinner?"

"It's about 1:30 in the morning, Victory," Tristan said.

"What? It can't be. I just lay down. I was waiting for you to come back with dinner." She looked over at the desk again, this time seeing the covered plates.

"I came back around seven and found you fast asleep. I thought you needed the sleep more than dinner." He couldn't stop himself; he ran his hand down her silky hair. It felt as soft as it looked.

"So you've been watching over me the entire time?" she asked, feeling a little stronger in the warmth of his embrace. She wasn't a woman who needed a man, but this felt right.

"I slept in the chair for a couple hours. It's not bad." Tristan shot her a sexy little smile.

"You didn't have to stay. Sleeping in the chair, you're going to regret it in the morning."

"Believe me, I've slept in much worse places. I wanted to make sure you were going to be okay."

He looked into her eyes. They reminded him of stunning emeralds, flawless and unique. He was beginning to be able to read her moods by looking into those unique eyes. He could see bewilderment and uncertainty shining through those wondrous gems. "I should go and let you sleep." He stood up and headed to the door.

"Tristan," she said uncertainly. He turned back to look at her, waiting. "Would you mind staying with me the rest of the night? You can sleep here next to me." She patted the side of the bed. When he didn't move or say anything she stumbled on. "I guess the encounter in the forest affected me more than I thought." She dropped her gaze to her hand lying at her side.

"Encounter." Tristan frowned. "Victory, you are one extraordinary woman," he said with a laugh. "Only you would refer to a near-death experience as an encounter."

He walked back to the far side of the bed. He sat down and took off his shoes. He pulled the pillows out from under the bedspread and stacked them under his head. He stretched out on the bed and slid his arm around her shoulders, pulling her close to him. Victory resisted for a second, then melted into his side. "Yes, you're right," he said.

"About what?" she asked.

"This is much more comfortable than the chair."

In only minutes, they were both asleep. It was the fastest Tristan had fallen asleep in a very long time.

* * * *

Tristan walked into the lab carrying two lattes and a couple of scones. He had woken up in her room, in her bed, alone.

"Morning, doc," he said nonchalantly.

She looked up from her microscope and gave him a shy smile. "Good morning, sleepy head. You looked so peaceful, I couldn't bring myself to wake you this morning. Besides, I have a massive amount of research to double-check." He handed her a latte and scone. "Thanks, I didn't get any breakfast."

"That's exactly why I brought you some." He took the lid off of his latte, blew on it, and took a drink. "So, where's our subject?" he asked, as he tilted his head toward the empty chair on the other side of the glass in the exam room. "And where's Max?" He looked at the corner of the lab and empty chair Max usually occupied.

Without looking up from her work she answered, "Apparently, there is something more interesting monopolizing Mr. Max. As far as our subject, they told me he was going through some health tests. And no, I don't believe it for an instant."

Tristan glanced over at Victory. She surprised him more each day. These guys weren't pulling anything over on her. For the remainder of the morning they worked side by side, like a real team. They were so busy and involved in their studies that they worked straight through lunch.

Tristan yawned and looked up from his computer.

"Hey, we missed lunch," he said, looking down at his watch. "You hungry? I'll make a run to the deli."

"Hmmm. Oh sure, I could use something. I'm not picky; get me whatever you're getting," she said, without stopping her work on the computer. She was so engrossed in her research, she never heard him leave.

A few minutes later she heard the door open.

"That was quick," she said, as she looked up and saw Max walk in, leading the test subject. The man looked as if he had been in a bar fight. He appeared covered with cuts and scrapes on his face and up both arms. His clothes were rumpled, like he had worn them for at least two days.

"Oh my! What happened to him?" she asked. Then she looked into his face and saw pure malevolence.

"He got to take a run last night; he needed to stretch his legs," Max said and pushed the man farther into the lab.

"You mean he was out running in the forest. I thought he was having health tests done." She never took her attention off him. She tried to make a mental connection with him but kept picking up a red haze of random thoughts.

"He did have an exam this morning after I brought him back. Mr. Braxton wanted to see if there were any physical changes."

Max took him into the next room and strapped him into the chair.

"He should be gentle as a kitten for now. The doctor gave him something to calm him down," Max said.

She looked at Max with contempt. "Tell me you didn't drug him. He won't be any good to me if he's drugged."

"Your problem not mine," Max said. He picked up the magazine he had dropped in the chair on the way in.

Tristan was heading back to the lab, his arms full with bags and drinks. Suddenly he inhaled a familiar scent emanating from the lab. He increased his pace and reached the door in mere seconds. He threw open the door, and he scrutinized the entire room in an instant.

"Hey, watch it," Max scolded a few feet from where the door had flown open.

Tristan took in a deep breath and pushed back the adrenaline threatening to erupt.

"Oh, sorry, I didn't know you were sitting there. It's kind of hard to juggle all this food and open the door. I guess I kicked it little too hard."

"You need to be careful next time," Max grumbled and focused back on his magazine.

Tristan walked over to the counter to where Victory was working and emptied his hands. He looked up into the furious scowl of the man strapped to the exam chair. His scent was familiar but not identical to the one he had tracked in the forest the night before.

"Tristan, are you okay?" Victory asked in a low voice.

"I think he could have been the one stalking you yesterday. His scent is familiar but not exactly the same," he whispered to her.

"By the looks of him, it was the first thing I thought. I know the thing that chased me was male, but this guy hasn't shown any aggression toward me, nothing but the same old pure hate," Victory said. "Of course his captures drugged him, which it could explain his lack of aggression."

"There's another explanation. Braxton could be using more than one specimen," Tristan said.

"Anything is possible, but I sure hope not. He concerns me enough. His genetic makeup is changing quickly. I don't know if his system will be able to adapt fast enough," Victory said.

Chapter Sixteen

"Hey Noah, where's Logan?" Tristan asked.

It was after midnight, and the two men were hidden at the far corner of the compound at a prearranged meeting site.

"He's out scouting the jungle layout. He figures the security grid can't possibly cover the whole forest," Noah said.

"I can tell you from experience it covers a very large portion of it."

He proceeded to tell Noah of his and Victory's ordeal the day before in the forest.

"So you think Braxton is using it as a testing ground, letting his specimens out into a contained setting," Noah said.

"I wouldn't be surprised. I can tell you I didn't see any cameras while I was out there. So I guess he is only concerned with seeing what is happening in the compound."

"Or maybe he figures most people would be too afraid to enter the jungle, and if they did, then they were on their own."

"That sounds like Lawrence Braxton; he is a cold-hearted son of a bitch. If someone doesn't serve his purpose, he throws them away like yesterday's trash," Tristan said.

"So have you gotten a chance to get an up-close view of where they are housing this guy they're using as a guinea pig?"

"Not yet. The building is separated from the rest of the compound and it is heavily guarded. It also has all the high-tech bells and whistles. More advanced than the rest of the compound."

"If you can find a way in, go for it. Wyatt really wants to know who this guy is and if he is the only one in there, or if Braxton has other men locked inside the enclosure. He would also like you to contact him ASAP," Noah said.

"I will. But I need to be within a few feet of Victory, and she has to have a clear mind. She's beginning to tap into her telepathic abilities. I can understand her thoughts, but she can only feel my tone or mood. In her mind, it's like relating to an animal, I guess."

"She's got the animal part right," Noah snorted. "Poor baby, sounds like a tough assignment, having to stay close to someone that gorgeous."

In the next breath he became all business. "The captain's getting pressure for some answers. It seems there are some very deep pockets involved in this organization, even deeper than we originally thought. But we haven't yet pinpointed the players. We still believe there is someone in the government involved, so this is still all staying on the down-low. Our group and General Roberts are the only ones aware of this mission. However, the general is getting antsy. He doesn't want to get caught with his pants down. He is pushing Wyatt for answers—yesterday."

"Got it. I'll try to make contact with Wyatt tonight. See you again in a couple of days."

The two men vanished into the night like a couple of ghosts.

Tristan moved stealthily through the compound. He got to the corner of the building next to the dorms and just before he made the turn he heard a man talking. He couldn't see the man because of the darkness and the distance, but he recognized the voice and his scent–Polo. Dave Anderson was on the island, one of Braxton's top men.

"Yes, sir. Max has finished briefing me about their progress," Dave said, as he spoke into his cell phone. "The girl is making headway, but it is going slower than we expected." There was a pause as he listened.

"Damn," Tristan whispered. He wished he could hear the other side of Dave's phone conversation. He stood a good distance away from Dave, so he dropped to his belly and inched his way to a closer corner of the building. "Shit," he muttered again. There was no cover between him and where Dave stood. He remained where he was and decided half a conversation was better than nothing at all.

"Jerry is still tailing Victory's sister Payton, we could always grab her to put pressure on the doc." Another pause. "Yes, sir. I understand; I realize we are trying to keep this project top secret, and the more people involved the greater the risk. I understand." A long pause and then Dave continued. "I asked Max about Morgan getting out of his cell. Seems he let him out it the hope he would track Collin down." Another pause. "Yes, sir, it worked."

Dave fell silent for almost five minutes. Tristan knew he still stood in the same place because he could hear the slight tap of his shoe.

"Mr. Braxton, these men are showing some mental issues. Morgan seems to be handling the process better than Collin. Victory hasn't had much trouble with him, only what we expected. I understand we have only started with the experiments, but we could find ourselves dealing with real problems if we can't keep them under control."

Another pause. "I understand. We will only delete a subject if we can no longer control them." Dave stopped tapping his foot. "I'll be out of here in a couple of hours. I have a few more reports to review. I'll check in with you when I return to the mainland. Good night, sir."

Dave started to walk in Tristan's direction. Tristan melted back into the shadows and waited for him to pass. In most situations he would follow Dave, but he'd promised to make contact with Wyatt. Now with this new information, it was imperative he update Wyatt double-time.

"Wyatt," Tristan sat in a chair in Victory's bedroom. He had let himself into her room at least an hour ago. Time quickly slipped by as he sat and watched her sleep; she looked so serene.

"Tristan. I've been waiting to hear from you for over two hours. Where have you been?" Wyatt asked with a note of concern in his voice.

"On my way back to the dorm I stumbled on Dave Anderson. I hung out and listened to a pretty interesting

conversation." Tristan relayed what he heard to his brother.

"There's no need to worry about Payton. We've got a guy on her 24/7. We have been trying to limit her to work and home. She's still really worried about Victory, but she understands you are with her, and you being there seems to comfort her. Do you have any idea who Morgan and Collin are? Are those their last names or first names?" Wyatt asked.

"I'm not sure. I guess you need to check both first and last. I'd start with the military, see if there are any AWOLs or missing. Then maybe check on guys who have gotten out in the past year or so, or even on leave."

"What makes you think they are military?"

"Just a hunch. The way Morgan handles himself for one, and if it was Collin who tracked Victory in the forest, he clearly had some training."

"Okay, I'll have Jack start there; it's as good as anything. How is Victory doing with all that's happened recently?"

"She seems okay. Considering she's been kidnapped, shipped to an island, and forced to do research on a project against her will. Oh, and let's not forget the madman killer who is forcing her into completing research in three weeks that rewrites what we know about human DNA. She is pretty upset with the way Braxton is rushing the project. He must have his endgame in sight."

"Or he's being pressured by the group. I mean, think about it. The Kaleidoscope Group has footed the bill to buy an island, move its residents to another island, and build them an entire town. They built a

state-of-the-art research facility and staffed it, along with bringing in men to use as guinea pigs. They are bleeding money. This group might be mega-millionaires, but they still want to make a profit. Make sure you keep track of Braxton. I'll do the same on this end," Wyatt said.

"Roger," Tristan said.

"And Tristan, watch yourself. This group is very astute and we already know they have endless resources."

"Don't worry, bro. I'll watch my back."

"Good. And check in with me a little more frequently."

Tristan opened his eyes and realized Victory was scrutinizing him.

"So, how's my sister?" she asked.

"Sorry, I didn't mean to wake you. Your sister is fine. How did you know I was talking to Wyatt?" He practically tripped over his own tongue. *"Geez Farraday, get a grip,"* he scolded himself.

"No, you didn't wake me. I felt a faint hum in my head."

"Son of a bitch. I'm really sorry, Victory. I didn't mean to hurt you."

"What? No you didn't hurt me. I think my brain has started to adapt to it. It feels like an electrode attached to my temple. It's kind of soothing actually."

"Huh. That's a big improvement from the headaches."

She was lying on her side watching him. "I suppose you haven't slept at all tonight."

"No, not yet; I've a lot to get done. It makes it much easier to get around without being seen if it's dark and most of the compound is asleep."

* * * *

She slid farther into the middle of the bed and patted the space she had previously occupied. "Come here and get some sleep." He gaped at her, the surprise evident on his face. "I sleep better when you're here." She didn't understand *why* she slept better, and she still didn't trust Tristan totally. But he had come and rescued her. He put his own life in danger, no questions asked, and it seemed she was developing a mental link to him. Maybe subconsciously some part of her had begun to have faith in him.

"I suppose I could use some downtime, and I seem to sleep better here," he said. Tristan slid in beside Victory, the bed still warm from her body.

"Sweet dreams," Victory said. She rolled over and snuggled her backside against him. She felt his whole body become tense, but within minutes he relaxed slightly, followed by a soft snore.

* * * *

The sun started to rise. Tristan opened his eyes and found himself entwined in Victory's soft, supple body. Her satiny golden hair fanned out across his chest. Unable to stop himself, he reached out and took her hair in his palm and let it fall through his fingers. He watched her as she stretched, opened her eyes, looked up into his and smiled at him. Tristan reached down and took her chin in his hand. He tilted her face up to him and brushed his lips tenderly across hers.

He instantly knew he'd made a mistake; he couldn't stop with a scant taste of her. He reached out, gently took hold of her waist, and pulled her into the heat of his body; once again, he claimed her lips, but this time with a lust that burned deep in his bones. Victory moaned with pleasure. He pulled her slightly away from him and looked into her longing gaze.

"Victory," Tristan groaned.

"Shhh." She placed her fingers across his lips. "Don't say anything."

Victory reached up for his face and kissed him. He could swear he felt her passion flow through her and into him. She pulled his body over the top of hers. The feel of her under him spurred him on.

Tristan raised himself above her and looked into her face. He placed his hands on the bed and framed her head between them. He bent toward her and kissed her once more on the lips and then traced his mouth down the soft curve of her neck. He slid one hand down her shoulder and gingerly cupped her breast in his palm. He could feel the heat of her burning through the flimsy cotton of her pajama top. He stroked her breast and was answered with a taut bud. He gently slid his hand over to her other breast and lavishly caressed it. He moved to the buttons on her pajama top, and he undid them slowly, the entire time falling into the abyss of the green pools specked with gold flecks that were Victory's eyes.

Tristan separated her top and took one of her pink nipples into his mouth. He licked and teased and enjoyed the bonus of her moans and responses. He kissed his way down her belly. He did so slowly, taking his time. He pushed her pajama bottoms down languidly as he lavished her body with kisses. He pulled away from her, relieving her of her pajamas. Tristan stared down at her in awe; the sight of her nakedness was even more enthralling than he could have imagined. Victory's angelic body was perfect, with exquisite breasts, not large but a perfect size to fit in his palm. Her waist, slender and slightly flared out at her hips; it drew his gaze down her long elegant legs.

"You are bewitching, Victory."

He discarded his shirt, ran his hands up her long legs, and placed a kiss on her belly. She shivered. Tristan traced feather light kisses down to her soft golden curls. He spread her legs apart and positioned his body between them. He thoroughly explored her with his tongue and took his time to find her sensitive spots. Tristan thrust his tongue deep inside of her, and started a slow lavish movement with his mouth bringing Victory off the bed. He laughed against her, and the vibration caused her to writhe off the bed once more. He pulled her hips closer to him to savor her. Wildly she reached for him.

"Not yet," he all but growled. "I've waited a long time to get you in this position. Now I have you here, I'm going to take my time and enjoy you."

"Tristan," Victory panted. "I can't take much more of your enjoyment. I feel as though I'm coming unraveled."

Again he laughed against her.

"Yes...you can." He felt her begin to tense; she started to pant with pleasure. He felt her wave of orgasm tear through her.

"Tristan, please…Now," she begged.

He enjoyed this side of her. He pulled away from her and again kissed his way up her body. He stopped at her breast. He suckled and nipped at her; he filled his other hand with her free breast and rubbed the taught tip between his thumb and finger. In an instant he felt her hands on his jeans, as she fumbled for the zipper and forced it down. She plunged one hand into the opening and found him hard and hot. She freed herself from his grasp. Victory peeled his jeans and boxers halfway down his thighs and took hold of him. Now it was Tristan's turn to moan.

* * * *

She giggled softly. Tristan pulled away from her and removed his jeans and boxers. He was lying on his back when Victory again took hold of him with both hands. Gently she slid her hands up and down his shaft. He was imposing and impressive. She continued to rub one hand up and down the length his shaft and gingerly filled her other hand with his sack. He felt so hot.

"Jesus, Victory, you're killing me," Tristan growled.

He fumbled for his jeans and pulled a foil-wrapped condom out of his pocket.

"Let me do it," Victory said. Tristan opened his hand and she took the condom. She sat up on her knees and straddled his hips. She opened the foil-covered condom, placed it over his tip, and looked straight into his eyes. Sweat broke out over his top lip. Never taking her eyes off his, she slowly rolled the condom down the length of his shaft.

Victory straddled Tristan. He grabbed her by the waist and rolled her over on to the bed. Victory gasped in surprise. Tristan was again blanketing her body, but this time he held himself slightly above her. She breathed hard as she looked at him. He maintained the position for a few heartbeats. Then he spread her legs apart with one of his thighs and lowered himself one slow agonizing inch at a time toward her. His tip finally touched her and she strained to impale herself on him.

He smiled down at her and lowered his head to her. He claimed her mouth at the very same instant he thrust himself to the hilt inside her. They groaned in unison. Tristan remained deep inside Victory, her muscles clenched, as he pushed himself deeper inside of her. He stayed there for another heartbeat, then began long slow strokes, fully filling her and totally withdrawing from her. She felt shots of electricity fly through her entire body. Then she climaxed hard and fast, followed as hard and fast by Tristan. The warmth and weight of him blanketed her. This was heaven.

* * * *

Tristan rolled on to the bed and took Victory with him, still buried deep inside her. He had found nirvana and he wasn't ready to give it up.

Just then Victory's room phone started to ring.

"Perfect," Tristan grumbled. He reached for the phone and handed it to Victory. She started to move off him, but he grabbed her and pulled her close. It took him completely by surprise that he needed this intimate connection to last few seconds longer.

She gasped and then steadied her breath. "Hello."

"Ms. Winters, this is Max. We have a problem here in the lab. I need you here immediately."

"All right," she said. "I'll be there in ten minutes."

"Fine," Max said and hung up the phone.

"Max wants us at the lab," Victory said and handed him back the receiver.

"I heard. He can wait a minute or two longer." A devilish smile played across Tristan's face.

Chapter Seventeen

Tristan and Victory walked into chaos. Her previously organized workspace looked like a hurricane had torn through it. There were papers on the floor, computers pulled from their outlets, broken glass, cracked storage cabinets, and chairs in multiple pieces. There were two additional men besides Max in the exam room. All three men were attempting to tie the test subject down into the chair.

Tristan automatically jumped in front of Victory to shield her from the threat of Max. "What the hell?" Tristan yelled. "Someone's not happy."

The men finally secured the test subject in the chair. All three turned to look at Tristan and Victory.

"Seems our client here isn't happy with his current situation anymore," Max growled as he entered the lab. "I've sent for the doc; our subject needs to be given something to calm him down."

"No," Victory said. "If you dope him up, he won't be of any use to me. You said you need some results. Let me try and calm him."

"Victory," Tristan jumped in. "I don't know if that's such a great idea."

Max looked from Tristan to Victory.

"Fine, but if you can't get him under control, and I mean now, I'll call in the doc."

"I can," she said. "I need to call him by his name." She stared straight at Max.

"The boss didn't want any names," Max said.

"I can't communicate with him if I don't even know his name," Victory hissed back, determined to stand her ground.

"Morgan." Max snapped at her.

She glared at him. "Is that his first name or last?"

"Just Morgan."

Great, Tristan thought to himself. If this was Morgan, that meant Collin was yet to be seen, and from what Tristan had overheard last night, he was going to be even harder to handle. For now, he would keep that piece of information to himself. No point in upsetting Victory, nor did he want to distract her.

"I need you and your men to wait outside." Before Max had a chance to reply, she continued on. "Your presence is irritating him. I have Tristan here if I need help."

Max stood silently and studied the scene; he looked from Morgan to Tristan to Victory. "All right. The boss wants results, so I'll give you a bit of leeway. But I'll be right outside," he said, and glared mercilessly at Morgan.

"I wouldn't expect any less," Victory snipped at him.

Max signaled for his two men to leave the lab.

"You do have a plan, right?" Tristan asked.

"Sort of," she said. Still smiling at him, she continued telepathically, so as not to be overheard. *"I have been trying to get him to respond to me telepathically over the past few days. I think I'm going to give it another chance."*

Victory headed to the exam room door.

"I'm coming with you," Tristan said.

She spun around and extended her arm, hand pressed against his chest.

"No. Please, Tristan. You need to wait here in the lab. He will see you as a threat and I won't get anything out of him."

Tristan narrowed his eyes and looked from her to Morgan.

"Okay, but if I see him so much as lift a finger in your direction, he's going to find out what kind of threat I can be."

"Thank you." She patted him with her still outstretched hand and smiled up at him.

God, she could melt his heart if he let her.

* * * *

"Wish me luck." She turned back and continued to the exam room. She could feel Tristan's stare burn into her back.

She opened the door, smiled at Morgan, and without turning her back on him, closed the door behind her.

"Hi, Morgan." Victory greeted him and remained motionless directly inside the doorway.

A look of surprise briefly crossed his face and disappeared as quickly—replaced with a look of hate.

"I'm sure you won't believe me. But I really want what's best for you."

He stared at her and made no response.

"Really Morgan, I want to help. I'm here against my will, and I have a pretty good feeling you are too. At the very least, you didn't know what you were getting yourself into. I want to help you."

"Right."

His abrupt response surprised her.

"That's why you shoot me up with this stuff and study me like a lab rat." His words came out as a snarl.

A low buzz started to reverberate in Victory's head and almost chattered her teeth. She put her hands up to her temples and pressed.

"That's not what happened, and you know it. I didn't give you the serum; I've been trying to help your body adapt to what they gave to you," she said aloud.

"If you want to help me, get rid of this stuff; it's making me crazy." His pain showed all over his face.

"Would it be all right if I took some blood from you?"

She needed to make this look real while she continued to communicate telepathically. Victory waited patiently until she saw a slight nod from Morgan. Then she started toward him.

"It doesn't work that way. That much I know for sure. The serum has bonded with your genetic makeup. With the research I have done both here and before Braxton kidnapped me, I know the best that can be done is to create a buffer which will slow down the process and hopefully give your body time to adapt to the change. With time I'm pretty sure I could come up with a solution."

Morgan continued to glare at her but nodded his head in understanding.

"Great. I thought this was going to be an easy gig. Now you're saying we're changed for good," he murmured.

"We?" Victory asked. The pain started to show on her face. "What are you doing?" She snapped and looked at Morgan dead on.

Morgan stared back at her, slightly surprised.

"You can hear it? I'm blocking any transmissions from leaving this lab. No one can hear us, doc."

Amazement briefly overshadowed her pain.

"You can do that? It could become very handy. But could you dial it back a tad; my head is throbbing." A second later relief flooded her. "Thank you, Morgan. Can we still speak freely?"

Morgan nodded.

"Before you explain any further, I would like to bring Tristan in on this conversation," she said.

Morgan remained motionless as he stared at her.

"He's here with me; he's a good guy."

"He's military," Morgan said. "He might be one of the guys who put us here."

"Yes, he's military. But really, he is here to help you. Trust me when I tell you, he wasn't involved with bringing you here."

Morgan sat quietly. He glowered through the glass as he sized Tristan up.

"Okay, what the hell," Morgan finally said.

"Tristan, can you hear me?" Victory threw the thought into Tristan's mind.

Tristan broke his glare from Morgan, glanced at Victory, and nodded.

"I'm fine. Morgan has agreed to include you in our conversation. Come in here and join us. He can put up a psychic force field so no one can hear us."

"Great, but we better make this quick." Tristan walked into the exam room. "I don't know how much longer Max will be content to hang out. I'm getting a clear scent of impatience radiating off of him."

"I understand. Morgan, tell us what happened," Victory said.

"My teammate, Collin, and I had hardly gotten back from a tour. We were told we would be performing strength and endurance tests for Braxton's corporation. We both volunteered; we figured it would be a piece-of-cake assignment. Right," he snorted.

"Before you came here, did you have any special skills?" Victory asked.

"I'm a sharpshooter in the Delta Force."

"No, I mean like a sixth sense?" she asked.

"I've always been able to feel when an enemy approached. Sometimes I could mentally push them away from my position. Is this what you mean?" he asked.

"Yes, exactly. The foreign DNA must be magnifying your natural ability. Then it reflects it back as a force field...very interesting. How about Collin, has he ever said anything about special skills?" Victory pressed, excited at a possible lead.

"No, nothing," Morgan said.

"That's it!" She had found the first viable lead. A pre-existing natural ability, it had to be the connection. "So Collin isn't adapting as smoothly."

"How did you know? No, he's not doing well. I think he is starting to lose it," Morgan said. "He got out of the compound the other night. Max sent me out after him."

Tristan jumped in for the first time.

"It seemed like the perfect time to get out of here; why come back?"

"My plan exactly. But on the way out the door, Max described my baby sister to a tee. Told me what she'd done that day and what clothes she wore. He even showed me a dated picture on his phone. Then he informed me if I didn't come back with Collin, he would have her shot. Shot. Terri is only eight years old, the bastard." Morgan was hot.

"I caught up to Collin as he started closing in on the two of you at the river. Sorry about him going after you. He seems to have periods when he's not himself, and recently they seem to happen much more often. I'm worried for him."

"Did you tell Max or anyone else we were out in the forest?" Tristan asked.

"No. Now it's my turn to ask a few questions. Why are you here, Military?" Morgan asked, as he scrutinized Tristan.

Tristan didn't know how much he should tell him, but he knew he had to give him something to gain his confidence.

"My mission is to keep tabs on Victory. To pull her out if the need arose. I'm also trying to get some inside information on Braxton and the people he works with."

"Do you have a way out?" Morgan asked.

"My team on the outside is working on a solution as we speak."

"They're here on the island?" Morgan asked.

"Yep."

"Then let's get the hell out of here," Morgan said.

"It's not that simple," Victory stepped in. "I need to gather all the research Braxton has. Together with my research, I'm certain I will be able to help you and hopefully Collin. If we leave now I'm sure I could reconstruct the research, but it might be too late for Collin and you."

"For now, we need to stick to what we have been doing. I'll work on getting all of us out as soon as we can," Tristan said.

The door to the lab swung open. Max came striding through.

"At least you settled him down. That's good. Now let's get back to work."

He opened the door to the exam room, and instantly Victory noticed the buzzing stop.

"We are working," Victory said. "I'm preparing to draw a new blood samples from Morgan." She pulled a syringe and large rubber band from her pocket. She tied the band around his upper arm and inserted the needle.

"Thank you," Morgan whispered in her mind.

She looked into his eyes. She felt the warmth of his words but not the words themselves. She made a leap of faith.

"You're welcome, Morgan. I'm going to do all I can to help you and Collin; I promise." She smiled at him and then withdrew the syringe, untied the rubber band, and left the room.

* * * *

"Wyatt, I've got additional information."

Tristan stretched out on a blanket next to Victory. They had taken their lunch to the beach away from the hubbub of the lunchroom.

"Good to hear from you, Tristan. What do you have for me?" Wyatt asked.

Tristan debriefed Wyatt on the morning's events.

"I believe the guy is for real," Tristan added before Wyatt had a chance to ask.

"I'll have Jack do some digging and see who assigned Morgan and Collin to Braxton. We've been running up against brick walls back here. We can't get a clear lead on who is connected to this group."

"Are you saying you want us to stay for the rest of the week?"

"At least for a few more days. The more information both you and Victory can gather, the better off we'll be. It doesn't look promising on my end at this point."

"Do you think Braxton is simply going to let us go home at the end of next week? And even if he does, we can't leave Morgan and Collin here."

"I don't know, probably not. Victory is too valuable to him. What I do know is, Braxton is not the kind of man who will allow Victory to leave if he feels there is anything she can still contribute to his cause," Wyatt said.

"I agree. We'll stay here for a few more days. Then I think we should pull the plug, no matter what."

"Sounds like a plan. In the meantime gather as much intel as possible and plan on pulling Morgan and Collin out with you. I've got a couple of outside guys I can call in; I'll put them on Morgan's sister. Take care, Tristan."

"Always," Tristan assured his brother.

Tristan looked over at Victory lying beside him. Her eyes were closed, and she looked so peaceful he thought she had fallen asleep.

"So, what's the scoop?" she said, her eyes still closed.

"Wyatt wants us to stick it out here for a couple more days, gather as much information as we can. Then we need to plan on pulling out and taking the two men with us."

She rolled over on to her side and propped herself up on one elbow.

"I can't leave. Braxton will do something awful to Payton. Besides, my time is up in ten more days. He promised to let me go home then, and he said he would leave my sisters alone."

"Victory, do you honestly think Braxton is a man of his word? Do you really believe he is going to let you get on a helicopter and leave? You're too valuable to him. At the very least he will try and convince you to come to work for him permanently, and at the very worst, he will kidnap you again."

He sat up and stared down at her. Tears gathered on her lids. The sight of her upset pulled at his soul.

"Then how am I supposed to keep my sisters safe, barring working for that maniac?" Her tears threatened to escape.

"Don't worry. Even if the team can't get to the bottom of the Kaleidoscope Group, we will make sure you and your sisters are taken care of."

A single tear escaped and trickled down her cheek. He reached out with his finger and wiped it away. Then he got to his feet and held his hands out to her.

"Come on, we need to get back. I'm sure Max has the lab cleaned up by now."

Chapter Eighteen

The compound was quiet, except for the sound of the warm, gentle breeze blowing in from the ocean, causing the palm trees to rustle in unison. The night was lit by the glow of a full moon. Not the optimal time to try to move through the compound without being seen, nevertheless Tristan had no other alternative. With the days numbered, it was imperative he step up his recon, full moon or not. Victory had not been pleased with the idea of him lurking through the campus, but he reassured her that this was what he did. It was a few minutes past midnight, and, like the last time he was out at night, the compound was devoid of all the usual inhabitants who filled the paths and buildings during the day.

As he crossed the yard from the dorms, he heard voices. He centered himself and honed in with his acute sense of smell. Tristan estimated the group probably stood somewhere near Collin and Morgan's building, inside the heightened security area. This meant they were clear across the compound. He could distinguish four others besides Max. He moved through the shadows to get closer to the group.

"Okay, I don't want any more repeats of the other night," Max snarled. "Neither Collin or Morgan are allowed out of their cells, got it? I don't care if they want to stretch their legs. Whatever idiot lets them slip by him won't live to regret it."

Tristan closed his eyes, slowing his breathing and listening. He picked up no other scents or sounds of humans between him and Max's little group. He opened his eyes, took one last look around, and shot off in the opposite direction, heading to the main office.

Having observed Max's routine over the past several nights, he knew he had at least an hour before the man would head to his office and suite. At this time every night Max visited a female employee's bungalow.

Tristan reached the target and surveyed the area surrounding it. It appeared deserted, and the office was dark, save for the insignificant glow of what looked like a small desk lamp. Tristan moved closer to the building, carefully checking the perimeter. He found no motion or heat sensors, he moved in closer and found an open window.

"Arrogant son of a bitch," he murmured to himself. "He thinks no one has the balls to enter his domain. Let's see what I can find, shall we?"

Tristan pushed the window open enough for his body to clear it, slid through, and closed the window behind him.

He stood in the office, out of reach of the glow of the desk lamp, and canvassed the room. The office was neat, which surprised him. There was a four-drawer filing cabinet on one wall, two overstuffed chairs, and a small table between them. A large desk dominated one-third of the room. He walked to the desk and clicked the mouse on the computer. To his astonishment, the computer came awake; it showed an open file.

"Dumb bastard." He shook his head; this guy was really something, all the easier for him. The file seemed to be his daily report to Braxton and the Kaleidoscope Group. He read the screen.

"Have men under control, will not be allowed to roam loose in the outer jungle due to Collins' unpredictable behavior. Morgan seems to be adapting. Winters made a connection with Morgan today. Her research should move along quicker now that she has developed a rapport with him. Believe to still be on target with primary goal, to develop a serum to be sold, with the purpose of creating the perfect soldier."

Tristan read through the passage again. It had been obvious from the start this group was up to no good, but this proved the situation even worse than he expected. He spent the next ten minutes reviewing more of the reports. Then he pulled a small thumb drive from his back pocket and began to copy all the files on the computer. While it worked, he went over to the filing cabinet and pulled out the top drawer. He checked his watch and estimated he had only about ten minutes until Max might return.

Tristan went back to the desk, reached into his pocket, pulled out what looked like a Chapstick, and rubbed it on the coffee cup sitting on the desk. A few seconds later, a print of a finger and thumb appeared on the coating. When they had dried, he peeled them both from the coffee cup and placed them inside a small Altoids tin. Then he pulled the thumb drive from the port, glanced at the door leading to the suite, and begrudgingly headed back to the window where he had entered. He would have to save the suite for tomorrow night. As he lowered the window to its original position he heard the click of a lock release. Crap, Max returned early tonight. He pulled away from the window and vanished into the night.

Victory left her bedroom window open as Tristan had instructed. Using her window to leave and return made it appear to anyone who monitored the room that Tristan had once again spent the night.

"What did you find?" came a whisper from her bed.

"I thought you were asleep. I'm sorry; I didn't mean to wake you," he said.

"No, I haven't really been able to sleep; I've been dozing. I take it went okay since you are back in one piece. So, what did you find?"

He lay down on the bed next to her and relayed what he discovered.

"They want to use my research to create an army." She was appalled. "My research is for peaceful reasons, to improve the bond between humans and canines. My long-term goal is to find possible combinations of DNA that will lead to curing diseases in humans and canines, not for destruction."

"Unfortunately, Victory, Braxton and the Kaleidoscope Group are only two of thousands of demented individuals and groups who exploit well-meaning research into something financially beneficial to themselves."

"Why can't they see the good this could produce? It could be a way to improve people's lives in the very near future."

"Because improving people's lives won't make them money now. The Kaleidoscope Group has no concern for the future; they want it now," Tristan said.

"Seems to me that finding cures to cancer would be a profitable venture," Victory said.

"Yes, someday. Except that's not what this group wants. Terrorism sells. They will take outstanding military personnel and others and make them indestructible killing machines. Create the prefect mercenaries. It gives people like Braxton a feeling of power—and *power* is what drives him."

"I need to stop him. I can't let him exploit my work," she said, with steel in her voice.

Tristan reached out and pulled her close to him. He tucked her shoulder under his arm.

"There's nothing more we can do tonight. We both need to get some sleep." He leaned over her and kissed her lips lightly. He pulled away to look into her face and was mesmerized by those bottomless jewel-green eyes. Tristan claimed her lips once again. He deepened the kiss, running his hand down her silky neck. He continued down her body, stopping as he gently molded her breast in his palm. Then he resumed his journey downward to the hem of her nightgown.

He skimmed his palm back up her soft smooth leg and lingered at her hip as he felt her heat for him increase. Tristan pulled the nightgown up over Victory's head and lovingly gazed at her perfect body.

"Maybe sleep can wait for a little while," he murmured, his stare blazing a trail down her curves.

* * * *

Victory found a cooler next to her computer upon arrival to the lab the next morning. It contained three vials of blood. She had a hunch these vials were from Collin.

"This isn't a good sign," Victory mumbled to herself as she stared into her microscope.

Every time she introduced the wolf DNA to the spun down blood serum, it immediately began to attack and break down the human serum. After she repeated this same test a number of times, she came to the conclusion that a person who lacked some type of natural heightened senses could not withstand this coupling. She must find a way to stop this breakdown, or Collin would not survive. The only way for the process to be successful would be to create some type of binder that could act as a bridge to join human and wolf DNA in harmony.

Victory finally looked up from her microscope. She put her hands on her waist and stretched the cramps from her back.

"I feel like a cup of coffee; how about you?" she asked Tristan.

Tristan looked up from his computer. After spending the last two weeks with Victory almost twenty-four hours a day, he was now able to read her demeanor; he knew something troubled her. She smiled slightly, still the smile didn't quite reach her eyes, those breathtaking jade jewels. There was sadness and concern in them, along with a paleness to her skin.

"Sure, you know me, when do I ever turn down a cup of coffee?" he asked.

They both got up and headed for the door.

"How long are you two going to be gone?" Max asked from his permanent fixture on his chair in the corner of the lab.

"Thirty minutes or so. I thought we could take our coffee down to the beach and take a walk; I need to stretch my legs and clear my head," Victory said.

"Don't be gone any longer. Mr. Braxton is coming out to the island. He's due early this evening, and he expects great progress," Max said.

"Great," Victory mumbled.

"You say something?" Max asked.

"I said no problem," Victory said.

They picked up some coffee at the lone coffee stand along with a couple of cookies and headed to the beach.

"Assuming the blood left in the cooler for me today is Collin's, it doesn't look promising," she said.

"So you have discovered something?"

"I've run the same test numerous times and gotten the same result. The foreign DNA attacks the human DNA; it breaks it down and destroys it." She started to feel the pressure of failure. "I don't know what to do, Tristan. This is why research needs to be done one baby step at a time. Each step is then tested and retested. This is a new dilemma for me. I have a person's life depending on me to find a solution to this problem."

"Even so you do think there is a solution?"

"Maybe not the solution Braxton wants. But everything has a solution; it simply depends on how long you have to find it and if you are willing to keep on searching," Victory said, as she took a sip of her cooling latte.

"Based on your research today, how long does Collin have?"

"I don't know. It depends on a multitude of factors."

"Such as," he prompted. He hoped if he kept her talking and thinking, she would eventually stumble on at least one path to follow.

"Such as, how much serum they injected into his system. How long ago they injected him. I would have to backtrack and figure out what the percentage of serum is to the percentage of human DNA. These are the obvious factors," she said.

"Then you could save Collin."

"Hopefully, possibly. It depends on how fast I can find some answers. You heard Max; Braxton is coming in tonight. That's a whole new set of circumstances; I have no idea what to tell him. There isn't enough time. Research takes time, trial and error, you know that. And if Braxton even caught wind of the idea my real focus is to try and help Collin, we would all be in trouble. He can't find out I am looking for a solution to this problem. We both know his only concern is superhuman soldiers."

"There's only one solution. You tell him the truth."

"The truth! If I tell Braxton what I believe, he may feel Collin is expendable," she said, looking bewildered.

"I never said you tell him the whole truth. Look, Braxton is an astute man. He's going to know if you are stalling or not. He's knows your background, Victory; he is aware how intelligent and diligent you are."

"So what are you saying?" Victory asked.

It still surprised him that such an intelligent person could not figure out how to lie or twist the truth to her own benefit.

"What I'm saying is you tell Braxton there is a basic cellular change taking place, only you're not sure what the outcome will be. Tell him the rate of change is different in each individual. Therefore, if he has another person infused with the serum, you need to study him or her," Tristan said.

"Oh, now I get it. Give him enough information, yet not so much he has the answer!"

"Exactly," Tristan smiled at her. "Have an answer to everything he asks you, but only enough to convince him you are truly making progress."

"I can do that. I'm so grateful to have you here with me, Tristan. I wouldn't be able to make it through if I didn't have your help."

She couldn't believe what she just said. When had Tristan begun to matter to her? The thought sent tiny shivers up her arms.

"Thanks, but don't sell yourself short, Victory. You can do anything you put your mind to, and you would survive this," he said.

She flashed him a wicked little grin. "Possibly, all the same you are a great fringe benefit." She reached down and took his hand.

He laughed. "It's nice to know I'm good for something."

"You make a good assistant too," she giggled.

"Come on. We need to get back before Max sends out a search party."

* * * *

Victory had been brilliant in her report to Braxton. If Tristan didn't know differently, he would have believed her entire report.

"I am aware the human DNA I was working with today is from a different person. To glean any real additional information, it would be extremely beneficial for me to study this individual directly," Victory said, and finished out her hour-long report. She only hoped she sold her story to Braxton.

Braxton sat quietly, elbows on the arm of his chair, fingers steepled together. The room was shrouded in absolute silence. Victory could hear the pace of each individual's breath, entering and exiting their lungs. A tiny sheen of moisture gathered on her upper lip. This could be the end. Braxton knew she had lied to him.

"Intriguing," he finally said after what seemed like hours. "It seems you have moved forward with your findings; I am pleased. However, it looks like you and your assistant may be our guests on the island for longer than we initially thought." He looked from Tristan to Victory. "I hope I'm not keeping you from anything important," he said directly to Tristan.

"Nope, I'm good; wherever the doc goes, I go," Tristan said. "Besides, this place is great."

"Max. See that Ms. Winters has access to our other specimen starting tomorrow." Braxton rose and started for the door. "Oh and Ms. Winters, I would like a complete report of all your findings and conclusions on both specimens by the end of this week." He left the building, Max hot on his heels.

"Specimens." Victory was furious. "They're people—people who have names, lives, and loved ones. The nerve of that man, who does he think he is?"

"Take it easy, Victory. Right now he's the one holding all the cards, but it won't be that way much longer," Tristan whispered.

"If he thinks I'm staying one day longer than three weeks, he's got another thing coming," Victory spat.

Tristan laughed in her mind. The feel of it warmed her whole body. "You sure are a wildcat."

She glanced at him and her cheeks flushed with color.

* * * *

Victory and Tristan walked into the lab early the next morning to find Max already seated in his usual chair.

"Morning, Max," Victory said.

She and Tristan had thoroughly enjoyed a night filled with extraordinary lovemaking lasting into the wee hours of the morning. The worries of the day faded away, if only for a short span of time, but at least her mood remained lighthearted. Without even realizing it, Tristan had become her anchor amongst all this chaos. She realized she was growing to trust him, as a friend. She didn't think having a sexual connection to him was the best idea, and she was positive falling in love with him would be a terrible mistake. She knew to her very soul he was not the type of man to love. He was a warrior at heart. The thrill of the mission was what warmed his blood. Tristan would not be fulfilled having a family and a nine-to-five job. What was she thinking?

Deep down, she still didn't completely trust his motives.

"Collin is in the exam room, like you requested," Max said.

Victory looked up into the exam room window to see a large man with light-blue eyes, light-brown hair, and a grim expression. His arms and legs were strapped tightly to the chair, although he still thrashed about and tried to free himself.

"He's upset this morning. Mr. Braxton brought a couple new tracking chips with him. Both Collin and Morgan got chipped this morning," Max said with a callous attitude.

"Are you saying he's not usually this upset?" Victory asked.

"Nope, he's been pretty much pissed about everything since he got the shot of serum," Max said.

"Great," Tristan said.

"I can call the doctor in to give him a sedative. I would have already done it except I didn't want you yelling at me 'cause I did," Max said.

"I don't know, Victory; maybe we should let them give him something to take the edge off. This guy is mega-pissed. I don't want him to hurt you," Tristan said.

"If he's sedated, the testing could be tainted, and he wouldn't be coherent enough to talk. No, I don't want him sedated. I need some time with him," Victory said.

"Your funeral," Max said with a slight laugh.

"Hey, that's not funny," Tristan shot back.

"Chill out. All I'm saying is watch yourself. Morgan's a pussycat compared to his friend Collin. I'm going to go get some coffee. I got two guys at the door if you need them," Max said, as he got up and tossed his magazine in to the chair he'd previously occupied.

"What—you are going to leave us here alone with him?" Victory threw back sarcastically.

Max continued toward the door.

"Yep. Mr. Braxton said to give you free rein."

Max closed the door and left Tristan and Victory alone, staring at Collin.

"Okay, I might as well get started," Victory said.

She pulled open a drawer, finding a syringe, a couple of vials, and her rubber band. She stuck everything in her pocket.

"First, I have to establish some trust with Collin." She headed for the exam room; Tristan was right behind her. She turned around to look at him. "You know the drill, Tristan. I need…"

"Don't even start. I'm coming in. I really don't like this."

"What? All I wanted to say is to please give me some space," she said with a smile. She thought it unwise to push the issue as she could tell he was on edge.

"Yeah, right," Tristan said.

As Victory opened the door, they were bombarded by random snippets of the day in the forest and flashes of pure rage. Victory felt dizzy. Tristan reached out to steady her.

"Victory, are you okay? I think we should wait for a while and give him more time to settle down," he said.

"I'm fine. I don't know if he is going to settle down. His mind is in a state of flux; he's confused, upset, and losing his self-control. His thoughts remind me more of a wild dog than a human."

"Great, just what we need, a really big guy with a really shitty attitude," Tristan said.

For a single breath, Victory's mind cleared. She threw up some mental barriers and proceeded forward. Tristan felt Victory withdraw from his mind. He knew what she was doing, and, although he didn't like being out of the loop, he realized it was the best for her.

"Hi Collin. My name is Victory, and this is my assistant, Tristan." Victory turned slightly to touch Tristan's arm.

Collin stared at them. "I know who you are, and he's no assistant. I tried to introduce myself to you that day in the forest, remember?" he snapped.

She stood her ground.

"I need to take some blood from you, so I can try and help you."

"Yeah, help me," he snorted. "Come on over here, and I'll show you how you can help me." He waggled an eyebrow.

Tristan grabbed her arm as she started to move forward. "Are you crazy? You're not getting anywhere near him. Let me get the blood." Tristan held out his hand. Victory hesitated and then thinking better of it, she reached in her pocket and pulled out all of the supplies.

As Tristan stepped closer to Collin, he saw him tense.

"Listen Collin, I'm going to get this blood, so we can do it the easy way or the hard way." Tristan continued on toward him. He reached the chair and wrapped the band around Collin's arm. He quickly located a vein from which to draw some blood. Tristan took shallow breaths, trying to keep the pungent odor of Collin's ever-increasing adrenaline from overtaking him, the entire time feeling Collin's body wind tighter and tighter.

"There, it wasn't that bad now was it?"

"What would you know about bad?" Collin hissed.

Tristan nearly pushed Victory out of the exam room.

"This guy is vicious," he said.

"It's not him; it's the foreign DNA, and it has taken hold of his system. Couldn't you feel the wildness in him? I could feel the uproar throughout his entire system. The wolf is trying to seize his actual essence," Victory said. "Did you feel it?"

Tristan admired Victory's telepathic senses. He had them with only with his brother, Wyatt, until she came along. Now, after a mere two weeks, he also had a link with her. Victory could telepathically speak to him, and he was able to project feelings to her. She was expanding his telepathic world.

"If you are referring to the overwhelming adrenaline he continued pumping out, then yes. I could feel waves of anger and pain roll off of him," he said.

"Pain, really, hmmm."

"What, are you telling me I felt something you didn't?" he asked.

"I think we complement one another. Each of us picks up different feelings that complete a whole picture," she said.

"You think. Or I could be reading his face." Tristan was skeptical at the possibility he could read a person's feelings.

"Give yourself some credit, Tristan; you have a gift. Like you said, I'm only an amplifier," Victory said.

* * * *

Hours had passed since Victory last looked up from her computer or microscope. "Crap," she said.

"Doc, what's the problem?" Tristan asked.

"I can't come up with the right combination to balance out the foreign DNA. I've tried over three hundred combinations." She looked exhausted.

"You know it's going to take some time. This isn't something that is going to happen in a few hours." He tried to reassure her.

"The problem is, I'm worried Collin doesn't have much time."

"You're doing all you can. We need to call it a night. Go get some dinner and relax."

"And tell me, how do you plan to relax?"

"I'm sure I can come up with the perfect plan," Tristan bantered back with a sly smile.

Chapter Nineteen

Tristan and Victory were woken by yells coming from the main courtyard.

"What's happening, Tristan?" Victory asked, as she bolted upright in bed.

"I'm not sure. Get dressed." He gathered his clothes and dressed quickly.

A rap sounded on the bedroom window. Victory gasped as she pulled the covers up to her chin. "Who's there?" she whispered.

"I can't make them out. There's too many people milling about to distinguish individual scents. You stay here, and let me check it out."

Tristan finished tying his boots and got up from the chair. Without turning on a single light, he slid out of the bedroom window.

"Tristan," someone whispered from the shadows.

"Morgan, is that you? What's happening?" He couldn't clearly see the man hiding in a nearby bush, but he could now differentiate Morgan's scent.

Morgan came out of the shadows.

"It's Collin. He broke out of his room again. Max is organizing teams to track him down. I thought you might be able to help me remove this asinine tracker Max implanted in my leg today." Morgan rubbed his upper thigh. "After we get it out, I plan on finding Collin and getting the hell out of here."

"No, you can't," Tristan said.

"Who the hell's going to stop me, you?" Morgan shot back.

"Take a breath, Morgan, and listen to me for a second. There are more people involved in this predicament than only the two of you. Victory and I need a couple more days to gather as much information as possible. Then we will have a plan including removal of the tracker, but this is not the time," Tristan said.

"Collin might die tonight if one of those idiots shoots him. He's losing it; he's not himself at all," Morgan said.

"That's another reason we have to stay. Victory doesn't have all the research she needs to help Collin. If you guys leave now, Collin will not survive long on the run. He's going to need help, and so will you."

"Okay, okay, I see what you're saying, but what about getting Collin out of the mess he's in now?"

"We'll get him out. You go back to your room and stay there. Victory and I will take care of Collin."

Morgan stood there for another second.

"I guess I should at least get out of here before one of those imbeciles finally realizes I'm gone and tracks me here."

"And go back to your room, please."

"All right. I'm leaving Collin's life in your hands. Don't make me regret trusting you." He stepped back into the shadows and disappeared.

Tristan slid back into the bedroom. He found Victory dressed. She sat in the chair on the far side of the room.

"It was Morgan," he said.

"I heard everything. Remember? Heightened hearing." She rose from the chair. "We should get going if we want to be any help to Collin."

Damn the woman's keen hearing. He needed to make sure he kept her ability in mind in the future. He headed for the door and motioned for her to go through. "We need to locate Max as soon as we possibly can. Between my sense of smell and your blasted ultra-keen hearing, it shouldn't be too hard."

The compound was buzzing. People flooded out of their rooms to see what all the commotion was about. Security teams were going from group to group, sending them back into their rooms. Tristan recognized one of Max's men.

"We can save some time. Isn't he one of Max's men?" He pointed at a man working with one of the groups a few yards away.

"Yes, he's the guy who stood at the front entrance of the lab yesterday while Collin was in the building."

Tristan jogged up to the man and grabbed him by the arm. "Hey, I need to speak with Max; where is he?"

The man turned and focused his attention on Tristan. "You need to go back to your room, sir. It's dangerous to be out right now; Collin has escaped and already attacked one of our men."

"I know he's out. That's why I need to locate your boss," Tristan said.

"Sir, return to your room; this is none of your concern," the man insisted.

"It is my concern. Mr. Braxton will be very upset if this hinders Ms. Winters' research. What's going on?"

The man scowled at Tristan for another minute, no doubt contemplating whether to believe him or not. "Fine. If you get into trouble, you're on your own. He took a couple men and headed into the forest. Collin is an idiot; he's got a tracker in him. Does he really think he's going to get away?"

Tristan returned to Victory. "Let's go; I'm sure you heard."

They ran through the compound and headed straight for the forest. They continued to run for a couple of minutes, and then Victory reached out and grabbed Tristan's arm.

"Stop, Tristan; we don't have time to run haphazardly. I can't concentrate on listening when I have blood pumping in my ears."

He stopped, barely breathing hard. Victory put her hands on her knees and took in a deep cleansing breath. She centered herself and listened to the sounds of the forest around her. Tristan followed suit and focused himself. Their surroundings closed in around them as they remained transfixed.

"That way," the two said in unison. They took off at a run, certain time was against them. Ten minutes later, Tristan reached Max with Victory hot on his heels.

Max whipped around, his gun held at the ready and pointed straight at Tristan's heart. "Dammit, man!

You're lucky I didn't shoot you. What the hell are you two doing here?" he demanded as he lowered his gun.

"One of your men told us where you were. We are here to help you locate Collin. Where is he now?" Tristan asked.

"A hundred yards or so up ahead," Max said. "Two of my guys are flanking him now. We should have him pinned shortly."

"What's your plan?" Tristan asked.

"He attacked one of my men. He's getting out of control. I have the authority to take him down," Max said with steel in his voice.

"No!" Victory shouted. "You can't kill him. I need him for my research. It will slow me down immensely if I don't have him to study. Call Braxton right this minute and ask him if he wants you to kill Collin." Victory was not about to let them shoot Collin.

Max thought about what Braxton's reaction would be if he killed Collin. Yes, he'd been given the authority, all the same Braxton might view it as his inability to control the situation. He could be the next one disposed of.

"Fine." He holstered his handgun and pulled another one from the small of his back.

Victory drew her breath in sharply as she watched him pull out an even larger gun.

"Tranq," he said. "I'll take him down with this. You two stay put." He looked down at the small screen he held in his other hand. "My guys have started to force Collin back this way." Max turned his back to them and started to walk away.

"What if one of the other guys shoots him?" Victory asked.

"They won't unless he attacks them." Max headed into the thick foliage hanging off the trees.

Tristan pulled Victory back to him as she attempted to follow after Max.

"No, Victory, we've done all we can. Now we have to wait and hope everything works out. The last thing I want is for you to get caught in the crossfire in the dark forest."

Huddled against Tristan's warm, solid chest, Victory listened intently. She heard the men slink through the vegetation off to her left. She reached farther and caught a low growl that she suspected to be Collin. He was reacting like a cornered animal, ready to strike. Then she heard a howl and for a split second, dead silence.

"You got him, sir; he's down," one of the men hollered.

"They got him," she said to Tristan. "Hopefully, with the tranquilizer gun, not a bullet."

"We'll know in a minute. All we can do is wait." Tristan rubbed his hands up and down her arms, trying to comfort her.

Minutes later, Max appeared from the overgrowth. "I tranquilized him, got him a split second before he took another one of my guys down. The team is getting him ready to take back to the compound. There's nothing more to see here; you two need to head back to your rooms."

"Can you bring Collin to the lab tomorrow morning please?" Victory asked. "I have more tests I need to run."

"Yep, will do; see you both in the morning," Max said.

"Do you really need to work with him tomorrow, or do you want to make sure he is okay?" Tristan asked her after they had walked for a while."

"Why Mr. Grant, you know me so well; both," she said with a smile. It was the first sign of relief she had shone since they heard the news of Collin's escape over two hours ago.

* * * *

Logan strolled into the cave. He was still in his cammies, and they were covered in foliage and dirt. "Honey, I'm home. What's for dinner?"

Noah rolled over in his sleeping bag and scowled at Logan.

"Dinner? I ate hours ago. What have you been up to? I can see it was something exciting since you haven't deloused," Noah said.

"Very exciting. Sorry to bring the outdoors in," Logan said with a smile. "But I didn't want anyone sneaking up on me while I was out bathing. It's quieted down out there now, so I thought I'll grab a cup of coffee and head out to the spring."

They'd lucked out this trip; usually they had to bathe in ice-cold water. This time, however, Noah had found a warm spring on one of his first trips out; it was almost like home.

"Don't keep me in suspense; tell me what happened." Noah got out of his sleeping bag and cut Logan off. "Back up, dirt boy; I'll make the coffee."

"Thanks, mom. Collin broke out again tonight. Tell ya, he's one sneaky bastard. Don't know what he was like before he got fused with a wolf, but he's freakin' good now. I saw him clear a ten-foot rock formation in a single leap. He ran through the forest doing at least fifteen miles an hour," Logan said.

"No shit."

"It took Max's team over two hours to track him down, and that's with a bloody tracker in his leg. He'd better be thankful for Tristan and Victory. Max and his team were so pissed; they were going to take him down. Tristan and Victory showed up at the same time they cornered Collin and saved his hide. It took some talking, but they convinced Max to tranquilize him. Speaking of Tristan, shit, he is the best tracker I have ever known, but, hot damn, with Victory working with him, those two are unstoppable. I pity the poor bastard trying to hide from them. It took them only fifteen minutes to track Collin down."

"Shit, I'm glad he's on our team. I love ya Logan, but if I ever need to be found, send Tristan and Victory. You stay back and make the coffee," Noah said, with a laugh. "Tell me about Max's team." He became serious again and all business.

"Six-man team including Max. He's the only one we have to worry about. Obviously got tracker in him, the other five can't find their dicks. Max treats them like a bunch of teenagers, not a military background among the bunch."

"Bet that pisses him off," Noah said with a smile a mile wide.

* * * *

"Good morning, Collin. How are you feeling after your little run in the forest last night?" Victory came into the exam room, clipboard and vials in hand. She crossed the room and put her items down on the table. "Do you have any idea how close you came to getting yourself killed?" She turned back and glowered at him.

"My jailers won't give me any PT time, so I decided to take some anyway." he said, a grim look etched in his face. "Why do you care? Oh, that's right, one less guinea pig to study," he threw back at her.

Victory studied him intently; she wondered what Collin was like before the wolf DNA got injected into his body. She would never know. This forced change in his personality would be permanent. Now it was her job to make sure he might have the chance to adapt to it. She wondered if adapting was what he really wanted. Unfortunately, the alternative was even worse. Sadness flooded her mind. This was the first time she had ever allowed herself think this way.

Tristan felt the ripple of anguish flow through Victory. He looked up from his computer and stared into the exam room and focused on her back. He pushed thoughts of comfort into her mind.

She turned back to the table in the exam room, her stare rising to meet Tristan's.

"Thank you."

He felt the words burn into his brain.

"I'm fine, really. I didn't mean to interrupt your work."

She felt him withdraw. For the first time, she was left with an emptiness after his withdrawal. Had Tristan become so important to her that she relied on his mental connection? Were these feelings she had toward him real, or were they the only things she could grab on to with all this chaos around her?

Only four weeks had passed since this man walked into her life, but she couldn't imagine her life without him now. No one, except for her family, had ever been this essential to her. Goose bumps ran down her arms; *oh my God, did she love this man?* The thought chilled her to her bones. Tristan was not the type of man who could love her. He would break her heart if she let him in.

"You sure you're all right, Victory?" Tristan asked, as he stuck his head through the doorway of the exam room.

With a quick shake of her head, in an attempt to push her last thought away, she smiled back up at him. "Yes, I'm working out a problem is all."

"Okay, Collin. Tell me, how are you feeling today?" She turned toward him and refocused her full attention on her task at hand.

"Like something is trying to tear me apart from the inside out," he hissed back at her. "I lose time."

"How do you mean?" Victory was ecstatic. They were actually conversing.

"What I mean is, I'm doing something, or I'm in one place and then I wake up, and I'm somewhere else, doing something I don't remember starting. So tell me, doc, is that normal for a person who's been injected with God knows what?" Collin asked.

"What's normal? Unfortunately I don't have anything to compare to, since you and Morgan are the first two humans I am aware of, who have been injected with canine DNA."

"Great, I'm blazing trails. Canine, huh? Guess it explains my constant panting and craving for steak," he snickered.

Victory couldn't help herself; she gawked at him. It finally dawned on her—she was actually conversing with the true Collin.

"What's the matter? Am I growing two heads?" he let out a little snort.

"What. No. Sorry. Collin, I need to take more blood; is that okay?" she asked.

"Human pincushion at your service." He held his arm out.

Victory took the blood, smiled at him briefly and left the exam room. "Where's Max?" she asked as she went back into the lab.

"He mumbled something about coffee. I think he's getting soft, last night wupped his butt," Tristan chuckled. "What did you say to Collin? He acted like a pussycat?"

She held the samples up, shaking them in front of him.

"Hopefully, these little guys are going to tell me," she answered, her face beaming.

"I don't get it, but whatever you said to him put our buddy to sleep." Tristan jerked his head in the direction of the exam room.

She looked back into the exam room. Sure enough, Collin's head lolled back, he'd fallen asleep or blacked out.

"Tristan quick; start the video in the exam room." She ran over to help him.

He did what she asked, no questions. Only after everything was up and running did he ask, "Are you going to tell me what's going on?"

"I had my first conversation with Collin."

He looked at her in confusion.

"The real Collin, not the DNA-induced Collin, and believe it or not, he's funny."

"I find it extremely difficult to believe. So what does that mean?" Tristan asked.

"It means he is fighting to stay in control, not always winning, but at least he's still trying. It gives me hope I might be able to help him," she said.

"Okay, doc; then let's get to work."

Collin woke up two hours later, spewing obscenities. It surprised Tristan that Victory was pleased.

"Tristan, can you go in and get three more blood samples from him, please. Max, you can take Collin back to his room after Tristan gets his blood."

"Great, he's in one of his bad-ass moods," Max groaned.

If he only knew, Victory thought. At last, she might have found a breakthrough, and she would take it to her grave before she let Braxton hear about it.

Chapter Twenty

Victory leaned against the headboard, knees bent, and typed furiously on her laptop. She was so consumed in her work, Tristan thought he could leave and be back before she would even notice. Although if not, he wouldn't want her to worry. He shook his head. He couldn't believe the thought crossed his mind. When had he ever given a second thought regarding anyone's feelings–except maybe his brother. Crap, this assignment was taking its toll, or could it actually be Victory? *No, it couldn't be—could it?* Did he actually have deep feelings for this amazing woman?

"Not the time, Farraday, there's work to be done." He grumbled as he bent down and began to lace up his boots. "Victory?"

"Hmmm?" she mumbled.

"I need to go out for awhile."

"Again tonight? You've gone out every night in the last week."

"You'll be fine; besides, you're wrapped up in your work," he said.

"That's not the point. I worry about you getting caught or hurt every time you go out at night," she said.

Wow, her words floored him. No one ever worried about him.

"Really? Don't worry about me. I'm one of the best at what I do for a living."

He rose from the chair and walked over to the bed. He leaned down close to her and placed his right index finger under her chin; he tilted her head up and bent down to kiss her. He could get used to this. Focus, he needed to focus, or he would get caught.

"See ya soon," he said and slipped out the bedroom window.

* * * *

Victory continued working for what seemed like hours. She was edgy and needed a break. She glanced at the clock on the nightstand and realized it was a little before midnight; Tristan left only an hour ago. She put the laptop down beside her on the bed and got up. Leaving the bedroom, she walked into the living room, where she grabbed a magazine and dropped down into an overstuffed chair. She haphazardly flipped through the magazine and found nothing that caught her attention. She needed to do something.

She got up from the chair, returned to the bedroom, and threw on a light jacket over her T-shirt and shorts. She searched the floor for her sneakers and found one under the bed and one clear across the room. She grabbed her room card and headed out the door.

The night was beautiful; she took in a deep breath and filled her lungs with the alluring fragrances of plumeria, orchids, and tuberoses. The sky was crystal clear and sparkled with millions of tiny stars. The moon shone so bright that the lit tiki lamps seemed to be overshadowed by its glow. Victory passed a few people strolling through the paths as she headed to the canteen. The island's canteen was located near the edge of the compound. As she walked in, it surprised her to find the place filled to capacity. Most of the small tables were full, along with the shuffleboard and darts area. She looked over to the far side of the building and noticed four pool tables, each buzzing with players. Victory walked up to the bar and was met by Andy, the boy who'd welcomed Tristan and her to the island.

"Ms. Winters, nice to see you. Have you and Mr. Grant settled in? Make sure to call me if you are in need of anything." He nearly yelled at her to be heard over the crowd; his voice blasted in her ears.

"Thank you, Andy. You seem to keep yourself quite busy," Victory said.

"Oh yes. I only work here two nights a week, but I do enjoy this job," he said. "What can I get you?"

"I would like a glass of Merlot. Is there anywhere quieter I might be able to enjoy my wine?" With her acute hearing and Andy's unnecessary yelling, she felt a headache coming on, a common side effect in these types of situations.

Andy grabbed a wine glass and uncorked a bottle of Merlot.

"Sure, you can go out to the veranda." He pointed to the door at the backside of the building.

"Great, thanks." She paid for her wine, said goodbye to Andy, and headed out to the veranda. She opened the door and found a large open setting. Small wicker tables topped with glass and oversized wicker chairs sporting huge pillows filled the area. Each of the tables was adorned with a crystal bowl filled with water, floating candles, and plumeria. The perfume of scented candles and flowers wafted throughout the veranda. She instantly thought of Tristan and wondered if this wafting fragrance would overpower him, as sound did her. She spied a chair and small side table at the far side of the veranda. She walked over and sat down. She looked out at the dark ocean, the lights of the stars reflecting in the breaking waves.

Victory cleared her mind of work and wrapped herself in the wonders of the night. Before she realized it, she began eavesdropping on the conversations going on around her.

"Sheesh," she scolded herself; she really must work harder not to do that.

She heard the mention of her name somewhere at the far side of the veranda. She refocused and honed in on the single conversation, at the same time blocking out all the other voices.

"Haven't you heard about it?" It was Max's second-in-command.

"No, give me the run down," the other man said.

"Max told me we would be pulling out the day after tomorrow," said the first man.

"Are we leaving Winters and Grant here?"

"No, stupid. Let me finish what I'm trying to tell you. We're taking Winters, Morgan, and Collin."

"Where are we going?" asked the other man.

"Max didn't say. It's all very hush, hush. All I know is it's another Kaleidoscope property," the first man said.

"What will happen with Grant? Is he being sent home?" asked the other man.

"The boss isn't happy with Grant. He thinks Grant will just be in the way after we move Winters. It wouldn't surprise me if Grant didn't finish the trip with the rest of us. Max loves tossing guys from aircraft; I've seen it before," said the first man.

Victory stiffened. Her first instinct told her to run, but she needed to stay and hear this out. Besides, if she got up now, the two men might spot her.

"Mr. Braxton is coming in late the same afternoon we are to pull out. He will take Winters with him. Max will have a second chopper; we'll be with him, along with Morgan, Collin, and Grant. Something tells me it's going to be a very short ride for Grant," Max's man said.

"It's about time something exciting is going to happen. This whole assignment has been pretty boring, except for the couple times we got to track Collin," the second man said. "Speaking of boring, I'm on watch in half an hour, I should leave."

"You mean to tell me you've been sitting here drinking beer and you've got a shift in thirty minutes?" The first man laughed.

"Yeah, like I said, it's been really boring, I'll be fine," he said, as he got up to leave.

"Not if Max finds out. You will find yourself with more excitement than you want."

The two men headed for the door.

Victory started to leave and then she thought better of it. The last thing she needed would be to run into one of them on her way out of the canteen. She sat patiently and sipped on her wine and glanced at her watch. Thirty minutes later she started on her way back to her room.

Victory unlocked her door, went into her bedroom, and found Tristan lying on the bed wearing only his jeans. His hair was damp from his recent shower. She looked at her watch. She'd been gone for two hours.

"Hey, where have you been?" He smiled up at her. "I was beginning to worry."

"Sorry, I lost track of time. Tristan, we're in real trouble," she blurted out as she struggled to remove her jacket.

He got up off the bed and went over to help her.

"Here, let me help; you're getting yourself all tangled up."

After he helped her get out of the jacket, he walked her over to the bed and made her sit down beside him.

"Now, take a deep breath, relax, and tell me what happened."

"I decided to go out for a walk around midnight. I got finished with my work for the night and was feeling slightly edgy. I thought some fresh air would do me good. I walked to the canteen. I hadn't been in there yet and thought a glass of wine would help me relax. The place vibrated with activity and the level of noise was more than I could deal with. I took my wine and went out back to sit on the veranda. While I sat there, I picked up on a conversation across the way. It was two of Max's men." She relayed the men's conversation to Tristan word for word.

"Are you sure they didn't see you?" He seemed more concerned for her immediate safety.

She shook her head in response. "They didn't see me. I started to get up right after they left the veranda and then I thought better of it and stayed to sip on my wine for thirty minutes."

"Good," he replied, with pure relief in his voice.

"What are we going to do Tristan? We have less than two days to get out of here." She was nearly in a panic.

"Don't worry. I knew the time would come when we would have to get out of here. That's one of the things Noah and Logan were assigned to work out— how to get us all off this island. It sounds like we will have to step up the timetable. Okay, when we met back at the campground, you said you work with plants and could make remedies."

"Yes, I've done it for years. They came in handy with my practice, and my family uses them on a regular basis. Why?" she asked.

"Great. I've used them too, but I'm sure you have more experience for what we will need. If you can tell me what types of plants you need, I can get them for you," he said.

"You mean you really are a botanist?" she asked with a look of surprise.

"Yes, I never lied to you Victory; I might not have told you the whole truth, but I didn't lie. We're getting off the subject. Can you tell me what types of plants you need?"

"Yes, depending on what you want to use the remedy for."

"I want you to prepare an odorless liquid that will cause someone to fall asleep," he said.

"I can do that, but it would be easier if we went out together. I take it you already have a plan," she said.

"I do. I will go out and get our morning lattes. Like I usually do, I'll pick up a coffee for Max, and I will put the remedy in his drink. While I'm gone, you will ask him to bring Morgan to the exam room. After Max is out cold, we get Morgan loose and head for Collin. Then we all head out to our rendezvous point where we meet up with Logan and Noah."

"There could be one problem with the plan," she said as she thought aloud.

"Really," Tristan grinned. "And what might that be?"

"How do we get through the gate where Collin is being held? You said it has a fingerprint scan at the gate."

"Yeah, that's right."

"I don't think your print will work. Morgan and Collin have gotten out of the compound. Why don't we use the same route they are using?" she asked.

"I wish. They are jumping over the fence." It still surprised him they could accomplish the feat.

"They jump a fifteen-foot high-voltage fence? I'm impressed, apparently the wolf DNA is improving their abilities," Victory said.

"Yeah, but we don't have the advantage of wolf DNA, not that I want it. Even so I have planned on a way to get in." He reached into his jeans pocket and pulled out a tiny tin of Altoids. He placed the tin in her hands.

"Are you trying to tell me I have bad breath?" she scowled at him.

"No, open it," he chuckled.

She looked at him and then down at the tin and opened it. Inside there were no mints, only a couple pieces of plastic or gum. "What is it?"

He carefully pulled one of the pieces out and placed it on his thumb.

"Meet Max's print."

"You have been busy working at night. When did you get his print, or more to the point, how did you get that?"

"I took it off a coffee mug he left on his desk in his office." He smiled at her, quite pleased with himself. "Of course, I've been working. What did you think I was doing? Never mind, don't answer that question. Although the truth of the matter is, I would've rather been in bed with you," he teased. "Speaking of which, it's been a long night for both of us. Let's try and get a few hours sleep."

"Sleep," she repeated and raised one eyebrow.

"Yeah, after we unwind."

He smiled at her as he grabbed hold of the tie holding her shorts up. Her shorts dropped to the floor, leaving her naked from the waist down.

Victory didn't move a muscle, bewitched by the pure lust in Tristan's dazzling violet eyes. He took a step toward her and placed a hand on each side of her waist, right below the hem of her T-shirt. Leisurely, he moved his hands up the sides of her body and stopped at her breasts. He stroked both buds, and her pulse fluttered beneath his hands.

He continued up until he could slide the shirt off of her. He brought the inferno that was Victory to him and claimed her mouth with a fervor that consumed him. He felt her hands pull down the zipper to his jeans and then surround his shaft. He stepped out of his jeans as he pushed Victory back to the wall.

He lifted her off the floor, and she wrapped her legs around him. He positioned his body directly under her and slid her down the wall at the same time he plunged up into her. She moaned with pleasure and wrapped her legs even more tightly around him as she thrust her hips to meet him, over and over. Tristan could swear he saw flashing colors flood his head. No one ever made him feel like Victory could.

Tristan carried her to the bed and the two of them fell into it.

"I like your definition of unwinding, Mr. Farraday," she whispered into his ear as she began to nibble on his earlobe.

She used his real name. Was she trying to tell him something? Maybe telling him this was very real to her? Hundreds of thoughts ran through his mind, but this was not the time to question her. Instead he simply responded, "I figured you would. I still feel wound up," he teased.

"We can't have that," she said and pulled Tristan over the top of her.

Chapter Twenty-One

After putting in a long day at the lab, Tristan and Victory headed out to take a walk in the jungle. With any luck he would locate the plants Victory needed to make her sleeping potion. Victory was familiar with much of the foliage indigenous to the island, but Tristan was an expert. She enjoyed watching him wander through the forest looking at all the different plants. He would point out unusual plants and tell her their names and some interesting properties. He found everything she needed, and then they headed back to the compound.

"I'll need to clean them before I make up the mixture. I'll head back to my room, wash them off, lay them out, and then I'll meet you for dinner," she said, as she headed in the direction of their rooms.

Around nine they sauntered out of the dining room, hand in hand. The compound was already quieting down for the night. Clouds came in from the ocean and blocked the glow of the moon.

"Looks like we have a storm heading this way," Victory said.

"It's the start of the season. On the upside, it will make it easier to get around the compound tonight. Morgan will be coming by in an hour," Tristan breathed in her ear as they walked up the path.

She slipped the key card into the door and pushed it open.

"I have a slight headache, Tristan; I think I'm going to take a couple aspirins and lay down."

"Sounds like a good idea; you've been pushing yourself too hard," he said.

"I'm trying to get some results for Braxton."

She walked into her bedroom with Tristan behind her; he shut the door.

"We're getting really good at playing our parts," she said with a grin.

"A couple of real actors," he said. "Mission accomplished; whoever is listening will believe we are in for the night and hopefully tune us out for the evening."

"Are you going to take out Morgan's tracker chip tonight?" She sat on the edge of the bed taking her sneakers off.

"No, I took a scalpel from the lab, and I'm going to give it to him tonight so he will be ready tomorrow."

"You mean he has to remove the chip himself?" she asked.

"That's the plan."

The thought of using a scalpel on herself sent shivers all over her body.

"Morgan is approaching." She turned her head toward the window.

"You're right; I caught his scent." He walked to the window, opened it, and waited for Morgan.

"Hey Tristan, we're ready for tomorrow on our end," Morgan said, and shook Tristan's outstretched hand.

"We're on. We got all the plants we needed today. Victory has gone into the bathroom to work on Max's sleeping potion. Here are a scalpel and one of my team's communication ear buds."

"Wow, that's pretty cool." Morgan held the tiny communication device between two fingers. "Give me the rundown on it."

"Press this little button and you will automatically be linked to the team. It's sound sensitive. When you speak, we'll all be able to hear you. Make sure you don't turn it on until I have taken the security grid down," Tristan said.

"Got it."

"How are things with Collin?" Tristan asked.

"He's getting jumpy and wants to leave yesterday."

"It's your job to keep him under control, Morgan. If anyone can do it, you can."

"Don't worry; I'll take care of him."

As if on cue, the compound alarm went off. At nearly the same time, the two men smelled smoke.

"You smell that?" Tristan asked.

"Yeah, I do. Damn it all to hell, it's Collin. He said he needed some entertainment, and he might go find a book. I told him to stay put and I would bring him back something to read. He's left the freaking enclosure," Morgan swore.

"Damn it Morgan, I thought you said you had him under control?" Tristan all but spat back.

"I thought I did. He promised me he would stay put, but he's getting more and more unpredictable each day."

Victory ran out of the bathroom.

"What's going on?" she asked.

"It's Collin; he's left his enclosure again, and this time he started a fire to add to the confusion," Tristan said.

"Now what are we gonna do?" Morgan asked. "They are probably out to shoot him this time."

Tristan answered without hesitation. "Looks like he's forced our hand; we leave tonight. We'll have to make some changes to the plan on the fly. Morgan, you track Collin down and then stick to the plan—meet us at the rendezvous point as soon as you have Collin secure. I hope you have some idea where he is going?"

"Like always, he'll head for the forest," Morgan said, as he too began to get antsy.

"Okay, you are going to have to kick it into high gear when you leave here. Give me twenty minutes to take down the grid and then put in your ear bud. After I get the grid down, we will contact Noah and Logan so they can make the necessary changes to our escape. Victory, you will be with me."

"I need to go to the lab first. I can't leave without all the research. I can't afford to start this project from scratch again. Morgan and Collin are running out of time."

"Okay, you go straight to the lab and then meet me near the loading bay. Do you know where the loading bay is?" Tristan asked.

"Yes. It should only take me twenty minutes to gather up my laptop and all the data."

"Morgan, you take off. Victory, go put on all-black clothing and head directly to the lab. Please, be careful."

"I'm out of here. I'll keep you updated as to my progress. After I secure Collin we will head for the rendezvous point." Morgan melted into the shadows.

"I need to leave," Tristan said.

"Go, I'll be fine. Change, lab, loading bay," Victory reiterated.

"That's it, and stick to the plan. Victory, please be careful." Tristan leaned inside the window, pulled her into his arms, and kissed her. "See you soon." With that, he too went off into the darkness.

Victory headed to the lab. The compound was chaotic with people trying to see what had happened, and others attempting to get the fire under control. She overheard people saying Collin had set the coffee shop on fire. He'd poured cooking oils and flammable cleaners on the thousands of books lining the walls which added fuel to the fire. The building was a total loss, with flames shooting over twenty feet into the air. The only hope now was to stop it from spreading. The scene was so intense Victory's movements were going unnoticed.

The lab was lit at the outside door with a small overhead light. Victory stopped, hidden by the shrubbery, and listened; she heard no one in the vicinity and looked around to make sure no one was near. After she made sure she was alone, she walked up to the lab and unlocked the door.

The inside was cloaked in darkness. Victory stepped into the building and reached out to switch on the light. She went straight to her workstation. She pulled the large backpack from her shoulder and placed it on the table, slipped in her laptop and the stack of files next to it, along with the thumb drives she had recorded. Then she went over to the cooler and emptied it of all the samples.

She was so absorbed, she never noticed a shadow quickly pass in the doorway. As she secured the contents of her backpack, she realized her mistake. She heard the slightest rustle of clothing behind her. Before she had the opportunity to turn to see what made the noise, she got hit from behind and crumpled to the floor unconscious.

* * * *

Tristan managed to disable the security grid in less than ten minutes. Collin's fire served as a huge distraction and actually helped him, as there wasn't a single man left inside the facility. He pushed the tiny button on his ear bud and popped it into his ear.

"Noah, Logan, this is Tristan."

"Roger," Logan said. "What the hell is going on in there?"

"Collin got impatient, decided to start the party without us," Tristan said.

"So he likes to play with fire," Noah chimed in.

"Yeah, I guess he does. Morgan are you there?" Tristan asked.

"Roger," Morgan replied slightly winded. "I haven't picked up Collin's trail yet, but I must be closing in on him."

Logan was at the far side of the compound scouting out the surroundings.

"The compound is clear and the escape route is secure. I have made initial contact with our chopper. Pilot estimates thirty minutes to rendezvous," Logan said.

Logan approached the helipad with caution when he noticed a small chopper sat on the tarmac. Man, they were in luck; he could pilot anything. They could all be off this rock in minutes. Of course it all depended on if Morgan could locate Collin in time. All of a sudden, the chopper came to life—the blades started to rotate and the control lights inside came on. There were no outside lights illuminated, whoever was piloting the thing didn't want to be seen. A terrible thought crossed his mind.

"Morgan, you there? This is Logan."

"Hey, Logan, I'm here," Morgan said.

"Collin doesn't happen to be a chopper pilot does he?" Logan asked.

"If it flies, Collin can pilot it," Morgan said.

"Shit, shit, shit," the team heard. Logan ran full out to the chopper. His only hope was to reach it before it was too far off the ground. He reached the chopper and jumped, and missed the rung by scant inches. As he jumped, he saw another person slumped in the passenger's seat.

"Logan, what's happening?" Tristan asked.

"God damn it all to hell. Collin took off in the chopper, and I'm sure he wasn't alone."

Tristan looked down at his watch; he'd been so involved with everything going on he lost track of time. Forty minutes had passed since he left Victory, and he hadn't heard from her yet. She probably lost track of time, knowing her, and became engrossed with her work. He cleared his mind and reached for her. There was no response; he couldn't feel her. There was nothing.

"Come on, Tristan; Morgan is already here at the rendezvous point. You and Victory have to get the lead out," Noah said.

"I'm heading back to the lab. I can't reach Victory."

Tristan took off in the opposite direction and ran for the lab. Three minutes later, he reached the building and found the door wide open. He quietly moved to the door. He filled his lungs with the night air and picked up Victory's familiar scent, lavender and chamomile. Then his heart nearly stopped as he caught the slightest scent of Collin. Tristan froze. He forced himself to keep breathing as he slowly walked into the lab.

The lab was empty. He turned on the flashlight and looked around. Victory's workstation was cleaned of her computer and files. He shone his light on the floor and saw it, a jade and gold earring—Victory's earring. A heart-wrenching scream tore through his soul, yet he didn't utter a single sound. The room started to spin and Tristan dropped to his hands and knees.

* * * *

Wyatt was in the Situation Room keeping an eye on the extraction that unexpectedly unfolded twelve hours ahead of schedule. He'd been busy reviewing the latest results when a wave of nausea hit him, followed by a blood-curdling cry thundering through his brain.

"Victory!"

"Tristan, what's happened?" Wyatt pressed. He'd never felt such a punch of pain or unadulterated terror

resonate from his brother. While on assignments, Tristan had been shot, stabbed, and tortured numerous times and never had Wyatt felt this anguish from him. *"Tristan, for Chrissakes Tristan, answer me."* Wyatt got no response. "Get me a bloody sat phone," he yelled to his team.

"Noah here."

"Noah, what's happening there?" Wyatt demanded.

"I'm at the rendezvous point with Logan and Morgan; we're waiting for Tristan and Victory to join us. Looks like Collin took off in a chopper, not sure where he's headed. Logan thought there might have been someone else in the chopper with him."

"Son of a bitch," Wyatt said.

"Sir?" Noah asked.

"I think Collin took Victory," Wyatt said. "Where's Tristan?"

"Last time I heard, he headed back to the lab to get Victory," Noah said.

"How long ago?"

Noah glanced down at his watch. "About fifteen minutes ago. They should've been back here by now."

"Something's wrong. One of you needs to go and find Tristan. And keep me updated," Wyatt ordered.

"Yes, sir, right away."

Noah switched off the phone and turned to the other two men.

"Something's up with Tristan; the captain wants us to track him down." Noah stuck his ear bud back his ear. "Tristan, come in. Tristan. Shit. No answer. I'm heading back to get him."

"I'll come with you." Morgan chimed in.

"No, you stay here with Logan; we need to get you out."

"Do you know where the lab is?" Morgan quizzed him.

"Not exactly, I have a general idea, and it can't be that difficult to find."

"If you have to look for it you're going to burn time," Morgan said.

"He has a point," Logan said.

"Fine, let's go," Noah said.

"Great, follow me," Morgan said and took off running.

"Hey, asshole, slow down," Noah said through his ear bud. "We don't all have dog genes."

"That's wolf DNA; get it right," Morgan teased as he slowed to human speed. "This way is a shortcut. The lab is at the end of this path."

Five minutes later Morgan and Noah were at the perimeter of the lab.

"Looks like the front door is open," Noah said.

"Yeah, that's not right. Something is clearly not right here. You wait here; give me thirty seconds to get around back, and I'll go in through the exam room," Morgan said, and headed for the far side of the building.

"Roger." Noah looked at his watch and squatted down in the bushes to study the area.

Morgan slipped around the building to the exam room door. Jesus, he hated this place, and here he was going right back in. He entered the exam room at the same time Noah came through the lab door.

The lab was dark, aside from the light shining in from the outside doorway. He could make out a large figure on the floor.

"Tristan?" Noah leaped toward the figure on the floor. "Tristan, are you hurt?" Noah grabbed one of Tristan's shoulders. Tristan swung around. He sprang to his feet and had Noah pinned to the wall in the same instant. "Tristan. Take it easy it's me, Noah."

Morgan took in the unfolding scene. He charged through the exam room door and headed into the lab with every intent of helping Noah. Noah saw him coming and waved him off. "Tristan, snap out of it. Where's Victory?"

Agony showed on Tristan's face at the mention of her name.

"Victory. Son of a bitch. Collin took her." A look of surprise showed on Tristan's face as he realized he had Noah pinned to the wall by his collar. He dropped his hands and stepped back. "I'm really sorry, Noah."

Noah shook his head and shrugged it off. "Don't give it another thought."

"So she was the other person in the helicopter," Morgan said, and stepped farther into the lab.

Tristan turned to Morgan, a menacing look shadowing his face.

"That's probably a good bet. And if the asshole puts even one hand on her, I will skin him from head to toe," Tristan said.

"We need to get out of here and back to the helipad. We've been here too long, and our chopper will be here any minute," Noah said.

"Down," Morgan snapped.

Both Noah and Tristan dropped to their knees the second the word left Morgan's mouth. In a flash they saw a small silver lightning bolt pass over their heads. They heard a slight gasp and then a thud behind them.

"Clear," Morgan said.

The men stood and turned. They looked down at a guy with a scalpel protruding from his neck. He still gripped his MP5 submachine gun.

"Holy crap, Morgan, you have one hell of an aim. You can be on my team anytime," Noah said. "I believe we should take the hint and not overstay our welcome." He bent down and pulled the MP5 free from the dead man's grip. "He won't have a need for this any more." He patted him down and found a pistol and radio. "These could come in really handy."

"Let's drag his body into the exam room. It will take them longer to find him in there," Tristan said, as he bent down to grab the man's legs.

Noah smashed the outside light above the lab door, leaving the lab enveloped in darkness. He closed the door and followed the other two men into the next room.

"Let's exit via the back door. Unlike the front entrance, the area around the back door is clear. It will be easier to spot any of Max's dickheads," Morgan said.

The three men left the building and headed back to the helipad.

Chapter Twenty-Two

"Mr. Braxton, I have some bad news," Max said as Braxton answered his cell.

"What?" Braxton snapped.

"Unfortunately Collin and Morgan broke out tonight, and to confuse matters, they started the coffee shop on fire. All the books burned to a crisp."

"Forget about the asinine books. Have you located them on their receivers?"

"I have one blip on the screen and I believe it's Collin. I think Morgan disabled or removed his tracker. I think the two men are staying together," Max said.

"Then why are you standing around talking to me? Go and find them," Braxton barked.

"That's where it gets tricky. They took the small chopper. The mechanics left it sitting on the tarmac."

"What?" screamed Braxton.

"How do I follow them? They took the chopper." Max ignored the man's tantrum.

"What do you mean, how? Call for the other blasted bird you imbecile! It's sitting inside the maintenance shack."

"Yes, sir. Should I take my team?"

"Yes," Braxton said. "For Chrissakess, contain the situation, Max. I would prefer you take them alive, if it's not an option, dead is better than loose. Take Victory with you. I'll call you later with a meeting place."

"Yes, sir. Should I still dispose of Grant?"

"Get rid of him any way you see fit. I don't want him to leave the island."

"I'll take care of him," Max said.

"I'm relying on you." Braxton cut the connection.

Max took two of his men and headed off in the direction of Victory's suite. He thought he would also find Tristan there. He knocked on her door. When he got no answer, he knocked harder.

"Ms. Winters, it's Max. I need to speak with you." Still no answer. He turned to one of his men and stuck out his hand. The man handed Max the master key card. Max opened the door to Victory's room.

"Victory? It's Max, sorry to intrude, however you are needed at the lab." He listened. Not hearing any response, he walked through the living room and opened the bedroom door. There were clothes scattered all over the floor and bed. All the drawers were pulled open, no other personal items were left anywhere. He studied the room, his glare stopping at the wide open window. "Shit," he sputtered.

He turned around and ran out to the main room and out the entrance door, going across the path and up to Tristan's room where he repeated the process with the key card. Neither Victory nor Tristan were there, either. "Christ." He spun around and faced the man behind him. "Organize a search party; we need to locate

Victory and Tristan as soon as possible. I want all five of you to each take a small group of employees, spread out, and cover this compound." Then he noticed there were only four of his men present. "Where's Ed?" he asked the group.

One of his men spoke up. "Ed contacted me a while ago. He thought he saw someone enter the lab."

"And you've waited 'til now to bring this to my attention, you moron? If I didn't need each and every one of you, I'd shoot you myself." Max pulled his walkie-talkie from his belt and bellowed into it. "Ed! Come in." No response came back, only the crackle of static. "Ed!"

"Should I go to the lab and see if he is still there?" the same man asked.

"No," Max barked at him. "I'll do it myself. All of you go and search the compound as I said, and stay in touch. Check in with me every five minutes, sooner if you find anything. You asswipes better find them, or I'll disappear you!"

The group dispersed, scattering throughout the compound. Max headed for the lab. He had a feeling he wasn't going to like what he found there.

As Max approached the lab, he noticed the outside entrance light was out. As he got closer, he realized it was smashed; glass littered the ground in front of the building. He pulled his pistol from its holster and tried the knob; it turned easily, another bad sign. He stood to one side of the door and cracked it open. He slid his body inside and pinned himself to the wall, pistol held at the ready.

Before the door closed, he wedged one foot against it, allowing the evening light to seep inside the pitch black building. He waited briefly for his eyes to adjust to the darkness. Not seeing any movement, he lowered his gun and flipped on the switches, lighting the entire lab. He found no one inside and it didn't look like anything was disturbed. Only then he noticed Victory's computer was missing.

He couldn't shake the feeling that something else wasn't quite right. His gaze dropped to the floor in front of the door, where he saw a few large drops of something dark. As he pushed the lab door farther open, the drops turned into a small dark pool of blood. Drag marks led from the pool through the lab and into the exam room. He walked across the lab to the exam room and switched on the light. At first glance nothing looked disturbed except for the streak of blood. He looked down at the floor and found Ed, under the table, scalpel sticking out of his neck. "Shit."

An hour later after combing the compound and having no luck locating Victory or Tristan, Max made a decision. He rounded up his men and headed in the direction of the helipad.

* * * *

Tristan, Noah, and Morgan met up with Logan a few yards off the helipad.

"Update," Tristan said.

"Our extraction is seven minutes out. They are coming in dark," Logan said. "What's the plan?"

"We need to locate Collin and Victory as soon as possible. He already has a substantial head start on us." Tristan looked at Morgan. "Tell me Collin didn't remove his tracker chip."

"Not as far as I know. I don't even think he knows he has one in him. We need to confiscate a receiver, so we can track him. Max gave one to each of his team," Morgan said.

"Okay. Logan, contact the pilot. Tell him to stand ready, but outside of the island's airspace. Noah and I will head back and find one of those receivers."

"Hold on," Noah broke in. He started to search his pockets. "Here it is. I thought this might come in handy." He pulled a small black box from his pants pocket. "I took everything the dead guy carried, even his half-empty pack of gum." He shook the box and tapped it against his other palm. "Shit," he said, as he continued to play with the box. "I must have damaged it in all the commotion."

In the near distance they heard a helicopter approach. Tristan spun around and looked at Logan.

"Logan, I thought you said the chopper was seven minutes out?" Tristan asked.

"I just finished talking to him. He's five minutes out waiting for instructions," Logan snapped back.

"Then who the hell is that?"

"Aw, hell." Morgan said. "It's got to be the island's other helicopter. It didn't even cross my mind; last time I saw the chopper, it was at the maintenance shack with parts scattered about."

"And exactly when was the last time you saw the chopper?" Logan asked.

"A couple days ago," Morgan said.

"It looks like someone got it up and running, and it's heading this way," Tristan said.

"We need to scatter and stay down," Logan said. He had kept a look out with his night goggles, and down at the bottom of the path, he saw two tiny flashes of light and two men heading toward them. "Two men, ten minutes out, heading our way. I can't tell for sure, but it looks like one of them is Max."

All four of the men melted back into the trees. They waited for the enemy to approach.

The glow of the helicopter came into view, its lights getting brighter and brighter as it advanced in the direction of the landing pad. Three men all armed with submachine guns were sitting on the edge of the chopper, feet on the skids, ready to blast anything that moved. Max and the other man passed Tristan's team, scant yards between them.

Max had a receiver in his hand and looked at the screen. "Son of a bitch, I've lost Collin's signal; how far did Braxton say the range of this thing was?" he asked the guy beside him as they kept moving to the chopper.

"Twenty-five miles," the man said. "Don't worry, sir; the helicopter Collin stole is equipped with a homing beacon. All our helicopters have sonic tags on them. As long as he's in our helicopter, we can track him, no problem."

"You better be right or you're dead." Max barked.

"Should we take them down?" Logan whispered through his ear bud to the team.

"Negative," Tristan whispered back. "We call in our own bird and follow them. There's too much firepower showing; it's not worth the risk. Their chopper is equipped with a receiver, we follow them."

"Yeah, and from what I've read, Max could track down Collin with his nose alone," Noah snorted quietly.

"Oh, sorry Tristan, I didn't mean anything by my smelly comment." Noah chuckled.

"Right, wait 'til this is over, wise guy, I'll show you scent tracking and your ass will be mine. Now stop wasting time and slither up there and tag that bird," Tristan said.

"Yes, sir, commander," Noah said.

"Any problems?" They could hear Max yell to his team over the sound of the blades.

"No, sir," one of the men responded, just as loud. "No sighting of Grant, either."

"We'll worry about him later. He's here on the island somewhere, and after we leave, there's no other birds left on this rock. Let's go."

He jumped into the passenger's seat and tapped the pilot on the shoulder. Seconds later the helicopter went airborne.

"Mission accomplished." Noah rejoined the group. "They won't be getting away from us."

As soon as Max's chopper disappeared into the night, the four men stood up.

"I contacted our ride; the chopper will be here in six minutes," Logan informed the group. "Let's go get our stuff," he said and turned back to Noah.

Tristan and Morgan headed for the tarmac to wait for their ride.

"Do you have any idea where Collin might be heading?" Tristan asked as they walked.

"Not really. I do know he is from Washington State. That's why he volunteered for this assignment with Biotec. He hoped to get some weekends off and take a trip home. Fat chance."

"Really. Do you happen to know where in Washington?" Tristan asked.

"I can't recall. Seems like he told me at one time, but I was probably only half-listening. Why, are you familiar with Washington?"

"That's where our team is stationed. We're on the peninsula across the sound from Seattle. Yeah, I know it pretty well. I've spent most of my off-time traveling throughout the state," Tristan said.

Noah and Logan came strolling up to the helipad, loaded with backpacks.

"Man, am I looking forward to taking a shower and sleeping in a real bed," Logan said.

"What a wussy boy. Are you getting soft on us?" Noah asked. "Here comes our ride; they're right on time."

Chapter Twenty-Three

Victory woke with a throbbing headache. She put her hand up to the back of her head and felt a golf-ball sized lump.

"Ouch," she hissed as her fingers hit an especially tender spot.

"Sorry about that. I needed to make sure you came with me, and I didn't have the time to discuss the matter," Collin said. "Here, this will help with the lump." He handed her an ice pack. "And this is for your headache," he said, and offered her a glass of water and some aspirin.

She took the items he offered, not wanting to upset him.

"So, may I ask where we are? I'm not familiar with this part of the island," she said.

"That's because we aren't on the island. I brought you out to my cabin. I know the place needs a little work," he said as he looked around the tiny interior. "No one will find us out here."

The room they were in consisted of a small kitchen and living area containing an overstuffed chair and small sofa. It also served as a makeshift bedroom. She sat on the edge of a bed across the room from the kitchen and put the glass and bottle down on the nightstand next to her. She saw one interior door, which she assumed led to what must be the bathroom.

"Why did you kidnap me?" Victory asked.

She felt uneasy; she didn't hear any other people outside, only birds. Just then she realized they could be completely isolated, with nothing and no one around for miles.

"Kidnap is such an ugly word. I didn't kidnap you. I am in need of your undivided attention and your expertise," Collin said.

"Is this how you treat someone whose help you need?" she asked. "If it is, then I should think you don't get much cooperation. You're no better than Braxton."

"No, it's not. For argument's sake, let's say I haven't been myself lately," he sneered. "I figured you did this to me, so who better to fix me."

"I told you I didn't do this to you. If it had been my decision, I would have never let them inject you or Morgan. There's simply too much research left to do before one jumps in with human subjects."

"Braxton obviously did not agree with you," he fired back. "Why didn't you stop him?"

"I tried to tell him, but it was too late. He's a madman and is only out to make money. I've researched the genetics of genus *Canis* for over ten years. I'm considered the leading expert in the field, and still I would not have introduced the serum into anyone's system."

"I guess that's why Braxton decided to solicit your help, because of your extensive research. And why I took you from the island, and why I brought you with me. You're probably the only person who can cure me."

"I can't cure you. The best I can do, with time and research, is to find a way to get both your DNA and the foreign DNA to cohabitate together. As far as Braxton soliciting my expertise, guess it depends on your definition. If you call threatening my family and kidnapping me soliciting, then you're right," she snapped back at him.

He glanced at her with complete surprise on his face.

"What do you mean? You and Tristan weren't employed by him?"

"No. Morgan said he told you about us," she hesitated, perplexed he didn't already know about their situation.

"He didn't. At least I don't think so. I can't remember," he replied and jammed his palms up to his temples.

"What's the matter?" Victory asked with sincere worry in her voice.

"It's this horrendous throbbing in my temples. I've been trying to fight it, but sometimes, no matter what I try, I can't stop it." He paced the entire cabin.

"How often does the pain persist and for how long?"

"No, not the pain, I can deal with the pain," he nearly screamed at her. "It's this devastating feeling of overwhelming rage. It's wild and fierce, and at times it completely overpowers me. When I lose control and the rage takes over, I blackout and lose time. I have to get out of here." Collin continued to pace the floor. "Lock the door and stay inside. Don't try to leave; we're miles away from anyone else, and the woods are dangerous, believe me." Collin walked to the door. "Victory, lock this after I leave; I mean it."

He walked out the door and left her there. The question remained, where was there? She walked to the door and contemplated making a break for it, but all she could see was forest. Not knowing how far the nearest neighbor or town might be, or even what country she was in, she figured for now her best bet would be to stay put.

She closed the door and threw the deadbolt. She turned and leaned back against the door, listening to the sounds around her. She caught the sounds of birds, squirrels, and a bear, scraping his claws on a tree. Then she heard the blood-chilling guttural growl of a wolf. For a split second the forest fell silent.

"Tristan, can you hear me?" Victory attempted to make contact with him. She wasn't sure how strong their connection might be, or what distance they could cover, but she gave it her best shot. *"Tristan,"* she yelled in her mind. Nothing. There was only silence.

* * * *

The SOCOM helicopter tracked Max's helicopter up the west coast.

"I think Morgan is right," Noah said. "Looks like we're heading straight up to Washington; now the only question is, where in Washington? I would prefer to not bring up the rear throughout this entire mission."

"What are the updates from Jack?" Tristan asked.

"Nothing new yet, but he should get back to us soon. You know Jack, he's a computer whiz," Noah said.

Tristan leaned his head against the headrest. He closed his eyes as he replayed the events of his last encounter with Victory. Silently, he cursed himself for his mistake. He should never have let her go to the lab by herself.

"Tristan."

His eyes flew open as he lurched upright.

"You okay?" Logan asked.

"I think I heard Victory," he said.

He closed his eyes and focused on Victory.

"Victory, can you hear me?"

Victory thought she felt an ever-so-subtle buzz in her temples. Could it be Tristan? Could he really hear her, or was it pure desperate hope? Whatever it was, she would try with her all to contact him.

"Tristan, Collin knocked me out from behind when I walked into the lab. I'm sorry; I didn't see him, and I was so distracted I didn't even hear him come up from behind me," she babbled in her mind.

There it was again. He couldn't understand everything she said to him, but he did get bits and pieces.

"Well," Logan prompted. "Are you getting anything?"

"I'm not getting all of it, but I can pick up pieces. She said Collin came up from behind her in the lab. Which in itself is surprising, Victory has a sense of hearing like no one I have ever known."

"Does she know where she is?" Noah asked.

"She hasn't said, or at least I haven't been able to pick up anything about her location. I'm going to try and contact her."

Tristan settled back and propped his head back against the seat. He filled his body with a few deep breaths and focused all his energy on reaching Victory.

There it was again. This time, Victory felt a very distinct push in her mind. *It's Tristan, it has to be him,* she thought.

"I'm not sure where I am. Collin said something about a cabin. He wants me to help him. He seems to think I can reverse what has happened to him; I've tried to explain the only thing I can do now, is to try and help him adapt to his life now."

Tristan blew out his breath; relief flooded his body. He knew she was safe and Collin needed her, so for now it would keep her safe, he hoped.

"She's okay. I feel a pain in the back of her head, probably where Collin hit her. All I understood is Collin believes she can cure him and something about a cabin." He looked at Morgan. "You know anything about a cabin?"

"He went out into the forest." Victory continued on. She didn't know what, if anything, Tristan could hear, but she relayed everything. *"He warned me not to leave. He said I would not be safe out there. He even told me to lock the door after he left. Tristan, I think he is having trouble staying in control, but he knew, so he left me. He didn't want to be near me for fear he might hurt me. This is a good thing. He is beginning to adapt, or at least acknowledge when the change is coming over him. Yet he is trying to stay in control. Maybe this will buy me more time to help him."*

Victory's head began to pound, between all the thoughts running through it and the large bump. She lay down on the bed and put the ice pack on her head.

"Shit," Tristan said. "I think Victory might still be in danger with Collin. She said something about him losing control. What about the cabin Victory keeps mentioning, Morgan?"

Morgan remained silent. At first Tristan didn't think he would respond.

"Nope, I don't remember anything about a—wait a minute." Morgan bolted straight up and looked at the other three men who stared at him. "His grandfather, I remember last summer we barely got back from a mission. Collin was really upset. His grandfather had passed away while we were deep undercover. He was dead and buried before Collin even knew about it. The two of them were really close. His grandfather raised him since the age of ten.

"Anyway, he got a letter from an attorney telling him his grandfather left everything to him. This included the main house in Seattle, all his investments, and a small hunting cabin. What really surprised Collin was his grandfather had already changed everything he owned to Collin's name, over one year before his death."

"So, where's this cabin?" Noah asked.

"I don't think he ever told me. But it shouldn't be hard to track it down. It's in Collin's name, that's a place to start," Morgan said.

* * * *

Victory was lost in a dark forest as she came upon Jeffery and his two friends. Bang, Bang! The gun went off. Jeffery withered to the ground; blood covered his crisp white shirt. "Jeffery," she screamed. She sprang up from the bed, tears running down her face.

"Who's Jeffery?" Collin asked. He'd stretched out on the small sofa. There were very few windows in the cabin, and Victory could hardly make him out in the early morning light.

"What time is it?" she asked.

"It's around six in the morning. Why, do you have a hot date?" he smiled. "You didn't answer my question…who's Jeffery?"

"He was a college friend of mine and the reason I currently find myself in this situation."

"I bet he'll get an earful when you get back," Collin joked.

"No, he won't. He's dead." Tears instantly filled her eyes again and threatened to spill down her cheeks. "I saw Jerry shoot him and there was nothing I could do to stop it."

She wiped her eyes and tried to wipe the scene from her mind. It suddenly dawned on her what Collin had said—when you get back. *It must be a good sign*, she thought; *he intended to let her go home, sometime.*

"Are you telling me I slept the entire night?" she asked.

"I don't know about the entire night. I've only been here for around two hours."

"Did you take the tracking chip out of your thigh?"

"What?"

"The chip, have you removed it?"

"What chip? I don't have any chips. What makes you think I have one?" he asked.

"Morgan told me both of you have trackers. Braxton instructed Max to place the trackers in your upper thighs. You don't remember?"

She knew it was not a good sign.

"No," Collin said, as confusion played across his face.

He got up from the sofa and dropped his jeans. Victory cheeks flamed a dark shade of pink, and she turned her gaze away from his direction.

"The douchebag. That's what this is," he hissed and rubbed his right upper thigh. "I thought I stabbed myself during one of my blackouts."

Collin picked up his jeans, fished a pocket knife out of his front pockets, and headed to the kitchen. There he snapped the knife open, placed it on the counter, and grabbed a lighter out of one of his kitchen drawers. He lit the lighter and ran it over both sides of the knife, sterilizing the blade.

"Would you like me to take it out?" Victory asked.

"I guess you would do a better job. Do you mind?"

"No problem." She got up from the bed and walked over to the kitchen. "It would be easier for me if you would lie on the table. The light is better and I can get at it easier."

Collin handed her the knife and got up on the table. Victory looked at the spot which she was sure contained the chip.

"This is going to hurt," she warned him.

"Don't worry; I've had a lot worse. Try to dig a bullet out of yourself. Now that smarts," he teased. "I'm ready whenever you are–shit," he snapped, as Victory stuck in the knife and scooped out the chip.

"Sorry. I figured, better to get it done quickly." She reached for a couple of paper towels to blot the bleeding. "Do you have any antiseptic and bandages?"

"In the cabinet in the bathroom."

"Here, keep pressure on this."

She headed for the tiny bathroom, found what she needed and returned to Collin. A few minutes later she had his cut cleaned and covered. She held out the chip. It was the size of a pen top. He took it from her outstretched hand, looked at it briefly, and then dropped it to the floor and smashed it with his foot.

"With any luck, good old Max didn't find out I left the island right away. But if he started tracking me a couple of hours after we left, then he already knows I'm on the west coast. Should give us a little breathing room, but let's not get comfortable. We will have to think about getting out of here in the next twelve hours. I'll need you to make a list of all the equipment you will need in order to find me a cure."

There is no cure. She almost told him once again and then thought better of it.

"I will need a lot of equipment, along with a usable lab. It's going to involve a great deal of funds and time."

"You let me worry about the money and the lab. All you need to do is make me your list," Collin said.

Victory knew she shouldn't stress or upset him. For now she thought it would be better to simply play along and hope Tristan would find them.

"Okay. Can I have my laptop?"

"Sure, I don't see a problem with that. There is no Internet service available anywhere near here," Collin said.

* * * *

"Son of a bitch," Max slammed the receiver against the dashboard.

"What's wrong, sir?" one of the men asked.

"We lost our signal. Damn it, Collin must have found the chip," Max hissed.

"We've crossed into Washington," the pilot announced. "Do I keep going or turn around?"

"Keep going; I know for certain he's in Washington. The only question now is where," Max said. "Okay, we head to Biotec; Dave is there, and he can help pinpoint Collin's location." He pulled out his cell phone and punched Dave's speed dial number.

"Hello Max, what's your status?" Dave asked.

"We lost the signal. I think Collin found his chip. We're on our way to you. I know he's in the state, but that's about as good as it gets. I need you to do your thing and get on your computer and see what kind of hidey-holes Collin has access to."

"I'll get started right away. Mr. Braxton is not on the premises right now, thank goodness. We need to try and keep this latest news from him. Needless to say, he's already hot about what happened yesterday. What's your ETA?"

"Thirty minutes. See you then. Okay, take us in to Biotec," Max said to the pilot.

* * * *

"They're dropping in altitude," Noah said.

"You think they located Collin?" Morgan asked.

"Not sure, all I can tell you is they will be landing soon," Noah said.

"Where are we?" Tristan asked.

"We're coming up on Seattle," Noah said.

"I don't think they found Collin and Victory; I think they lost the signal and are probably going in to Biotec to get some help. Victory was there when you told us about the chips, remember, Morgan? I'll bet she told Collin about his and he destroyed it. She's trying to buy them time."

"Smart woman," Logan said.

Chapter Twenty-Four

The SOCOM offices were humming. Wyatt had called in the second team, so the place was filled to capacity. Wyatt walked over to Jack's desk and asked, "Anything?"

"Not yet, sir; there are over two hundred McBains in the state. He did list his grandfather's house in Seattle as his home base."

"We know he wouldn't take Victory to Seattle," Wyatt said.

Jack's Bluetooth vibrated. "What do you have for me, Noah?"

"Your wish is my command. Victory must have told Collin about his tracker. We believe he has removed and destroyed it. This should slow Max down a bit," Noah reported. "Morgan's memory has improved, and he has recalled that Collin's granddad owned a hunting cabin."

"Does he know his name?" Jack asked.

"Collin D. McBain."

"So Collin is named after his grandfather," Jack said.

"That's a good guess. His granddad left everything to him. Even had the titles of all his properties put in his grandson's name a year before he passed away. Morgan said Collin does not have a middle name," Noah said.

"Okay, so where is this hunting cabin located?" Jack asked.

"Come on, Jack, we can't steal all of your thunder," Noah said.

"Great. Okay, let me get this into the computer and see what I come up with," Jack said as he disconnected.

"Seems Victory has bought us some time," Wyatt said.

Jack looked up at Wyatt. "Captain, sometimes you and Tristan give me the willies," he said and shimmied his shoulders in an example.

"Plug in Collin's name and cross-reference it with his grandfather, and let's see what you get for properties owned." He sat down in the chair across from Jack's desk.

"Got him," Jack said a couple minutes later. "Collin McBain owns a small place in the foothills of Mount Baker, Washington. The title got transferred into his name sixteen months ago by a Collin D. McBain."

"That's good enough for me," Wyatt said.

"Do you want to contact Tristan, or should I call Noah back?" Jack asked, raising one of his eyebrows.

"Call Noah; you have all the details," Wyatt said with a smile on his face. Even after all this time he could spook Jack. Wyatt loved it. Because in situations like their current one, it served to lighten the mood more times than he could recall. "I want to leave Tristan's 'channel' open. He's been picking up snippets of Victory's thoughts."

Noah's phone vibrated. "Yeah, Jack, what do you have for us?"

"Collin D. McBain transferred title to a place in the foothills of Mount Baker to a Collin McBain, approximately sixteen months ago. It's pretty isolated by the looks of it, and it's surrounded by forest. Got a pen?"

"Shoot." Noah jotted down the address. "Great, thanks Jack. Got him, foothills of Mount Baker, isolated in the forest, sneaky bastard." Noah relayed the coordinates to the pilot. "Looks like our closest helipad is located in Nooksack. We'll need to land there if we want to pick up transportation," Noah said.

"Let's do it," Tristan said.

* * * *

Max's team, plus three new guys, loaded into the helicopter to head out to Nooksack. He felt much more comfortable about going into this with three additional men, especially since two of them had some military training and the third was Detective Howard. They would be landing in Nooksack in forty minutes, and his team was edgy.

* * * *

Tristan and his team landed in Nooksack. The SUV they had reserved while still in the air sat on the tarmac.

"Noah, you drive; Logan, you're his navigator. Morgan, you and I will take the back. Let's park the vehicle a couple miles from the cabin and make sure it's well-hidden. We're not sure how close Max and his team are, but I am sure he will be hot on our heels, and we don't want to tip our hand," Tristan said as he jumped into the back of the SUV.

"What's the plan?" Logan turned and looked at Tristan.

"Morgan is going to try and talk Collin out. You'll need to do it fast; can you handle it?" he asked, as he looked at Morgan.

"If you would've asked me last month, I would have said absolutely. At this point, I would say it is fifty-fifty now," Morgan said.

"You're still our best option. Let's get going." Tristan said, and smacked the back of the driver's seat.

* * * *

Fifteen minutes later Max's helicopter touched down on the same tarmac in Nooksack. Two SUVs sat on the tarmac a few yards away.

"You three come with me," Max said. He pointed to Howard and two of the new guys. "You five take the second vehicle and follow us." They loaded all their gear, jumped into the SUVs, and headed out of town.

* * * *

A strong buzz started in Victory's head. It must Tristan, and by the strength of the buzzing he was close by. Victory nearly choked on her sandwich. Geez, it still startled her when he made contact. She coughed, picked up her coffee, and took a sip.

"You okay?" Collin asked.

"Yes, I'm fine. It went down the wrong tube," she said and she patted her chest.

"Tristan, I know you're close," she sent as clear a thought as she could manage. *"We're both in the cabin at the table eating."*

"The cabin is right up ahead," Noah said to the group. "Time for the details, Tristan."

"Let me go in alone; you guys cover my six and stay keep back. The last thing we want to do is spook him," Morgan said.

The three teammates looked at one another; cautious nods went around the group.

"Okay," Tristan answered for the team. "But Victory is our primary concern. If he threatens her, all bets are off."

"I understand, however I want to get Collin out of this in one piece, too. So give me some room, please," Morgan said.

"Let's do this. We'll have company soon," Tristan said.

Morgan started in the direction of the cabin. He made sure he stood out in the open to make it easy for Collin to see him coming.

Collin suddenly stopped eating. He swung his head in the direction of the door.

"Damn it all to hell," he said. He could smell Morgan, and he wasn't alone. He put his fork down and stared at Victory.

"What's the matter?" she asked trying to act confused.

"They're here," Collin said.

"Max?" she asked, genuine fear creeping into her gaze. He couldn't have beaten Tristan here, she prayed.

"No, Morgan, and he's not alone," he said.

"That's good, Collin; they want to help you, as do I." Relief filled her.

"Collin," Morgan yelled from the front yard. "I know you're aware we're out here. Come out so we can talk face-to-face. We're here to help you." Morgan stood still, holding his ground, arms out low in front of himself, palms up. "Collin I know you can hear me, and I know you know I'm not alone. Tristan and his team are here to help you."

Team? Now Collin's interest spiked. *What kind of team?* He looked at Victory with a menacing stare.

"What kind of team?" he demanded.

She sat not saying a word and felt the pressure of his stare.

"What kind of team, Victory? I know you know. He came to the island with you, only he's not your assistant is he?" Collin said.

"No," she finally forced from her lungs. "He's part of a SOCOM team. He was already on Braxton's trail. Tristan and his team were following Jeffery. I came on the scene when Jeffery asked me to meet him."

"Jeffery, your friend who got shot?" He continued before she had a chance to respond. "Now I get it." Lights went off in his mind. "Tristan's mission was to protect you and gather information."

"Collin please, come out and talk to me." Morgan pleaded again.

Collin got up from his chair and Victory started to follow.

"No, you stay right there," he said pointing at her. "I don't want you to get injured accidently. I still need your help."

He walked to the front door but left the screen in place to help camouflage his body.

"Morgan, it's good to see you. I'm glad you made it off the island. I would have taken you with me, but I didn't have time to find you. It seems you have made your own friends. Were you going to leave me there?" He was starting to lose focus. "Son of a bitch," he said curtly. He couldn't lose it now.

"What are you saying? I would've never left without you; you got impatient, Collin, you jumped the gun," Morgan said.

"Right," Collin snorted.

Victory sat very still at the table. She could actually feel the wolf try to emerge. She was finally certain that Collin's triggers were stress and adrenaline, not a good combination for a military man. She also knew he wasn't able to totally control it. She could feel his internal struggle. She wanted to contact Tristan but was afraid to put out any ripples in the atmosphere.

"We've been a team forever, Collin; you know down deep I would help you no matter what. Why else would we be here now. You need help; you can't do this on your own," Morgan said.

"I'm not alone; I have Victory, and we all know she's the one with all the answers."

"She can't help you if you don't give her the tools to do the job. She needs a laboratory and equipment. Please Collin, listen to me." Morgan could feel that he was running out of time.

Collin threw open the screen door and took a single step out onto the porch.

Victory tried to pinpoint the position of the rest of Tristan's team. She listened intently. Were they all out of range if Collin pulled the pistol from the small of his back? Then she heard it; a twig snapped. Tristan and his men had remained completely still; someone else had entered the vicinity—Max and his team.

She jumped up from the table.

"Tristan get down; Max and his team are right behind you. Collin, Morgan get down now," she yelled as she ran toward Collin.

Morgan dropped to the ground. Shit, he was out in the open, and he didn't have a damn gun. As if he read Morgan's mind, Collin pulled the gun from the small of his back and tossed it in his partner's direction, and then he turned and jumped back into the cabin.

Three shots smashed into the door, in the exact spot Collin's head had been only seconds before. He dove in Victory's direction and took her down with him. She slammed to the floor, Collin blanketing her. She felt the wind completely knocked out of her lungs.

"You okay?" he asked as he crawled off her and back to the door, slamming it shut.

"It's Max; he's here," she said, as she fought to draw air into her lungs.

"I figured that much out. Thanks for the heads up."

"We need to go out and help them," she said as she started to stand.

"No, Victory. You stay right there. Do not get up and do not move. We're not going out there; it would be suicide."

He crawled back to the kitchen area, pulled opened the cabinet doors, yanked out another pistol, some ammo, and a couple of knives. He jammed everything into different sections of his jeans. Then he crawled back over to Victory.

"Head to the bathroom."

"The bathroom, why?" She stared at him.

He gave her a push to the back of the cabin.

"We're going out the window."

"Great. What about Tristan, Morgan, and the guys? We can't simply leave them," she said.

"They can take care of themselves. Believe me, they're all trained for this; keep moving."

He gave her another shove. Once in the bathroom, he shut the door behind them.

"I'll go out first to make sure it's clear, and then you follow. Do you understand?"

She hesitated and looked back at the bathroom door.

"Okay," she finally answered.

In a flash Collin jumped out of the window. *"Tristan."* She had to make sure he was okay. She felt warmth fill her mind; thank God. *"Tristan, Collin is taking me out the bathroom window. We are leaving the cabin."* She hoped he understood what she said.

Tristan had heard her loud and clear. He wasn't sure going with Collin was a great idea, but then he didn't want her staying here, either. Things were heating up, and it was getting ugly fast. He sent warm reassuring thoughts back to her. He felt as if his heart was in his throat. He hated the idea of someone else keeping her safe. It should be him who kept Victory out of danger, but he had his hands full at the moment.

"Victory," Collin whispered loudly now. "Get your ass out here now."

The last thing she needed to do would be to upset Collin.

"All right, all right, I'm coming."

276

She popped her head out the window to judge the distance to the ground. It wasn't far at all. She went back into the bathroom and shot both of her legs out the window, followed by the rest of her. She landed on the ground like a cat, on all fours and quietly. She searched the area and looked around for Collin. Where did he go? He was right here only a second ago. Then she spotted his boot sticking out of a group of rhododendrons.

Tristan had snuck up behind one of Max's men when Victory had contacted him. He stopped and melted into the surrounding foliage. This was not a job he could complete while communicating with her. After he felt her leave his mind, he returned to the task at hand.

The man Tristan approached had Morgan pinned in the yard. He was firing his MP5, showering the ground. Morgan returned a few rounds, but he did not have the ammo the guy had and therefore shot sparingly, just enough to keep his enemy's head down. Tristan silently slithered on his belly and stayed as close to the ground as possible. He crept closer and closer to the unsuspecting man. Tristan stopped when he was about an arm's length away, reached into his back pocket, and retrieved his pocketknife. In one smooth motion he popped his knife open and jumped on the man in the same breath. He sliced his throat from ear to ear and then melted back into the forest. Morgan looked back and caught only a brief glimpse of Tristan's attack, it happened so fast.

The hairs on the back of Noah's neck stood straight on end. He swung around the same time a man jumped out at him brandishing a nine-inch knife. The man waved the weapon around in small circles in front of him and then lunged at Noah. Noah ducked the oncoming attack and threw the man over his shoulder.

"Had enough?" Noah asked.

The man got to his feet, shaking his head to clear the stars.

The knife lay on the ground halfway between Noah and the other man. The man glanced down at the knife and then back up at Noah.

"You don't want to do that," Noah cautioned the other man. It was evident to Noah this man had little training in one-on-one combat.

The man took a dive for the knife. Noah beat him to the prize. He stomped on the knife with one foot; his other leg swung forward and made contact with the man's head. The man's head whipped back instantly, snapping his neck, and his body dropped lifelessly to the ground. In the same fraction of a second, Noah heard the distinct click of a safety being released directly behind him. As his body continued down to the ground, he grabbed the knife, spun toward the sound, threw the knife, and dropped back to the ground. There was a wet gurgling sound; the knife had found its mark. Noah looked down at the man on the ground, knife protruding from his throat, eyes open but unseeing.

"Clear," Tristan shouted.

"Clear." Both Noah and Logan responded at the same time.

"Clear," Morgan said.

"How many?" Tristan questioned. "I got two," he added.

"Two," both Noah and Logan replied.

"One," Morgan answered; after all, he'd been pinned to the ground for half the fight.

"Max?" Tristan asked.

Max was nowhere to be found.

They all walked to the house.

"Are Collin and Victory still in the house?" Morgan asked.

"No, Collin took Victory out the bathroom window. Max must have taken off after them while we were playing around with his men."

They all ran around to the back of the cabin. There they could see the broken shrubs where Collin and Victory had slid out of the window. Off to the far side of the cabin they noticed a separate set of prints.

"We need to track them down. Should we fan out?" Logan asked.

"Give me a minute," Tristan said. "Let me see if I can locate their scents. Everyone freeze and be quiet."

He stood in silence and inhaled deep breaths. He changed direction with every breath.

* * * *

Collin and Victory were still trying to put distance between themselves and the fighting back at the cabin. Using their ultra-keen hearing, they could both hear someone tracking them.

"He's still after us," Victory said.

"I know. It's Max and he's not going to give up until he finds us," Collin said. "We should find a place to hide; you can't outrun him."

"Where do you suggest?"

279

"There's a cave at the top of this hill. Let's aim for it," Collin said.

"A cave? We'll be trapped there if he finds us," Victory panted.

"Don't worry. I don't plan on being bait; I have a plan," Collin said.

"Tristan, Max is hot on our heels." Victory tried frantically to connect with Tristan. *"By the sound of it no more than five minutes behind us."*

* * * *

"Christ Almighty," Tristan hissed.

"Can't locate them?" Logan asked.

"I have a very faint scent. There have been too many people and so much movement the scent is not very strong. Victory is trying to communicate with me; I can feel her, but she's unfocused and I can't understand what she is telling me."

Tristan stood as a statue, then, without a word, he started up the mountain followed silently by the other three men. He started to pick up his pace as the strength of Victory's scent cone increased.

Chapter Twenty-Five

Collin and Victory reached the cave.

"You get inside and hide," Collin said to her.

Victory gawked at Collin. "And where are you going?"

"Up there." Collin pointed straight up.

"That's sheer rock and at least fifteen feet straight up."

"Is that all? Piece of cake. I'll wait there for Max; you stay out of sight."

"What are you going to do once he shows up?"

"Don't worry. You need to get in the cave, Victory; we're running out of time," he said, and gave her a gentle push.

She studied him for a few seconds.

"You better be careful," she scolded him as she entered the cave.

Collin waited until she was out of sight. Then he focused on listening for Max, who was only a minute or two behind them. He squatted down, and in one smooth motion propelled himself straight up. He stood on a small ledge and looked down at the very spot where he had stood an instant before. He lay flat on the edge of the cliff and waited.

* * * *

Max walked out of the forest and stood in a small clearing. To the right of him, the side of the mountain, and slightly to the left of him, a narrow trail seemed to wrap around the mountain. He could see the trail was empty and he knew he was very close behind Collin and Victory. The only place left was the small cave he saw in front of him.

"Collin, Victory, come out of there peacefully, and no one will get hurt," he yelled into the cave. "I know you're in there. Don't make me come in and get you."

As he spoke he took a couple of steps closer to the opening of the cave.

"I don't have time for games. Get the hell out here now. Victory, you don't want anything to happen to Tristan do you? If you don't come out, I will shoot him on sight."

Max took another step forward just as a tiny shower of debris rained down from above. He looked up, but the sun had started to set and blinded his view. Instinctively he jumped back, but not before Collin slammed him to the ground. Max's gun popped out of his grip and both he and Collin scrambled to retrieve it.

In the same instant Victory appeared in the opening of the cave. She would not have Tristan shot because she was a coward. She stopped cold; riveted by the scene in front of her.

Collin reached the gun first, with Max right on top of him. Both men had their hands on the weapon and struggled to secure it. They fought and rolled, kicking and wrestling with one another. Victory frantically searched for some way to help Collin. Her face paled as she noticed the two men were mere inches from the edge of the cliff. The drop to the next ledge was as least one hundred feet down.

"Collin, the cliff!" Victory shrieked.

"Get back," he all but snarled at her.

The gun disappeared between the two men and went off a split second before they rolled off the cliff together.

"Victory!" Tristan burst through the overgrowth and saw her on her knees, her back to him and her head bent low.

"Oh God, Victory, where are you hit?" He dropped down behind her and placed both hands upon her heaving shoulders.

"Tristan," she turned to him, tears streaming down her face. She threw her arms around him and wept into his shoulder. "It's not me; the gun went off and then they were gone."

Tristan looked over the edge and saw the two men lying very still about a hundred feet down on a ledge.

"Who had the gun?" he asked her, still looking at the horrific scene below.

"I don't know. They were struggling with the gun. It was between them I think. The gun went off and they were gone."

Morgan, Noah, and Logan entered the clearing. Morgan ran to the edge of the cliff. He could see the two men; neither one moved. There was a large pool of blood, but Morgan couldn't tell who the blood belonged to.

"Shit. Collin!" he yelled. He turned to look at Victory. "Was he hit?"

"I'm not sure," she said.

"I'm going after him," Morgan said, as he pulled the backpack off himself and yanked a rope from it.

"I'll go with him," Logan said.

"I'll run back to our SUV and grab the first-aid kit," Noah said. "I'll call for medevac retrieval on my way."

"Wait right here," Tristan said to Victory. "I want to make sure the guys get down all right." Tristan stepped away from Victory and lowered himself down the rope a few feet. He carried both men's packs on his back.

Victory's heart pounded in her ears as she watched the men try to help Collin. Out of nowhere a powerful arm wrapped around her waist, another covered her mouth, and she got yanked clear off her feet and back into the darkness of the cave.

Tristan returned back up the rope and found Victory was nowhere in sight.

"Victory, did you leave something in the cave?" he said, a tingle of uncertainty running down his back. "Victory?" he yelled her name.

"I'm coming out," she said, from right inside the opening of the cave. Tristan thought he picked up a trace of terror.

Victory appeared at the entrance of the cave. Her arms were pinned behind her, tied at the wrists, and a gun held at her right temple. Tristan couldn't make out who held the gun, but he knew the odor—Ken Howard.

"Ken, what rock did you crawl out from under?" Tristan asked.

It took every ounce of his willpower to stay focused on the task at hand and not succumb to the panic threatening to overtake him.

"Very cute, Grant," Howard said.

"It's Farraday," Tristan corrected. He was trying to stall, to give himself a minute to formulate a plan. He hoped Noah was still listening, or at the very least, Logan would come back up the rope.

"Farraday, huh? I told Braxton there was more to you than met the eye. Of course, he didn't believe me. He said you completely checked out, and you were as you appeared. Goes to show my instinct is better than the damn computer," Howard hissed.

"What do you want, Howard?" Tristan asked.

"I want you to untie that rope," he replied and nodded to the ledge. "I've got what I came to get. Now stay right where you are, if you want her to stay in one piece."

"Let's talk about this. You're outnumbered. You won't get away with this," Tristan said, as he turned back, faced the edge of the cliff, and untied the rope dangling down to the men.

"Oh, but I will. There is a helicopter on its way as we speak," Howard said with a grin.

Howard pulled up on Victory's restraints; she grimaced in pain but refused to give him the satisfaction of crying out.

Tristan pushed at Victory's mind, only to find pain, sorrow, and fear. He tried again, with more intensity this time. She looked up at him, anguish reflected in her eyes.

"Focus, Victory. You're not alone; I'm here, focus," He saw a slight glimmer of awareness.

"Tristan, I can hear you," came her response.

Confusion passed over his face, *"Victory?"*

"Yes, I can hear you," she repeated.

"Enough with the stalling, Farraday. I want you to toss your gun and knife off to your right."

Tristan made no attempt to move.

"If you don't do as I say this very minute, I will blow her pretty little brains out and then yours. I'm leaving, and Victory is coming with me," Howard said.

* * * *

Noah swore a blue streak as he tore through Collin's cabin. With his ear bud in and still activated, he heard the complete exchange between Tristan and Howard. He'd already placed the call for a medical evac; they would have help in fifteen minutes. By the sound of things, it would be far too late to be of any help to Victory.

While Noah updated Jack, Wyatt ordered him to search Collin's cabin and to retrieve all of Victory's research, including her laptop, before he started back up the mountain. He knew his captain was right; they couldn't allow her research to fall into enemy hands. But shit, Tristan needed his help *now*.

"Finally," he snapped.

Of course, it had to be the last place he looked, inside an old fishing cooler. He opened his pack, yanked everything out of the cooler and shoved it all into his pack. He flew out the door and at a dead run in the next heartbeat.

* * * *

Tristan decided the safest thing for Victory would be to do as Howard wanted.

"You'll never get away with this, Howard. Like I said, you're outnumbered. We'll have you before you even start down the mountain."

In the far distance Victory thought she picked up a faint, whoop, whoop sound.

"Who said anything about going down the mountain?" Howard asked.

"There's no place for a helicopter to land. The closest place is back by the cabin," Tristan said.

Then they all heard a whooping sound, increasing in intensity. The helicopter came into view and hovered over the scene. Tristan glanced up and saw a man leaning out the open door, feet on the skids, MP5 pointed directly at him. A rope dropped from the open door and dangled a foot in front of Victory.

"As you can see," Howard said, with a sadistic smile on his face. "It's not landing."

He shoved the gun into the small of his back, kept a tight hold of Victory's restraints, and with his empty hand reached out for the rope and fastened it safely around himself. He yanked on the rope and grabbed Victory around the waist. They both rose into the air.

"Tristan, I have a clear shot," Noah's voice boomed through Tristan's earpiece.

"No, Victory is not attached to the rope. You hit Howard, she drops. Besides the damn MP5 will cut us both down," Tristan said.

Tristan stood there, powerless, as he watched Victory once again slip through his fingers. *"Stay strong, Victory; I will find you,"* he pushed into her mind.

* * * *

"I trust you, Tristan." Telling him so surprised her as much as it did him.

While the scene between Tristan and Howard had played out, Victory had refocused on Morgan and Logan. She listened as the events unfolded one hundred feet below them.

"I know you will find me. But first you must save Collin. Max is dead. Collin is critical. You must save him. I will be all right."

Howard was dragged into the helicopter and released. He laid Victory on the floor.

"You have it?" he asked the man who had pulled them up. The man nodded.

"Do it now," Howard said.

Victory felt a prick in the back of her shoulder.

"That should make moving her much easier," Howard said. "How long will she be out?"

"Should last for at least eight hours," the man said.

It was the last thing Victory heard as her world faded to black.

* * * *

"You're a dead man, Howard," Tristan yelled as he helplessly watched the helicopter increase altitude and fly off into the distance.

"I'm really sorry Tristan. I was all the way back at the cabin when I heard you through my ear bud. I hightailed it as fast as I could," Noah said.

"It's not your fault, Noah. Howard, the dirty cop, must have staked out the cabin and followed Collin and Victory right up here."

"Tristan," Logan yelled from below. "We need a medevac right now if we hope to save Collin."

"What about Max? Victory said he's dead," Tristan shouted back as he pulled the sat phone from Noah's pack.

"I already made the call, Tristan." Noah looked down at his watch. "ETA is five minutes."

"Max is dead. His head landed square on a rock, but he broke Collin's fall," Logan said from below.

"All right, first we get you all up, get Collin ready for transport, and make sure he gets the best possible care. After we take care of him, we locate Victory," Tristan said.

"I pity the poor bastard Howard," Noah said. "He doesn't know what it means to be a marked man by you. His days are on this earth are numbered."

* * * *

She trusted him. Tristan still couldn't believe she said it. Victory trusted him. He knew she'd grown to like him over the last month and enjoyed his company. Even though they were both acutely aware his lack of honesty when they first met had caused Victory to distrust him. He would find her, and he would kill Howard.

Thirty minutes later everyone loaded on the medical evac helicopter and headed to the nearest hospital.

"Tell me the chopper that rescued Howard and took Victory is the same one he and his team took off in from the island?" Tristan asked his team.

"I think it is," Noah said, as he dug through his backpack. "What the hell."

"What's the problem?" Logan asked.

"The receiver must have dropped out of my pack when I dug out the phone. I wasn't watching what I was doing. I searched the cabin and then hauled ass back up the mountain."

"Wyatt?" Tristan said, using their telepathic connection.

"I'm here, Tristan. Give me the status; I know about Collin," Wyatt said.

Tristan relayed the events of the day and ended with the loss of the receiver.

"Let me get with Jack and see what he can do. I'll have him call you. I'm going to start to work on our next plan of attack. I want your team back at SOCOM."

"Wyatt, I don't want to waste any time locating Victory."

"Consider it an order."

"Yes, sir."

"Tristan, don't worry. We'll get Victory back."

Noah's phone rang. "What's up, Jack?"

"I've located the helicopter you tagged."

"How?" Noah looked at Tristan, who smiled back at him. "Those two give me the creeps sometimes," Noah said, shaking his shoulders up and down.

"Tell me about it," Jack said. "Anyway, the helicopter is heading west, looks like they are going back to the complex on San Juan Island."

"Right back to where we started. This guy has got some balls," Noah said. He relayed the conversation to the team.

Chapter Twenty-Six

Everyone's eyes were glued to the screen on the wall of the Situation Room as Jack reviewed all the information he had acquired.

"We know Braxton is out of the country. Our best guess is he is meeting with the Kaleidoscope Group, probably to inform them of their loss on the Hawaiian island. We have monitored all types of communication; nothing has come out of there."

"You think Braxton is unreachable?" Logan asked.

"Either unreachable, or they have instructions not to contact him," Wyatt said.

Jack was busy on the computer as his fingers flew over his keyboard.

"I've picked up some cell phone texting. They expect Braxton back on the island late tomorrow afternoon," Jack said.

"Kinda sloppy, don't you think?" Noah asked.

"Probably," Jack said. "But they're cocky bastards, and they're playing the odds. They have such a large number of facilities; they probably assume we are chasing our tails trying to figure out which one they took Victory to."

"Okay, guys," Wyatt jumped in. "Our preliminary plan is to night drop the three of you on to the island. We need to work out all the details, which includes mapping out the security grid and layout of the complex. There's no time to let you leave and grab some R&R, however I want the three of you to have some downtime. Go over to the officer's barracks and get some sleep." Wyatt looked down at his watch. "It's five now. You have six hours to sleep and shower. Then I want you back here. We'll have a hot meal waiting for you when you return. You can eat while you get filled in on the mission. I want wheels up at oh-one-hundred."

Wyatt recognized the look on his brother's face and knew he would be in for an argument. He decided to defuse the situation by making the first move.

"Have you been able to reach Victory yet?"

"I've been trying, but I'm not getting anything. Best guess is that sack of shit Howard drugged her. I lost all contact with her as the helo went out of sight," Tristan said.

"She'll come too soon. Go take a break," Wyatt nodded his head toward the door.

Tristan started to argue as Logan tapped him on the shoulder.

"Come on, Tristan. You've been on your feet for the last forty-eight hours. You need a break. Victory is going to need you at the top of your game," Logan said.

At exactly eleven in the evening, the team once again assembled in the Situation Room. Everyone was enjoying the spread Jack had catered in, everyone except Tristan who was itching to start the mission.

"Wow, Jack," Logan said, between mouthfuls of prime rib. "You can cook for me anytime."

"Okay, Jack," Wyatt jumped in before the two started ragging on each other. "Let's hear the rundown."

"As you are all aware, we already had the basic layout of the island and compound from your first mission a few weeks back. I was tasked to dig deeper and make sure we weren't missing anything crucial. Frankly, I am surprised by their security, nothing outstanding, not like on their Hawaiian island," Jack said.

"Let's hear it," Tristan said abruptly. He was edgy and ready to go.

"You're aware of the electric fence encompassing the compound. Treat it with respect; it won't merely knock you on your ass, it will stop your heart. Nothing on the grounds, however there is both heat and motion detection in every building. Doors have electronic locks, nothing fancy, number pads. They have a four-man security team; they rotate out every five hours with about a fifteen-minute overlap as the teams change." Jack stopped to take a sip of his coffee.

"What time is the next change?" Logan asked.

"They are due to change teams at midnight, about thirty minutes from now. By the time you reach the island, there will only be the four-man team, who will be about two hours into their shift."

"Probably done with their initial grounds check and settled into their warm, cozy chairs with a cup of coffee," Noah said.

"Don't get sloppy," Wyatt said. "We want you in and out of there before anyone knows."

"Yes, sir," Noah said.

"Noah, you are in charge of bringing down the building security and getting those doors open. Then, you get a fix on the boat launch and make sure the team has a clear retreat to it."

"Logan, I want you to get into Braxton's office. You need to locate any and all information you can about Kaleidoscope Group and any additional research on the genetics study."

"Tristan, you find Victory. Remember, this is not a grab and go. Victory is your first priority; your second is to obtain any information regarding Kaleidoscope Group. Any questions?" Wyatt asked.

"No, sir," they all answered in unison.

"Good. Then get yourselves ready to go. We have a brand new C-27J Spartan idling out on the tarmac, wheels up in thirty minutes. Good hunting men." Wyatt said, as Tristan, Noah, and Logan left the room.

* * * *

The three men were all sitting in the C-27J Spartan, heading for San Juan Island and the Biotec complex. They were all dressed in black from head to toe. All three of the men leaned their heads back against their seats, eyes closed.

"Victory," Tristan pushed. *"Come on, Victory; wake up."*

Victory felt the chemical pull trying to keep her down. It would be so easy to succumb to the feeling of floating. She started to slip back into her dream world.

"Come on, Victory," Tristan pushed harder.

"Tristan," came her slurred thoughts.

"I'm here. Are you hurt?" he asked.

She opened her eyes and looked into the blackness enveloping her. She took stock of her body but remained still on the bed.

"No, I do have a whopper of a headache." She could feel the relief in Tristan. *"Really, I'm fine. I have no idea where I am, though."*

"You're back at the Biotec complex on San Juan Island. What do you hear?"

Victory took in a cleansing breath and cleared her mind. She closed her eyes and reached out with her hearing. *"It's pretty quiet. I hear snoring down the hall, and what sounds like a man on a cell phone—yes, he's talking to a wife or girlfriend."*

"That's your friendly guard, and it sounds like he's being lax," Tristan said. *"We are approximately twenty-five minutes from the island. I need you to get yourself ready to leave. But no lights."*

"Got it," she said.

"I need to update the team. I will contact you right before our HALO jump."

"HALO jump?" she asked.

"Yes, we are coming in via air, approximately thirty-five thousand feet up, so we won't be heard from the ground. From that height, we will be doing a HALO jump: High-Altitude-Low Opening. Be careful Victory, and stay put," he said, as he severed their connection.

Victory felt a real sense of emptiness after Tristan withdrew; this was not a good thing. What would happen after this whole nightmare ended and she returned to her normal life? Would she still feel this gaping hole in her mind…and yes, in her heart? She shook the thoughts from her mind; this was neither the time nor the place to examine these issues. She attempted to orient herself. Her eyes had started to adapt, and she could see numbers a few feet away from her. She finally made out a clock, and it looked like the time was one in the morning.

* * * *

"ETA five minutes," said the pilot.

"Yes," Logan said. "Time to dance."

The three men had previously checked and rechecked their gear. Now the team pulled on their oxygen masks, checked their gauges, and put on their helmets. They walked to the tail of the plane where Noah pushed a button and watched the floor of the plane open up to the inky night sky.

"Go," came the command from the pilot.

Noah looked at Tristan and Logan; all three gave the thumbs-up sign. Noah took three steps forward and free fell from the plane, followed closely by Logan.

Tristan stepped up to the open space to take his turn.

"Tristan, abort," Wyatt said.

Tristan stopped mid-stride. *"What's up Wyatt?"*

"Jack has received confirmation that there is a helicopter approaching the island. It's due to land in twenty minutes," Wyatt informed him. *"We believe Braxton is on that aircraft."*

"Probably a good bet, but we can't abort. Noah and Logan have already jumped." Tristan fell from the plane, *"and I'm right behind my team."*

"Then for Chrissake, get yourselves down there and stay out of sight until you verify the arrival of Braxton's aircraft," Wyatt said.

"Roger that." Tristan severed their connection. He checked his altimeter. At fifteen thousand feet, he removed his oxygen mask and contacted his team.

"Noah, Logan."

"What's up Tristan?" Noah said.

"Logan?" Tristan repeated.

"I'm here," Logan said.

"I got an update from Wyatt right before I left the plane. Apparently we will have company in ten minutes. We need to hit the ground, stow our equipment, find a place to hide out, and regroup."

"Roger," both men said.

They landed a few yards from the helipad and were lucky to find a supply shed nearby. The team had barely stowed their equipment and found hiding spots when they saw the lights of the helicopter come into view.

The lights encircling the helipad came on as Logan shut the shed's door. "Gets your blood pumping, doesn't it?"

The helicopter touched down and then the motor shut down, the blades spooling to a stop. The passenger door opened, and Dave Anderson stepped from the craft. He held the door as Braxton stepped out behind him.

"Give me thirty minutes and then bring her to my office," Braxton said.

"Yes, sir," Dave said.

The two men headed for the main building. The pilot stepped from the helicopter, made a quick check around the air craft, and followed.

"How are we going to play this?" Logan asked.

"We stick to the plan," Tristan said, "with a few modifications. Braxton wants to meet with Victory; he is probably going to lay out the ground rules. It's two in the morning; I'm sure it will be a fairly short meeting. Logan and I will shadow them to Braxton's office. Logan will wait until Braxton leaves the office to proceed with his search and seizure. I'll follow Victory back to her room. After Dave leaves, I'll get her out."

"Victory," Tristan reached for her.

"Are you here?" she asked. A few minutes before she had felt Tristan's adrenaline rush, it flooded her body as if she herself jumped from the plane. She knew the very fraction of a second he had jumped out of the plane.

"Yes, but we have a slight change of plan. Braxton and Dave Anderson arrived on the island, nearly on top of us. Dave is on his way to pick you up for a meeting with Braxton."

"Terrific," she said.

"Play along. I'll be close by. After Dave returns you to your room, I'll make my move."

Victory heard the tapping of buttons at her door.

"Seems my escort has arrived," she said, as she sat up in her bed.

Dave opened the door and turned on the lights.

"We meet again, Ms. Winters."

As the room flooded with light, she realized she was in the same room they had put her in the first time she'd been kidnapped and brought to the island.

"Unfortunately," she said. "What do you want?"

"Pull yourself together," Dave nodded to the bathroom. "Mr. Braxton wants to see you."

"At this time of night? Doesn't the man ever sleep?" she asked.

"You have five minutes," he said, as he sat in the chair next to the desk.

"Good evening, Victory," Braxton said as Victory entered his office. In his normal fashion, he did not look up to greet her but remained fixated on his computer screen. "Take a seat, please. Dave, wait right outside. This shouldn't take long."

Victory sat in one of the wingback chairs, hands clasped in her lap, and waited for Braxton to begin.

"Seems Detective Howard was correct," he said.

"About?"

"Tristan Grant, or should I say Farraday, is not as he appeared. His background check turned out to be impeccable, which leads me to believe he is connected with the government. Tell me, how did the two of you meet?"

Victory sat quietly and did not respond to Braxton's question. For the first time, he looked up and made eye contact with her. Something was different about her, he thought. Victory seemed to have a sense of calm or self-assuredness. He could easily change that.

"No matter. He's not here now. I admit the two of you put a slight crimp in my plans but nothing that can't be fixed. You will continue with your research. I am obtaining new specimens as we speak."

Flames nearly shot out the top of her head, and her stomach clenched at the thought of another person being burdened with his serum.

"Like I told you back on the island, this serum is nowhere near ready to be used on a human."

"Yes, yes, still you have to admit, it does make you produce results."

"They know you have kidnapped me. Someone will find me eventually," she said.

"No, they won't. No one will even look for you. Detective Howard is currently involved in staging your death. Tragic really, you were in a plane crash early this morning on your return to Seattle. Regrettably the plane crashed into the Pacific Ocean, and your body could not be recovered. Such a loss, you had so much to contribute to the world of science," Braxton said with a sadistic sneer.

She sat glaring at the man. He truly was a madman.

"What makes you think I won't try to escape or contact my family at the first opportunity?"

His sadistic smile spread. "Because whoever you call will be dead within twenty-four hours. If you escape, I will kill both of your sisters. Now, enough with this game, you are scheduled to leave here in seven hours; we'll be taking you to your new lab and home."

He pushed the button on his desk and Dave reappeared.

"Take Ms. Winters back to her room. She needs a good night's sleep before her journey. I won't require your services any further tonight, Dave."

"Yes sir, Mr. Braxton. Let's go Victory," Dave said.

Victory remained in her chair. For a moment she wished she could see Braxton's face when he found out she had ruined his plans once again.

"Victory," Dave repeated.

She rose from the chair and started for the door.

"You will have your specimens in two days," Braxton said from his desk. "I will personally be checking on your progress in one week."

Victory did not turn to acknowledge Braxton's comment; she continued to the door, Dave on her heels. For the first time, she noticed a small glass plate on the wall to the left of the door. The plate had two buttons, one up and one down. Three feet to the left of the plate she saw a split in the wall.

As she walked down the massive marble hall to the elevator, she heard the minutest of sounds behind her. It sounded like a door creaking.

"Tristan?"

"We're here Victory, in the stairwell," he answered.

Victory filled him in on the conversation between herself and Braxton.

"They put me in the same room I was in when I was first brought to this place. It's on the basement level, no windows obviously, room zero sixteen."

"Did it look like Braxton would be in his office for awhile?"

"I don't think so; he looked tired, and he cut the meeting short. He told Dave he wouldn't be needed any more tonight. If I were to venture a guess, I would say he will head off to bed shortly," she said. *"There is a door in the wall right next to his office door. My*

thought is it's a private elevator, maybe to his personal suite."

The door to the elevator opened and Dave escorted Victory back to her room.

"Someone will be back in seven hours to retrieve you. I would advise you to get some sleep. Tomorrow will prove to be a very long and trying day."

Without waiting for her reply, Dave closed the door and the electronic lock snapped back into place.

"What do you think?" Logan whispered to Tristan.

Tristan focused on Braxton's office and took a deep breath in through his nose.

"He's doing a lot of moving around in there. Victory said there is a door that looks like an elevator right next to his office door, probably his personal suite." He took another breath. "His scent is getting stronger; wait, the scent is dissipating. I think Victory is right, there is an elevator. Give him a good thirty minutes and then move up to the door."

Chapter Twenty-Seven

Noah watched the screens in the main monitor room. So far no one from the security team had shown up, but he knew it was only a matter of time.

"Tristan, what's your status?"

"I'm on the basement level. Logan is up on the top floor giving Braxton some time to hopefully fall asleep. He should contact you in fifteen minutes to deactivate the door."

"What about you? Have you located Victory's room?" Noah asked.

"Zero sixteen, but don't take it down yet. I'm waiting for the guard to doze off or get up for a bathroom break," Tristan said.

"It better be damn soon. I'm overstaying my welcome here." As if on cue, the door to the security room began to open. "Shit, I'll get back to you; I've got company." Noah silently shut the door to the broom closet and hoped the guy wasn't a janitor coming in to clean up.

The man entered the room and carried a walkie-talkie. After he scanned the bank of monitors dominating the area, he spoke into the walkie-talkie.

"Base, this is Jim. I've completed my sweep; everything is quiet. Can I take my dinner break now?"

A metallic voice came through the walkie-talkie. "Yeah, okay. One hour Jim, no more. I want you back in the monitor room in sixty minutes, not ninety; got it?"

"I got it. What's the rush? Nothing is happening," Jim said.

"You're right and I want to keep it that way. Dave Anderson and Mr. Braxton are on the island for the night. I don't want them to catch us with our pants down. Your sixty minutes starts now, over." The walkie-talkie went dead.

"Well, shit." Jim stuffed the walkie-talkie back in his shirt pocket and left the room. In his haste he failed to turn off the lights. Noah waited patiently in the closet. Five minutes later the door opened and Jim switched the lights off. "Numbnuts," he grumbled. "Now I will only have forty-five minutes by the time I make it down to the mess hall," he mumbled as he walked down the hall.

"Tristan, Logan, come in," Noah said into his mouthpiece.

"Status, Noah," Tristan said.

"Almost ran into our friendly security guard. Seems his boss is a bit edgy with Braxton on the island. We only have fifty minutes to reach the boat launch. After that they will have eyes on the monitors."

"Go ahead and pop the lock on Braxton's office," Logan said. He saw the lock plate turn from red to green. "I'm going in."

"Is there any way to slow the guard down?" Tristan asked.

Noah thought for a moment as he debated his choices.

"I could try and shut down the elevators, make it look like a malfunction. Except it will probably only buy us about fifteen to twenty minutes."

"Do it," Tristan said.

Tristan started to worry his guard would never get up from his seat. Finally the guard's walkie-talkie beeped and he pulled it from his breast pocket.

"This is Don," he said into his device.

"Hey, Don," said Jim on the other end. "Want to meet me in the mess hall?"

"Sure," Don said. "Nothing is going on down here. The girl must be sound asleep by now. Give me five minutes."

"Make it snappy. I have orders to be back in the monitor room in fifty minutes, seems the big boss is on the island," Jim said.

"Roger, I'll see you in two," Don said, getting up from his chair and heading for the elevators.

"Noah, hold off on tampering with the elevators. My guy, Don, is on his way up to have dinner with Jim. Give me five minutes and then release Victory's door," Tristan whispered.

"Crap, Tristan, you sure like to cut things close. I literally have my hand on the button to cut the power. Her lock will be down in five," Noah repeated.

"Victory, I'll be at your door in five minutes."

"Yes, I heard," she said, with a smile in her voice. *"This room might be nicely decorated, but the décor can't disguise the fact it's still a cell. I never want to see the inside of this room again."*

Tristan opened the door from the stairwell and headed for Victory's door.

Five minutes on the dot, room zero sixteen's lock plate turned from red to green. Tristan grabbed the knob and opened the door. He stood in the doorway, the lights from the hall flooding the pitch-black room.

From out of the darkness Victory jumped into Tristan's arms. Utter surprise and joy filled him as he lifted her off her feet and kissed her with a desperate need. Something told him that he would never get enough of Victory.

"I knew you would find me," Victory said breathlessly.

"Never any doubt," Tristan said, as he gently placed her back on her feet.

"Don't mean to interrupt," came Noah's voice through Tristan's ear bud. "But we only have forty minutes to get clear of this place."

"We're on our way out," Tristan said. "How's it going, Logan?"

"Braxton is tucked away, with sweet dreams I'm sure. It's been slower going than I would have thought. All of his files are encrypted, which isn't a shock, but geez, they are all large files. It's taking more time," Logan said.

"How long until you're finished?" Tristan asked.

"I need at least another twenty minutes."

"Twenty minutes, no more. At twenty minutes and one second your ass had better be heading out the door; read me?"

"Loud and clear," Logan said.

"You're going to be cutting it very close," Noah said.

"That's how I like it."

"I'll stay back and cover Logan's six," said Noah. "You have a clear shot to the boat launch, Tristan. I'll keep you updated if anything changes. There's one blind spot; it's right after you hit the tree line. There isn't a single camera until you reach the other side of the trees, so I'll have no surveillance."

"Got it. Thanks, Noah. I'll expect you two in thirty minutes." He looked at Victory and said, "Time to go."

"I'm right behind you," she said.

They were at the exterior door in under five minutes. Tristan put his arm out and blocked Victory from moving forward.

"Hold on," he whispered. "Noah?"

"You're still good to go," Noah said.

Tristan turned the handle and glanced around the courtyard. The grounds were dimly lit, save for the glow from the overhead lights at each of the doorways. He reached into his pack and pulled out two pairs of night goggles. He turned and handed one to Victory; the other pair he strapped around his forehead. Victory silently followed his lead.

"Ready?"

"As ever." Victory nodded.

"Okay, when we move, we move quickly. You stay right on my heels." Tristan took one more look out the door. "Let's do this."

He stepped out the door and moved to the edge of the courtyard. Tristan and Victory skimmed the sides of the buildings and moved silently around the courtyard. When they reached the last building, he stopped her with his outstretched arm.

"You're clear." He heard Noah's voice come through his ear bud.

He looked back at Victory; she nodded, indicating she had heard Noah. Tristan acknowledged with a single nod, and soundlessly, the duo shot off across the open greenbelt. Tristan was thankful for the darkness enveloping them; he tugged his night goggles over his eyes, and Victory followed his lead.

Minutes later they were at the edge of the forest. Tristan continued to run; he slowed his pace slightly to allow for the uneven ground. He stopped when he could see the boat launch.

"You wait right here, Victory. I need to make sure we're still clear."

Victory nodded her head in understanding. Tristan turned and started for the launch. He looked down at his watch and noticed twenty minutes had already passed. By now Noah and Logan were making their way out of the building, and he and Victory were on their own.

Victory heard the softest sound behind her, the sound of footfalls as they stepped on the pine needles covering the ground. She began to turn expecting to see Noah and Logan; in the same heartbeat, she caught the sound of a gun loading. She continued to turn in the direction of the sound, but as she did so, she changed her direction and threw herself between the sound and Tristan's back.

At the last instant, Detective Ken Howard realized what Victory intended to do. He attempted to divert his aim to his right, but the bullet still caught Victory. She let out the tiniest of cries as she crumpled to the ground.

Tristan swung around as he caught Howard's scent. His body refused to respond quickly enough as he saw what Victory attempted to do. Instantaneously his mind screamed, *"Victory, no!"* as he saw her fall to the ground.

"Christ almighty." Howard said, as he stepped out from behind one of the evergreen trees. "You two are really starting to piss me off." Howard raised his gun once more and pointed it at Tristan's head.

Howard dropped to his knees, shock on his face. He looked down and saw a red spot growing on his chest just before he collapsed.

Logan came running through the trees, followed by Noah. Tristan ran back to where Victory lay.

"God, Tristan, I'm sorry. I took the shot as soon as I could," Logan said.

"I know." Tristan said. "Go get the boat ready to go."

Logan and Noah took off.

Tristan dropped to his knees beside Victory. He saw the blood pool next to her left shoulder. He felt a sudden wave of nausea overcome him. He rolled Victory gently over onto her back. She lay there, unresponsive. Her face pale in the moonlight.

* * * *

"Victory," he said, in the smallest of voices. "Victory, you need to wake up, please."

A painful sensation blanketed her body, and it made Victory want to drift off into unconsciousness. Somewhere far off, she heard Tristan beckon to her. Ever so slowly, her lids fluttered open. Tristan's body filled her view. He pressed something into her shoulder, and it took all her will to keep from crying out. She looked into his deep violet eyes and for the very first time…saw fear. She smiled up at him. "I'll be okay," she moaned.

"Looks like the bullet went straight through your upper arm; I can't tell for sure if it hit the bone," Tristan said. "What in the hell made you do such a thing? Don't you ever pull something like that again, do you understand?" Tristan was beside himself at the thought of her jumping in front of a bullet for him.

"I can't promise you," she said with a weak smile.

* * * *

Tristan could have easily reached out telepathically to Wyatt and let him know about Victory's injury. But the last thing he wanted right now was to have Wyatt inside of his head. In the same instant he realized he loved Victory with his whole heart and soul, but he wasn't ready to share his revelation with his brother.

Tristan buried his face in Victory's hair and inhaled the unique scent that was only Victory. He knew in the depths of his soul he would never get enough of her scent; it had permeated every last cell of his being.

"God, Victory, I thought I lost you." He whispered into her hair. "I don't know what I would have done without you. I love you."

She pulled weakly away from him; unshed tears sparkled on her lids. "You love me?" she questioned softly.

"With everything I am. I want…no, I need you in my life. Please say you feel the same. Say you will marry me?" he asked, as he looked at her with all the love he felt shining in his eyes.

"I do. I will." She smiled back at him. Pain flooded her body, and she grimaced at her feeble attempt to touch his perfect face with her injured arm.

Logan ran up from the boat launch. "Can we move her?" he asked, unsure of Victory's injuries.

"Yes, it's a shoulder wound. Nothing life-threatening, but she will need medical attention as soon as possible," Tristan said.

"Good, we need to get out of here; we're out of time. I have some morphine and bandages in my pack." Logan moved in to help Tristan pick Victory up.

"I've got her," Tristan said. "Make sure you keep the path clear. Howard?" he asked as an afterthought.

"He's gone," Logan said.

"That's good, because I would have killed him. Only it would have been extremely painful and very slow." Tristan gingerly lifted Victory into the safety and warmth of his arms.

Chapter Twenty-Eight

"It's so great to have you back home safe and sound, sis," Payton said. She stretched out on one of the rattan overstuffed chairs with her feet propped up on a huge circular ottoman she shared with Victory.

The sky was a deep ocean blue, not a cloud to be seen. Victory looked around the patio and noticed all the chairs were occupied with Dobermans. Of course, her ever-faithful Dax lay right next to her sharing the love seat. He had barely left her side since the moment she returned home. She could feel the uneasiness ripple through him. She knew her injured arm didn't help matters. The bullet had grazed her humerus and caused a bone fracture. She was in a hanging cast with her arm bent at a ninety-degree angle; the cast started at her shoulder and ended a few inches below her elbow.

"It's wonderful to be home," she said. "I still can't believe all that has happened over the last two months. Sometimes it doesn't feel real, like I watched it happen to someone else."

"It most certainly was real. Look at the cast on your arm. And believe me, Willow and I worried about you every minute of every day. I am unbelievably grateful you came back to us in one piece," Payton said.

A car door slammed in the front yard and all the Dobermans leapt from their chairs to go investigate. All but Dax, who didn't take his gaze off Victory.

"It must be Tristan," Victory said with her eyes still closed as she soaked in the warm rays of the afternoon sun. She knew if it had been anyone else, the dogs would not have only gone to greet them, but would have alerted the entire neighborhood.

A commotion started behind her as all the dogs playfully leapt and nipped at each other.

"Okay, guys," Tristan's husky voice scolded lightheartedly. "Yes, I'm glad to see all of you too. Settle down now before someone bumps into Victory." Almost instantly the group dispersed, each dog going back to its assigned chair.

"If you want to sit and join us, you had better hurry before all the seats are taken." Payton giggled.

"My chair's saved." Tristan acknowledged Dax with a quick rub between his ears and then reached under to scratch his neck. Dax responded by laying the total weight of his head in Tristan's palm. Tristan went to the other side of the love seat and wiggled in next to Victory.

"Hello, my fiancée," he greeted her as he tilted her face up to his and gently kissed her lips.

"Hello my fiancé," Victory said savoring the kiss.

"I brought you something," Tristan said. He pulled a tiny black box from his pants pocket and opened it. Inside sat a spectacular, two-carat, square cut diamond; the band was also encrusted with diamonds. "Thought it time I made it official."

"Oh Tristan, it's the most stunning ring I have ever seen," Victory said, choking back her tears. She looked at her swollen and bruised left hand; there was no way she would be able to wear the ring.

"No worries," Tristan said reading her mind. He removed the ring from the box, picked up her right hand and slipped on the ring. "There. You can change hands after the swelling goes down in your hand."

She held up her arm; the diamonds caught the afternoon sun, all aflame on her hand.

"Wow, it really is breathtaking," Payton said.

"We're taking a short break," Victory said, as she eyed the group lounging.

"Yes, a break," Payton piped in. "We have been hard at work, booking caterers, florists, music, bakers…"

"I get it." Tristan cut her off from what seemed like it would be a never-ending list. "I've got news too."

"Tell us," Victory said.

"Collin has been moved out of the ICU."

They had been back for ten days. In that time Collin had undergone two surgeries.

"The doctors say he will make a full recovery. They plan to keep him for another week or so; after the week is out, he will be moved to another facility for physical therapy."

"Is he safe?" Victory asked.

"Yes. They have him at a military facility, under twenty-four hour guard. Besides that, as far as Biotec is concerned, he died along with Max when he fell from the cliff. Neither bodies were recovered." Tristan winked at Victory.

"And then," Victory prompted. "What does the government plan to do with him after? They can't leave him to fend for himself. There is still so much we don't know. The doctors might believe he will be physically recovered by then, except we all know better. We still need to deal with the foreign DNA running through his body. If a buffer isn't discovered, and I mean soon, the Collin who once was will not exist, assuming he survives the transformation."

"He's being taken care of," Tristan said.

"They can't lock him up again, or we are no better than Braxton," Victory said.

"Hear me out," Tristan said. Victory quieted and looked up at him. "They are working on a proposal right now. The government is going to offer The Winters Corporation a unique opportunity."

"Really, that's great, but what about Claremont?" Victory asked.

"They aren't being left out. Claremont will be invited to assist in this new venture; of course, the entire proposal hinges on you being the liaison between the two companies," Tristan said with a smile on his face. "Looks like the Winters women will be working together."

"What about the other man?" Payton asked. "Morgan, wasn't it?"

"Morgan has actually been very involved in this whole process. He will join Collin in this upcoming project," Tristan said.

"Have they found Braxton?" Victory asked.

"Not yet. He and the Kaleidoscope Group have gone underground. We know their pockets are deep.

I'm not sure how long it will take us to locate them, but we will."

"If you locate them," she corrected.

"Don't worry; we will. Everyone has to surface sometime, even Braxton. We have the most-qualified technicians working on decrypting Braxton's files, but so far no luck. In the meantime Wyatt feels it would be best for you, Payton, and Willow to stay close together," Tristan said with concern in his voice.

"It's settled then," Payton said. "I've tried all day to talk Victory into the two of you moving in here after your honeymoon." Payton waved Tristan off before he had a chance to protest. "Don't worry, there's plenty of room. You two lovebirds can have the carriage house. We remodeled it only four months ago. It will be perfect."

Victory remained silent and looked at Tristan.

"I think that's probably a great idea. We need to enclose your property with a security fence. There will be a security team on the grounds day and night. With the three of you living under one roof, it will make it much easier to maintain your safety."

A smile lit up Victory's face as she threw her right arm around Tristan's neck.

"Really, you wouldn't mind?" She hadn't realized how happy she would be about moving back home. Then another thought crossed her mind, and she drew back from Tristan. "What about Willow? Does she still have someone watching her?"

"Night and day. Don't worry, Victory. One of the guys will be flying over and will personally escort her home. She will be in good hands. Now let's hear more about this wedding."

Asia's head popped up off the arm of the lounge chair she'd been sharing with Kes. Her ears were stiffly erect and her eyes were a smoldering black. She vaulted over Kes and off the lounge in one stride, running full out to the front of the house. All three of the remaining Dobermans looked up from their spots. Dax glanced up into Victory's face and saw a flash of terror. He jumped down and headed for the front yard, followed closely by Parker and Kes.

"What's up?" Tristan asked. "Was it something I said?"

"I'm not sure, I think someone is in the front yard," Victory said.

In one smooth motion, Tristan reached down into his pants leg and retrieved his Walther .p38 from his ankle holster and headed to the front yard. He turned slightly, and never breaking stride, he said, "I'm sure I shouldn't have to say this, but you two stay put." As he reached the corner of the house, they heard the dogs yipping and howling. "What on Earth?" he muttered.

Almost drowned out by the chorus of Dobermans came a whimsical laugh. The herd of dogs rounded the corner, jumping up and down, and totally surrounded a striking blond-haired woman. Her resemblance to both Victory and Payton was obvious.

"Willow!" Victory and Payton cried. They sprang from their perches and ran to join the group, tears streaming down both of their faces.

"Holy Hell," Noah said, as he brought up the rear. "I've been in a lot of scary shit before, but none of it compares to being the target of a bunch of charging Dobermans. I almost wet my pants."

Everyone started to laugh, and the tension of the past few minutes faded away.

"What are you doing here, Willow?" Victory asked. "I thought the earliest you could come home was next week?"

"I couldn't wait. I left my assistant in charge of the project," Willow said as they hugged.

"Trouble," Noah chimed in. "When this woman gets an idea in her head, there's no stopping her. I could barely keep up with her."

"Seems to run in the family," Tristan said, as the two men stood in awe and looked at each of the three women.

"She's gonna keep you on your toes, man," Noah laughed, watching the three women.

"Tell me something I don't know," Tristan said, as a grin lit up his face.

About the Author

Joanne was born and raised in Sherburne, New York, a quaint village surrounded by dairy farms and rolling hills. From the moment she could read she wanted to explore the world. During her college years she slowly crept across the country, stopping along the way in Oklahoma, California, and finally Washington State, which she now proudly calls home. She lives with her husband and Dobermans, in their home located on the Olympic Peninsula with a panoramic view of the Olympic Mountains.

Joanne writes romantic suspense, paranormal, and contemporary romance. She loves to submerge herself in the world of her characters, to live and breathe their lives and marvel at their decisions and predicaments.

She enjoys a wide variety of books including paranormal, suspense, thriller, and of course romance.

Joanne is a PAN member of Romance Writers of America, (RWA), Kiss of Death, (KOD), Greater Seattle Romance Writers Chapter, (GSRWA), and past President of Peninsula Romance Writers, which was Debbie Macomber's home chapter.

You Can Find Joanne Here~

Email: joannejaytanie@wavecable.com
Website: http://www.joannejaytanie.com/
Blog: http://www.authorjoannejaytanie.blogspot.com/
Facebook: https://www.facebook.com/pages/Joanne-
     Jaytanie-Author/146892025475388
Amazon Author Page:
     http://www.amazon.com/Joanne-
     Jaytanie/e/B00C3458YE
Twitter: https://twitter.com/joannejaytanie
Pinterest: http://www.pinterest.com/joannejaytanie/
Linkedin: http://www.linkedin.com/pub/joanne-
     jaytanie/61/52b/532/
Goodreads:
https://www.goodreads.com/author/show/7063660.Jo
     anne_Jaytanie
Barnes & Noble:
http://www.barnesandnoble.com/s/Joanne-
     Jaytanie?store=allproducts&keyword=Joanne
     +Jaytanie
Amazon UK: http://www.amazon.co.uk/Joanne-
     Jaytanie/e/B00C3458YE
Smashwords:
     https://www.smashwords.com/profile/view/Jo
     anneJaytanie
Romance Books 4 Us:
     http://romancebooks4us.com/Joanne_Jaytanie.
html
AUTHORSdb: http://authorsdb.com/authors-
     directory/14114-joanne-jaytanie

75951427R00177

Made in the USA
Columbia, SC
28 August 2017